C000072288

ABOVE ALL, HUMAN

NATALIE DEBRABANDERE

ISBN: 9781693009549

DEDICATION

For my warriors…
Anne B. and Julie P.

X

ACKNOWLEDGMENTS

Thanks to Peter again for a wonderful design!

And to all my readers: as always, thank you for reading and reviewing in all the good places.

I appreciate you greatly!

CHAPTER ONE

Army Captain Crystal J. Thor had never expected to find herself staring down the barrel of a loaded gun after retiring from the Forces... Still, on that snowy night in Manhattan some years later, just after starting her security shift at a busy women's shelter on 42nd St, fate decided otherwise. The guy was huge. At least six-foot-four, bulky and muscular. At first, Crystal had no idea how he could have got inside what was supposed to be a secure building; but as she walked into the main lounge area, and discovered the intruder standing there with his gun in hand, she also spotted the terrified woman huddled in the far corner, who was still wearing her coat and hat. Her name was Karin. She was a new resident, only twenty-two years old. As Crystal glanced her way, Karin threw her a pretty desperate look, fear but also guilt and regret written all over her face. In response, Crystal nodded almost imperceptibly.

"It's okay, Karin," she murmured.

"Shut the fuck up!" the man snarled.

Crystal remained calm and she returned her gaze to him. *He must have walked in straight after Karin, and forced her to lead him up the stairs... Not a hard thing to achieve for a guy his size, really.*

1

He would have appeared intimidating at the best of times, let alone now, armed with what Crystal instantly recognised to be a 9mm Glock 17 Gen4. It was a serious weapon, popular among NYPD duty officers. She herself favoured the SIG Sauer P226 DAO, which was also widely in use by law enforcement. As an Army officer who had served in the Special Forces for five years, she was licenced to own and carry any kind of weapon she may have liked. Unfortunately, whenever on duty at the shelter, she had to leave her trusted Sig inside a safety locker the entire time. To Crystal, the rule made absolutely no sense. In fact, it had to be the most foolish, idiotic, dangerous regulation she had ever been asked to comply with. But when she made her opinion known to the director of the shelter, the woman shrugged.

"The sight of you walking around with a gun attached to your hip makes the residents nervous," she claimed.

This was simply unhelpful bureaucratic bullshit, as far as Crystal was concerned, and she pointed it out to the director as politely as she could.

"With all due respect, that's not been my experience," she said. "And not allowing me to be armed might put the residents at even more risk than they already are. I am the security officer, after all…"

In response, she was told that the rule was there to stay, and that if she did not agree with the way this ship was being run, she was free to leave. Crystal never enjoyed being told what to do by idiots. This time too, she struggled not to simply say, *'Fine, good riddance'*, and slam the door on her way out. The thought of not being able to afford the new campervan of her dreams held her back from storming out though. She needed this job… She had been saving for a while to get out of New York; she planned to head to Montana, and the mountains that she loved, but she was a few thousand dollars short of her required budget.

There was also the fact that she liked the women at the shelter, all warriors in their own right. The desire to protect and to serve that had led her to join the army in the first place was still alive and kicking inside of her. Captain Thor did not walk out on people, on jobs, or situations. She was not a quitter. So now, as she continued to study the intruder who still had his gun pointed at the centre of her chest, she remembered her backup weapon, the concealed tactical dagger strapped to her right calf. Given half a chance, she could do as much damage with it as with her handgun, if not more.

"Hey, buddy, why don't you drop the gun?" she said in an easy voice, as if talking to a friend. She did not want to spook him into a rage. "We can start again if you like, no harm done."

"Get me Darlene," he muttered.

Crystal kept her eyes on him.

"Who?" she asked innocently.

He was sweating pretty hard, and she also noticed that his index finger was not resting on the trigger itself, but on the side of the guard. *He's nervous, but in control,* she concluded. This was good, given how sensitive triggers could be. His stance indicated that he knew how to handle a firearm. Then, she spotted something else. The beads of perspiration on his forehead and his uneasy, suspicious darting eyes told her that in spite of his size, or his weapon, he still did not feel safe. *All right, then...* Crystal almost smiled when she realised that, and as a familiar bubble of deep calm and concentration enveloped her, helping to sharpen her vision, clear her mind, and relax her muscles in anticipation of imminent action. She may be retired, at least in the eyes of the military, but she was still a fighter. That would never change.

"Darlene Jackson," he grunted. "My fucking wife! Get the bitch here now!"

3

Even if Crystal had been a traitor, the kind to lead a lamb to slaughter, she could not have delivered the poor woman to her would-be executioner. In perfect timing, Darlene Jackson had left the shelter the previous night, bound for Florida under an assumed name. A brand-new job and a bright new life awaited her there, away from this crazy beast. He fixed her with a hard stare.

"Did you hear what I said?" he repeated.

"Sure," Crystal replied. "No problem."

She kept her eyes on him. So, this was the self-proclaimed loving and caring partner who had beaten Darlene so viciously that when she showed up at the shelter that first night, all she could do was collapse on the floor as soon as she was through the door. Her right arm was broken. So were several of her ribs, which made it hard for her to breathe. She struggled to speak. She could barely open her eyes due to severe swelling. After a while, she managed to explain that he had deliberately punched her in the face and chest, repeatedly, until she passed out from the pain. He could have killed her. Crystal still could not get her head around why, instead of a lengthy prison sentence, he was given a warning and a restraining order. It was unfair, unjust, and now, she could truly appreciate the lack of effectiveness of the measure. Crystal felt a rush of warmth and satisfaction at the thought of Darlene, who had managed to escape. She was long gone now, and safe in her new life, but newbie Karin did not know that. For Crystal, it was a great opportunity. She wanted to get her out of this room, and out of harm's way, as quickly as she could before something happened and it became ugly.

"Karin," she said, and the woman jumped in sudden fright. She looked petrified. Crystal flashed her a reassuring smile, as if this was business as usual. "Can you get Darlene over here, please," she said.

4

Karin stood frozen in place, staring at her with wide-open eyes, as if she did not understand a single word of what Crystal had said.

"Tell you what, just go and find Ruth," Crystal repeated in a calm voice, referring to the medical assistant on duty. "Tell her that we need Darlene, all right? Ruth can find her."

She kept a careful eye on the armed guy as she spoke. Still sweating; still in control, for now. Crystal did not think that it would last for much longer. She was desperately eager for Karin to get moving. At long last, the woman seemed to wake up from her daze. She looked as if the real, urgent message in Crystal's words finally got through to her; *Just go and get some help, for God's sake!* She nodded her assent, promptly took a couple of steps away from the intruder, and toward her. She was not far from the door now, and safety. For a few seconds, it seemed as if she might be able to get out and away. Crystal held her breath. *Come on... Come on!*

"Not so fast," the man growled.

Damn... She stiffened at the command, and the recognition that he was starting to lose patience, and his temper with it. He moved to go and stand between Karin and the door, effectively blocking her way. Crystal's hopes for the younger woman were quickly dashed.

"Hold it, goddammit!"

He grabbed her roughly by the forearm, causing Karin to let out a painful yelp, and threw her on the couch as if she weighed nothing.

"Don't you fucking move," he warned.

He was surprisingly quick and light on his feet for someone of his size, as Crystal was able to confirm with his next move. In a flash, he was in front of her, his weapon raised and pointed straight at her forehead.

"Easy," she snapped, forgetting that she was not the one in charge.

He was not close enough yet for her to be able to tackle him, although she might have attempted to do it if Karin had not still been in the room. She might have to soon, regardless. The shelter was operating at full capacity that night, as it so often did. Ten women were officially registered at the place, and most of them liked to come in and spend some time in the lounge after dinner; to talk, work, or watch TV together. Crystal could not afford to wait for much longer to take action.

"Stop dicking around, girl," the guy spat at her.

His face had turned red, evidence of his growing anger. She could see a bulging vein pulsing ever harder across his forehead. Too bad he looked so fit and healthy, otherwise she would have hoped for a heart attack to bring him down.

"She goes out, next thing you know, I got the whole SWAT team on my ass, uh?" he said. "I ain't that fucking stupid, bitch. Nobody leaves this room."

When Crystal did not reply, he narrowed his eyes at her.

"Get it?"

"Yes, yes... No problem."

She worked to sound appropriately scared, and not like she was thinking of all the many ways she could kill him with her bare hands if she were so inclined. She even managed a flustered smile to prove that she really was no threat to him; incredibly, it had an effect. The guy relaxed his grip on the handle of the gun; almost imperceptibly, but Crystal was paying attention, and she noticed. *How naïve can you be?* she thought; but she was pleased, and not too surprised. After all, he was used to abusing and dominating women. As long as she behaved as if she thought he could do the same to her, and made him believe that she was afraid of him, he would feel in control and forget to be careful.

More often than not, over-confidence and arrogance led to big mistakes in this dangerous game he wanted to play... And he clearly had no idea that he was facing a professional. Crystal was only waiting for him to slip up, and for her moment to pounce. He pointed to the phone affixed to the wall.

"You get on that, and call my wife. Don't make me ask you again. Let's go!"

"All right, all right," Crystal cowered. "I'll do what you say. Please, don't hurt us."

She moved slowly across the room. He kept his eyes on her and the gun pointed at her head. No longer watching Karin now, which was a really good thing. Crystal slowed down even more, inching ever nearer to the phone but seemingly never reaching the damn thing. With a bit of luck, he would lose his temper at some point and try to grab on to her. Maybe to hit her or shove her forward... To force her to speed up in any way he could. She wanted him to do just that. He had to come a lot closer for what she had in mind.

"Hurry the fuck up!" he ordered.

"I'm sorry." She leaned a hand against the wall for support, pretending to be short of breath. "Please... Put your gun down. You're scaring me. I... I can't..."

He took a step forward, fuming now.

"Pick up the phone. Pick it up, NOW!"

Crystal nodded, but she still did not move.

"Sorry... Sorry! Please, just give me a second!"

Hand flat over her chest, and breathing hard, she watched his face change. Rage was taking over nicely now. She almost had him. Almost... But not quite, unfortunately. In fact, she had run out of time. All of a sudden, a piercing scream echoed across the room.

CHAPTER TWO

Abigail Christensen was not a woman who enjoyed labels of any kind attached to her, although she was happy to go with a few in her line of work. She referred to herself as Congresswoman, Presidential Candidate, and last but not least, Amazing Lasagne-Maker. It was a good trio. On that day in Santa Rosa, California, she was on the campaign trail, and she was actually happy when the last meet-and-greet of her busy schedule came to an end. Not that she was tired... But something had happened that same morning which she had not shared with her team yet, and it weighed heavily on her mind. Usually, she thrived on meeting people. Abigail was a popular representative in her home state of Colorado. Since starting her campaign, she had also proved a firm hit in every town and city that she visited. She had recently qualified for the next round of democratic debates that would take place in just a few weeks. As a PAC-free candidate, she did not accept money from big corporations, and just relied solely on individual donations to support her campaign. At a glance, her vision for America if she was elected was bold. Representative Christensen had ambitions for a Foreign Policy of prosperity achieved through friendship and cooperation, not radical and bloody regime change. Once in office, she planned to reform what she considered to be a broken justice system. Healthcare for all would be a priority on the agenda, as well as education.

Again, she planned to make it totally free and available to all. She would end the failed so-called war on drugs, relax paranoid laws on immigration, and facilitate the exchange of goods and people. She supported diversity and full equality for everyone in all areas of society, regardless of someone's gender, colour, race, religion, food choices, sexual preferences, and whatever else might be used to create separation. On a more personal note, Representative Christensen also happened to be the number one most famous lesbian in the world at this particular moment... Between her radical political views and her fiery personality, it would have been difficult to say which was the most shocking or controversial for some far-right minded individuals.

"Hey, Abi; all good?"

Russell Stark, her campaign manager, came to sit in the car next to her. A thirty-year-old Yale graduate, he had, against all expectations, chosen to spend his first twelve months out of school sailing the world on a second-hand yacht. The boat never leaked enough to sink; 'Just to make my life interesting', he often laughed when he described his experience as a sailor. He had won the mono-hull fair and square at a game of poker that took place at a Burning Man event, and set sail for Hawaii the very next day. 'The lure of adventure... I just had to do it; you know?' He was a great guy, clever and talented, and Abigail loved working with him. Now she gave him two happy thumbs-up in reply to his question.

"Well done today," he added. "That was a tough crowd."

"Oh, but you know there is no such thing as a tough crowd, my friend," she teased. "Only inflexible speakers, right? This being said... Thanks."

"Right," Russell chuckled. "That was a nice touch finishing your speech with a mention of the war in Iraq, by the way."

"Yeah, I think it worked..."

9

"For sure. It was good to remind everyone that so many politicians who let it happen at the time now say that we should never have got involved... People loved it when you highlighted the notion that we need to have the courage to speak out against the system when it really matters, not years later when there's no risk to one's career."

"Thanks, Russ," Abigail repeated, smiling softly. "I think I should thank you, actually, since it was your idea to conclude with that topic. As per usual, you got the tone of this Town Hall just right."

He blushed in reaction, which tended to happen whenever she or anyone else on the team paid him a genuine compliment. His nickname was 'Red' on account of this quirky habit, which for a strapping six-foot-four who looked like Paul de Gelder, was unusual to say the least. But Russell was a lot softer and more sensitive than his muscular appearance would suggest. Now he leaned forward in his seat, and as he kept his eyes trained on her face, scrutinising, his smile gradually faded away. Abigail raised an enquiring eyebrow at him.

"What's up, my friend?" she asked. "You look preoccupied. Has Google been messing up with our advertising account again and interfering with our campaign? Or is it something else?"

She was referring to an outrageous so-called 'malfunction' of her Google account following one of the most watched debates, when her page was shut down for six hours for no apparent reason, preventing millions of voters from finding her online, and of course, registering their support and new donations. Now, her campaign lawyers were suing Google for fifty million dollars in damages, which was absolutely justified. Abigail had also gone public on every corporate media channel to denounce the Internet giant's blatant attempts at interfering with her freedom of speech.

'This is about manipulation of people's perception at the deepest level," she declared. "The hijacking of minds is the most insidious means of cheating. Who needs Russian bots when Google and Facebook are pulling the strings right here at home, right? I'll say it again: it doesn't have to be this way. The power is in our hands, not with the elite! Sure, they seek to control us and everything else... But stick with me on this journey, and I promise you that we will create a much different world... One in which freedom, opportunity, justice, respect, and equality for all really do prevail!'

This impassioned speech alone had gone a long way to repairing the damage that the Google incident had caused to the campaign. Supporters flocked to Abigail's website to sign up and donations soared. Not surprisingly, some quarters seized on the opportunity to slap a 'Mad Conspiracy Theorist' label on her back, screaming all over the Internet that she was just a female version of the crazy Alex Jones, and David Icke as well, nothing but 'a dirty dyke!'. Definitely not someone who should ever be allowed to lead the American people... But never mind that. It would take a lot more to make a dent in Abigail's shiny armour.

"Talk to me, Russ," she insisted when he did not reply.

"No, it's not Google," he said, looking chagrined.

"What's the matter, then?"

"Well, I'm still none the wiser about what happened to you this morning at the hotel, is what," he muttered. "I mean, you were on the phone for a good twenty minutes, and you looked as white as a sheet when you came out of your room..."

He shook his head, worry flashing across his quick blue eyes.

"Also, you got all introspective and quiet on us afterwards and refused to talk about it. I can't remember a time when you did not want to discuss something, Abs. Not ever!" He rested a gentle hand on her shoulder. "Abi; you're not sick, are you?"

She smiled and patted his hand in reassurance.

"I am well, don't worry. I was just waiting for the right time to fill you in, that's all. Trust me, you'll be glad you didn't have to carry that stuff around with you all day when I tell you."

His expression shifted from anxious to curious.

"What is it then?" he repeated intently. "What happened?"

"Where are Sam and JoAnn?" Abigail enquired, making him hiss in barely contained impatience. "I want them both to hear this, and I want to get a move on out of here too."

As she spoke, Abigail threw a quick glance around the car, ensuring that no one was lurking too close. They travelled in a new-model Ford Explorer XLT covered in campaign stickers that was great for advertisement, and made them easy to spot. It was not uncommon for people to come up to the vehicle after a meeting, wanting Abi to pose for an extra photo with them or sign an autograph. It was all part of the game, and as expected; she never refused. Right now, they were parked in front of this latest Town Hall venue, a popular city-centre coffee-shop whose owners were ardent supporters of her campaign. As Russell got on his phone to check with his two colleagues, Abigail spotted a lone guy standing on the corner. She frowned. He was dressed in faded jeans, a black T-shirt, and a tipped-down baseball cap that made it hard to see his face. He just stood there leaning on a lamp post, watching the car. *Doesn't look like the type to want a selfie much...* Abigail kept her eyes fixed on him, cool but alert. Even before deciding to run for the top job in the country, she had been appropriately aware of security requirements in her choice of career, but never overly concerned about it. Now it was a little different, of course, and especially after this morning's call. *Then again,* she reflected, *he might just be a shy guy who's curious about what we're doing.* The man finally ambled away, and she relaxed.

"The girls are on their way," Russell informed her.

Right on cue, the additional members of Abigail's *On-the-Road* team jumped in the car; Samantha Colson, event organiser and designated driver, and JoAnn Li, Press Officer.

"Sorry we're late, but we have a good excuse."

The two women carried what looked enticingly like take-away boxes, and a delicious aroma soon filled the entire vehicle. Abigail felt her mouth water.

"Oh, yes," she exclaimed, leaning forward. "Is that what I think it is?"

"Yep," JoAnn laughed. "I said we had a long drive ahead of us tonight to get to the next venue, and the café owners insisted we take a few pizzas. Fresh from the oven."

"Needless to say," Samantha pointed out, "they didn't have to work too hard to convince us. They gave us coffee, too!"

"That's brilliant," Russ exclaimed, as she handed out the cups. "People can be so kind, uh? If nothing else, that's what I'll take from this entire trip. It would be easy to take one look at the world right now, and lose heart on account of how messed up it seems to be... But underneath all that are real human beings. Generous, smart, friendly people who crave the sort of change we are looking to bring."

Abigail nodded, moved by the emotion in his voice.

"You're right," she approved. "People are great. And so are you, guys."

She enjoyed everything connected to this life on the road; the easy freedom that came with living out of a single suitcase, waking up in a new place every day, getting to meet amazing people along the way. She loved criss-crossing the country with her message of hope and empowerment, and delivering it face to face to those that she truly considered to be not just her fellow citizens, but her brothers and sisters in Humankind as a whole.

Abigail held unusually expansive views in that regard, for sure. She also cherished those intimate moments with her own crew. Sometimes, when they were running low on sleep and energy, which was inevitable from time to time on the campaign trail, pure enthusiasm and passion alone kept them going. Abigail's team had faith in her and their shared purpose. This was not a job to any of them, but a deep calling actually, primal and true. The thought of the mission to be carried out kept them smiling and their spirits high, always. And of course, a steady supply of coffee and pizza never hurt either...

"Where to, Madam President?" Samantha enquired. "Just so you know, Bodega Bay is only forty minutes from here, and it would make a great spot for a picnic."

"Let's catch a sunset before we hit the road proper," Russell agreed enthusiastically. "What do you think, ladies?"

"I'm with you!" JoAnn approved.

Abigail's chest tightened at the thought of the hard talk that she was going to need to have with them. She was not worried that anyone might want to quit as a result, but she hated the idea of putting her people in danger, and if they stuck with her on this path, well... Of course, they all knew when they signed up that this was not going to be your average campaign. The risks involved in taking part were real. Abigail was not surprised at the first signs of things heating up now... She had just hoped to have a bit more time. But never mind, hey: *when the going gets tough...*

"Boss?" Russell nudged her shoulder. "You still with us?"

Abigail nodded and she flashed him a smile. *You bet I am.*

"Let's hit Bodega and enjoy that pizza," she declared. "I do fancy a tailgate dinner."

CHAPTER THREE

The two startled residents reacted at exactly the same time and in the same way; by letting out an ear-splitting scream that must have scared the living daylights out of all the other women in the building. The two had just walked in with a cup of tea and a piece of cake, looking forward to a relaxing evening of TV and companionship. Needless to say, the sight of the giant armed man standing in front of the couch put a serious damper on their expectations. Screaming seemed like the most appropriate way to react to this violation, and so, they did. For Crystal, it all ended up being just right. The man took his eyes off her for a second; bad mistake, and it was all she needed to unleash her offensive. In one lightning-fast move, she kicked the gun out of his hand. The Glock slid under the sofa. *Great.* The guy was fast to react though. He launched a swift foot aimed at her head that might have knocked her out if he had made contact. Crystal was quick enough to duck, but this was a nice warning to her that the man could fight. *Whatever.* She was not one to underestimate her opponents anyway. For a brief moment, he looked surprised to find her still standing. She could not help but smirk.

"That all you've got?" she said.

Enraged, he turned on her like a wild dog, foaming at the mouth. She blocked his next strikes and punched him in the face, hard. He stumbled back and shook his head to clear his vision.

15

"Fucking bitch!" he growled.

"You're welcome. That was for Darlene, by the way."

There was some commotion down the hallway. Crystal was aware of one of the residents, who was still screaming, but this time at someone else to call the police. *Yeah, in your own time,* she thought. Anyhow, she was not planning on waiting for the cops. Part of her enjoyed toying with this thug, but she needed to put him down now. She would have done so with her next move, if the most extraordinary thing had not happened...

"Stop!" Karin cried at the guy. "Don't move!"

Crystal had all but forgotten about shy Karin, huddled on the couch in terror, until the woman chose that very moment to step forward. And not only that, but she was holding the guy's Glock in both hands in a death grip; shaking like a leaf, mind you, eyes wide and looking dazed. Crystal did a sharp double-take at the sight of her. *What the hell are you doing...?* Karin may have thought that she was helping, but she was too close to him, too inexperienced, and in the throes of a typical panic reaction. All he had to do was step forward, grab onto her wrist, and snatch the weapon out of her hand. Easily done; it took him less than a split second to achieve. *Shit,* Crystal thought. He whirled around, finger heavy on the trigger now, aiming for her. But if he thought that she was just going to wait around to get her head blown off, he had another think coming. She had moved even faster. All he must have seen of her was a blur as she crashed into him. He fired one aimless shot, inadvertently, right before she plunged her knife into his arm, pinning him to the floor. He screamed in pain and absolute fury. He clearly was not done fighting yet, though, and Crystal suddenly wondered if he might not be high on some kind of drug. She had him flat out on his stomach in a paralysing choke hold. She had stuck her knife through his arm. Anybody else would have given up by now.

16

"Drop your weapon," she ordered.

He hissed in response, and thrashed under her as if he were possessed, trying to free himself from her uncompromising grip. He even tried to raise his arm and point the gun in her direction. Crystal tightened her hold over his throat and gave her dagger a nice painful twist.

"I said drop it, or I'll cut your arm off."

She would never have done that, of course. As it was, she had been careful with the knife not to hit the major artery in his limb. A nice fleshy spot would get her the result that she was after just as well. She did not want to mutilate him, but she had no issue with inflicting maximum pain until he started to obey her. In the end, he really had no other choice left but to do so. Whimpering now, his breathing short and ragged, he finally opened his fingers, and let go of the weapon. Crystal grabbed on to it quickly, and pressed it against the side of his temple.

"Do I have your attention?" she asked. "Are you listening?"

With his face pressed into the carpet, still breathing hard in genuine pain, he managed to produce a weak nod in response; he was well and truly beaten this time, and compliant at last.

"I'm going to get up now." Crystal spoke quietly against his ear, in a calm and steady voice loaded with menace. "If I see you move even just a finger, I will put a bullet through your skull. I'm serious, make no mistake about that. Got it?"

He gave a muffled grunt, and went extremely still. Crystal knew that he was taking her seriously at last, even though she was still bluffing. She got up and shot a quick glance behind her.

"Karin, are you okay?"

The woman lay on the floor, crying, as she held onto what would turn out to be a broken wrist. Crystal looked to the door for any kind of help available. All the women were gone, but the medic on duty hovered in the doorway, watching her intently.

"I called the police, Crys," she announced. "Can I come in and do my thing?"

She was carrying her emergency kit and chomping at the bit to get involved. At least, it seemed like it. Ruth Peterson; twenty-years-old, bright and enterprising, was shipping off to Army Basic Training in just a few days' time. As soon as she had found out about Crystal's background in the military, or to be more precise, the tiny tip of the iceberg that was not classified, she had adopted her as a mentor and all-round adviser. Crystal was fine with that, although hero worship was not her thing, and she was quick to discourage it with Ruth when she spotted the first signs of it. Still, it did not stop the young woman from looking at her with undisguised admiration most of the time, and even more so right now, of course. Crystal nodded in her direction.

"Yeah, come in. Can you help with this one here first?"

She had pulled her dagger out of the guy's arm, and he was bleeding a fair bit.

"Sure thing," Ruth confirmed in a firm voice.

As the young medical officer approached, Crystal squatted next to his head, and she reminded him of her presence.

"I'm still here. Still watching you," she warned.

She saw him flinch, and cower involuntarily. Yep, she was fine with that answer. Ruth did not linger anyway. She was nice and quick, focused and efficient in her work. She cleaned his wound and dressed it up in record time, ignoring his pathetic sniffling, and then she hurried to take care of Karin, with whom she was infinitely warmer and more gentle. Meanwhile, Crystal kept her promise, and she stood watch over the injured guy until the police arrived. Only then did she let go of his weapon, and give it to them. Two officers cuffed the guy and got him up. As he stood, his arrogance seemed to make a speedy comeback. On their way out the door, he shot Crystal a nasty glare.

"I'll see you soon," he grunted. "Real soon."

"Oh, is that a threat?" she asked with a pleasant smile.

"You fucking..."

He almost said it, but suddenly shut up when it must have dawned on him that she was pushing him to incriminate himself in front of law enforcement officers. His face turned livid with rage. Crystal just shrugged. She was not interested in giving him more attention than he deserved now that he was under control, and could no longer hurt anybody.

"Have fun in jail," she simply said, as the police took him away.

Free to focus on the people who really mattered now, she went to check on Karin. The woman was in the middle of giving a full statement to the last remaining officer, and she started to weep all over again as soon as their eyes met. Crystal flashed her an instant, gentle smile.

"Hey, don't cry," she soothed. "It's okay, Karin."

"Oh, my God, I am so sorry, Crystal! He was waiting at the door and he grabbed hold of me as soon as I got there... He made me type in the code, and take him upstairs... All the while, I was thinking of ways to warn you, but I..."

"Really, it's fine," Crystal interrupted. "He was armed, and there's no way you could have stopped him on your own. Don't worry. It's over now, and I'm just glad no one's been hurt..."

She glanced at the woman's wrist, massively swollen, all black and blue... It looked painful, and she gave a sympathetic wince at the sight.

"Well, at least not fatally," she reflected. "How's she doing, Ruth?"

"Okay, but she'll need an X-Ray just to be on the safe side."

"Right," Crystal nodded. "Uhm, Officer; any chance she can ride with you?"

The female cop was amenable to the idea.

"No problem," she approved. "I'm headed straight back to the station, and the hospital is on my way. I can drop you off if you like."

"I'll go with you, Karin," Ruth offered.

"Great," Karin said in relief. "Thank you both so much."

Everything was falling into place, and as everybody relaxed a bit more, Crystal stood up, satisfied as well. She was planning on spending time with the other residents now, to check that they were all okay, and to reassure them that they were safe. As long as she had a say in the matter, there would not be a repeat of tonight's incident at the shelter. Not ever, that was for sure. She was also going to stop by the safe in the office and retrieve her Sig Sauer from it. Whether the Director liked it or not, she would be armed and ready when on duty from now on. Crystal remembered that she had better give the woman a call too, and fill her in on the events of the night so far.

"All right," she said. "Good stuff. I'll be…"

She was not able to finish her sentence. The words just died on her lips, as a sudden unexpected wave of dizziness washed over her, making her sway on her feet and stumble forward awkwardly. Crystal landed straight into the arms of the police officer, which, under different circumstances, and after a beer or two, she may have been more than happy to do. Certainly not now, though… Her legs failed her without even the slightest hint of warning, and every ounce of energy that she had before drained from her body. For a second there, she felt as if she might faint.

"Crystal, what's wrong?" Karin exclaimed.

"Hey, you okay?" the officer enquired in a calmer voice.

Crystal struggled to take a deep breath. *What the hell?*

"Mmm… Yeah," she mumbled. "I'm fine."

Truth be told, she was not in the least, and she also had no idea what the problem might be. She was grateful for the cop's immediate assistance, as the officer guided her toward the couch to sit down.

"Did he hit you?" she asked. "Are you hurt?"

Crystal shook her head, even as her vision blurred.

"No," she murmured, frowning hard. "Not hurt."

Hell, she was the one who had provided the pain, surely not the other way around. As a specialist combat instructor, and a talented martial artist, Crystal rarely if ever found herself on the receiving end of blows. Retired or not, she was still as sharp and fit as ever, and her skills were definitely on point. *Just breathe,* she told herself. She felt slightly better now that she was sitting down anyway, certainly alert enough to become aware of young Ruth's wandering hands on her body, prodding in places where she should not be investigating.

"Hey, get off," Crystal muttered impatiently.

She was wearing jeans, a pair of Reebok desert boots, and a loose, comfortable hoodie. It was black, probably the reason why no one had spotted the obvious any sooner. Ruth flashed her a confused look when she eventually did.

"What?" Crystal winced.

Ruth pulled up the front of her bloody jumper.

"This!" she exclaimed, pointing at her stomach. "Don't tell me you can't feel it!"

Karin looked, gasped in renewed agitation, and she turned white all over again; the cop let out a low, admiring whistle.

"Ooh," she commented. "That's got to hurt a hell of a lot."

Crystal stared in surprise at the deep laceration across her own side. Only then did she remember the one shot that the man had fired as she tackled him. *Damn...* The bullet had only grazed her, thankfully; singed a good chunk of flesh, but nothing worse.

She had not felt anything in the heat of the moment, but as her adrenaline wore off suddenly, and all at once, Crystal did feel her entire side start to tighten up, and burn as if someone were applying a flame thrower to it. The officer was right about it; it hurt like pure hell. Crystal looked up at Ruth, trying not to flinch at the same time.

"Oh, yeah…" she grunted. "Unlucky, uh?"

CHAPTER FOUR

Back for just a single day of hard-earned rest in her hometown of Denver, Colorado, the woman who hoped to become the next President of the United States still had no knowledge that CPT. Crystal J. Thor even existed... Although she would, soon. For now, after a great night's sleep in her own bed, and an early-morning run on the beautiful trails that started right behind her house, Abigail stood in the kitchen, frying pan in hand, making a batch of blueberry pancakes.

"What time's our flight to the East Coast tonight, Russ?" she asked. "Late afternoon, or something?"

He glanced up at her from his laptop.

"Bang on six o'clock. Hope it's on time."

"And we're going to Chicago first, right?"

"Yes. Then on to Detroit, Pittsburgh, and Philadelphia." He gave a half-smile as she delivered his pancakes and put a bottle of maple syrup in front of him. "Thanks, Boss."

"You want some more, or is that okay?"

"That's perfect. Smells and looks amazing, too."

"Great. Then stop acting so gloomy," she instructed.

His shoulders slumped at the soft rebuke, but it was true. Russell had been extremely subdued since Abigail had told him and his two colleagues about the call that she had received, over pizza in Bodega Bay. It was not good news, but still...

"Russell," Abigail added in a gentler tone. "Are you okay, really? Anything I can do to help?"

He shook his head, and gave her a grateful smile.

"No, I'm okay, Abi. It's just that I still can't get what Senator Birch said to you out of my head. My God! It's hard to believe, hey?"

Abigail sat down opposite him with her own plate, and she reached for the syrup. There were no real actual days off for her and her favourite campaign chief at the moment. Breakfast was as good a time as any to discuss strategy or current problems.

"Oh, I can believe it," she said. "Sure; it makes sense."

"But to threaten you with Kennedy…" he sighed.

"Like I said, Senator Birch was not the one issuing threats, Russ," Abigail reminded him. "But he is well aware that Foreign Policy, Healthcare, Education, and the Environment are not the only topics on my agenda, far from it. Since I've begun to make increasingly meaningful connections with high-ranking military officers who are willing to talk about what is really going on behind the scenes, it seems I have attracted the attention of some powerful people as well. The nasty kind. That's all."

Russell stared at her, his pancakes still untouched.

"Well, I'm glad you can rationalise it in this way, but as far as I'm concerned, if what Birch says is true, this is about a lot more than just people paying attention. You know?"

Abigail gave a quiet nod. Of course, she did.

"We knew this would happen. Right?"

"Right," he agreed reluctantly.

"All right, then. We'll be fine, I promise. Smile, and eat your pancakes."

Encouraged by her easy confidence, he took a bite, closed his eyes, and gave an instant grin of pure delight.

"Good?" she asked.

"Heavenly!" He laughed. "Thank you for looking after your staff so well, Madam President."

"Welcome. Good to see your gorgeous smile again, Red."

"Hey, stop trying to make me blush."

"Oh, but it is so entertaining," Abigail teased.

He chuckled, and carried on in a much lighter tone.

"No more doom and gloom, I promise," he assured her. "It was a shock to hear you relate Birch's warnings the other night, but I meant what I said to you back then, Abi. I'll be with you all the way, every step, no matter how hot, risky, or uncomfortable it may get."

She touched his arm, and rested a hand over her own heart at the same time.

"Thank you, Russell. I deeply appreciate it."

"This being said," he continued, "I think you need serious protection now. We've had this conversation before, and I know that you're not keen on the idea of having an armed guy follow you around 24/7, but as you tell me and the team so often, none of this is about us personally."

"Well quoted," she murmured. "It is about the mission."

"And as such, we need you safe and sound to keep it going. I say, let's not make it any easier for the men in the black suits to put a stop to your efforts. All right?"

She was grateful to him for not repeating the exact same words that her concerned and esteemed older colleague Senator James Birch, seventy-one, had said to her over that tense phone call. The man had more than fifty years of public service to his name, and a wealth of experience and wisdom to draw from in matters of state and politics. He also had a bunch of useful and loyal friends in high and classified places himself. Abigail knew he was on her side, that he could be trusted, and she did not take his warning lightly.

'You're definitely on their radar, Abigail,' the Senator had told her, after informing her that he was on a private encrypted line. *'They're watching you; you know? I'm sure I don't need to explain that these people will stop at nothing to protect their own interests. Think JFK, and enough said. If you become a problem that needs to be dealt with; disabled, or terminated, they will act swiftly and powerfully to do so. Their words, not mine... You understand. Be careful out there, kid. But keep going. You have my full support, especially since I know what you're really going for'.*

Abigail suppressed a cold shiver at the lingering memory of that tense phone call between them. She knew Birch well enough to realise that he would not have reached out to her in this way unless he absolutely felt that it was justified and necessary. Now, Russell was right. Worrying about threats and what *'They'* might want to do to her was no help at all, but focused action would go a long way to making her feel empowered and in control about it. She took a deep breath, and looked him in the eye.

"Okay, Russ," she declared. "I take your point, and it's time for me to make a change. In a way, I guess it's a sign that we're making progress in the right direction. So, do you have those security files you said you prepared for me with you now?"

"Sure."

"Let's take a look at them."

Russell seemed quite relieved. The last time he had brought up the topic of private personal security with her, Abigail had been a lot more reluctant. He moved quickly over to her side of the table, and pulled several folders out of his bag.

"I've been through loads of files already, and these are my final top three," he announced. "These guys are ex-military; all highly-qualified officers who enjoyed a brilliant career, but left somewhat disillusioned after realising the real truth behind US involvement in conflict abroad."

Abigail nodded, and she poured them both a generous dose of extra coffee.

"So, no rogue assassins among them then, you're sure?" she enquired. "No undercover CIA spies or Google agents on your list, I take it?"

Russell did not chuckle or even smile. He knew she was not joking, and he agreed. These were genuine concerns to take into account when deciding who to bring into their core inner circle.

"None of that as far as I could check," he promised. "And I was thorough with my research, trust me."

"I do," Abigail nodded, smiling briefly.

She reached for the first folder, which belonged to an Army officer named Jason Knapp, and quickly scanned through the information it contained. Nothing unusual to see there. His was a typical soldier's path, in a way. She glanced at his picture. *Yep, typical GI-Joe.* Impatiently, she grabbed the second folder, which, apart from a few minor details, was identical to the first.

"Says here that both these guys left the Forces to start their own private security business," she noticed.

"Yeah, that's right."

Abi looked up to meet Russell's gaze.

"So, how do you know they were disillusioned?"

"I spoke to them on the phone. They kind of said so."

"Really?" Abigail was unconvinced. "Mmm. Okay."

The last file was pretty much the same as the other two, and although she could see why Russ had selected the three men, she could not help but feel disappointed with the selection.

"So; which one?" he prompted.

"Mmm..." she winced, again. "I'm not so keen, Russ."

"Yeah, I can tell," he nodded wryly. "What's the problem? These are all great guys, you know? Well-trained, experienced, and with a solid mindset. I'd say perfect in all the ways."

"I know," Abigail replied. "Let me have another look."

She picked up the first folder again, but her reluctance was obvious.

"What were you hoping for?" Russell enquired curiously.

"Oh..." Abigail gave him a wan smile. "I guess some Han Solo character, a rebel-type soldier with a big heart and a cheeky smile who'd swoop in to save the day..."

"Are you describing your ideal bodyguard, or the woman of your dreams?" he joked.

Abigail was the one to colour lightly this time.

"Yeah, whatever," she muttered. "I guess given a chance to prove themselves, any of these guys would be able to fit in well with our group. I trust your judgment on these things, Russ, so why don't you pick one?"

"Are you sure?"

"Yeah, I'm sure..."

As he took the folders from her, Abigail spotted one more just peeking out of his bag.

"What's this one?" she asked.

"Oh, just another possible, but despite all my best efforts, I couldn't reach her on the phone to talk to her, so I didn't include her in the final cut."

Her? Abigail reflected, interested. She pulled the folder out, and did a sharp double-take at the sight of the one word printed on the front.

"*THOR?*" she said.

"That's her last name."

This time, Abigail could not help but give a slightly dazed, delighted smile in response.

"You selected a soldier named Thor to maybe become a part of our team, and join us in our efforts to overthrow the Military Industrial Complex, and all the rest of it?"

28

Russell looked at her blankly, obviously missing the deeper connection.

"Russ, you know that I have European Nordic roots, right?" Abigail told him.

"Yes... And?"

She did not enlighten him straight away, but opened the file instead, and stared at the two pictures on the inside page. The first one was the official service record snapshot that in this case, as pretty much always, pictured a stern-faced, unsmiling officer in uniform. Nothing too unusual about that, although the one difference that captured Abigail's attention was the woman's eyes; charcoal-black, perfectly focused, enticingly deep... Her intensity was palpable.

"Okay..." she murmured.

The second photo must have been taken out in the field. The background seemed somewhat desert-like, and Abigail was pretty sure that it was not Arizona... In the picture, the woman was standing in between two other soldiers who looked Middle-Eastern in appearance. Dressed in well-worn and dusty combat gear, a pair of Oakley sunglasses hiding her eyes this time, she was smiling directly at the camera. No helmet; short dark hair sticking out, as if she had been sleeping rough for a while. She looked fitter than the two guys, remarkably at ease, with an air of quiet confidence about her that made Abigail eager to find out more. She flicked to the officer's bio.

"Special Forces," she mused out loud. "Army Ranger duty."

She carried on reading, and her eyes stumbled over a single sentence.

"It says she was injured in Afghanistan while on a mission behind enemy lines..." Abigail looked up to Russell with an enquiring frown. "What the hell is a *'troublesome extraction'*, you think?"

"In Army speak, I'd say it's probably a clue that someone fucked up," he answered. "And that soldiers ended up getting hurt as a result, or even dying."

The file gave no further detail about that, nor as to the exact nature of the woman's injury. There was also no clue as to what she might be doing now, back on civvy street.

"I knew this one would catch your eye," Russ remarked with a teasing smile.

"Yes, and for all the right reasons actually," Abigail replied. "I would rather hire somebody who's not looking to do the job but motivated by our true purpose, than a bunch of professional security guys who'll only view it as a business opportunity. Not many women graduate from Army Ranger School; she must be pretty special. If nothing else, I'd like a second look at your wild card. Can you find her?"

"Of course, I'll get right on it. Just out of curiosity, why did you seem so taken with her last name? What's it got to do with your Norwegian ancestry?"

Abigail smiled, looking both amused and still amazed.

"Oh, quite a lot," she replied. "In ancient Norse Mythology, Thor is a hammer-wielding god linked to thunder and lightning, storms, strength, and guess what else?"

"No idea," Russell shrugged.

She flashed him an intent look.

"The protection of mankind. How about that, uh?"

"Nice," he grinned. "No kidding, you're serious?"

"No kidding," Abigail replied. "And you know what, Russ; I don't believe in coincidences. Let's track her down, and see if Captain Thor lives up to her famous name."

CHAPTER FIVE

Ruth looked surprised but excited when she opened the door to her Brooklyn apartment two days later, to find the woman that she considered her personal private hero standing there. Crystal was not known to pay her co-workers social visits after hours.

"Hey, Crys!" she grinned. "What's up, my friend?"

"Hey... Can you do me a quick favour?"

"Sure! What do you need?"

Sheepishly, Crystal opened her jacket to reveal the bloody washcloth that she was holding pressed against her side. Ruth's eyes grew wide.

"What happened to you now?" she exclaimed.

"I popped the stitches by accident. Can you fix it?"

"Of course. Come in. And what do you mean, 'by accident?"

Crystal walked in, automatically throwing a practiced look around the apartment. Although it may have seemed like it, she was not admiring the tasteful décor or checking out the eclectic collection of brightly-coloured Aztec rugs on the floor. She was just committing the layout of the place to memory, and checking to see where additional exits and windows might be, as she had been trained to do. Of course, intruders were not likely to come bursting through, nor was she to have to bail out in a hurry... Still, old habits die hard, especially the life-saving ones.

"Excuse the mess," Ruth apologised.

31

"Not at all. Excuse me for showing up unannounced..."

Ruth led her to her tiny bathroom, and invited her to take a seat on the side of the bath.

"You did well to, Crys," she assured her. "They would have made you wait ages if you'd gone to the hospital. Not their fault, mind you; just too many patients, and not enough doctors and nurses... Anyway, don't worry. I could do this sort of work with my eyes closed."

"Please, don't," Crystal muttered.

Ruth grinned at her exaggerated reluctance. She was pretty damn sure that a woman as tough and cool under pressure as Thor always appeared would not be afraid of needles.

"Let me have a look," she offered. "I promise it won't hurt, or at least not too much. Strip, Soldier."

Crystal shrugged out of her winter jacket and pulled her T-shirt over her head, keeping her Nike sports bra on. She caught Ruth's gaze on her body as she looked up; polite yet inquisitive, searching, and darkly serious as she flashed over the major scar that ran across her chest. *Yeah, well...* It was significant, all right. Crystal could not blame her from lingering a moment longer. Ruth looked mildly shocked and deeply curious, as she followed the scar's path with her eyes. It was a good half-inch wide, and thick, although paler now than it appeared at the beginning, in the early days when it used to be a nasty shade of purple. It started just under her left collarbone at the junction with her shoulder, and continued in a diagonal slash down to a point below her right breast. Crystal gave a low exhale. She had been without protective body armour at the time; she rarely discussed the reason why, or the circumstances that had led to her injury. As their gazes met, and Ruth bit on her lip in open wonder, she gave her an easy, confident smile in lieu of further information.

"Body's a bit battered," she said. "But still useful."

"Sorry, Crystal," Ruth murmured. "I didn't mean to stare at you like this."

"Why not?" Crystal shrugged, unperturbed. "Isn't it part of your job, after all?"

"Actually," Ruth chuckled, as her good mood returned; "I think you're right about that. Hey, you think they'll give me abs like yours in Basic Training?"

"I doubt it. These are limited edition. Hard to get."

"Ha! Good answer; I guess I'll make my own, then."

"Now; eyes up, recruit. Focus on the job, not my abs."

"Okay, let's see..." Ruth narrowed her eyes at the open wound and gave a disapproving shake of the head. "Yep, you need your stitches put back in. All three, actually. How did you end up breaking them? It was an accident?"

"Kind of," Crystal said. "Lifting in the gym."

Ruth flashed her a puzzled glance, and she put on gloves.

"Didn't someone advise you not to train too hard when you were at the hospital, at least for a few days?" she asked. "They really should have done."

"Yeah. They did... I forgot."

"All right, no problem. I'll sort you out."

Crystal was quiet as Ruth began to work, expertly piercing her skin with the needle, pulling the thread through into a solid stitch to close the wound. It was not painful, just uncomfortable. Crystal had experienced far worse in the past, and she remained stoic throughout.

"I feel so nervous, you know," Ruth admitted when she was almost done. "I know it's silly, but I just can't help it."

Crystal knew instantly what she was referring to, and she was not worried.

"It's normal to be nervous at first," she replied. "I was, too."

"Really? Even you? Wow!"

33

Ruth sounded surprised, hopeful; like she had been waiting to tell Crystal about the nerves for a long time, and as if it was a huge weight off her shoulders to finally admit it.

"Sure," Crystal shrugged. She rolled her eyes and flashed a crooked smile. "*Even me,* whatever the hell that's supposed to mean."

The young woman started to blush.

"Well, you know..." she reflected, her tone unusually timid. "My family aren't supportive of me joining up, and other than you, I don't know anyone else who has; especially not a woman. It's been great spending time with you at the shelter, talking to you about the Army, and observing how you conduct yourself."

"Oh? And what's that like?" Crystal enquired.

She was curious, and genuinely without a clue.

"You're focused, confident, and strong," Ruth replied. "Just like I always thought an officer should be. You're kind, patient, and you treat everyone with the same respect. You always give brilliant advice, too, and... And, uh..."

"What?" Crystal prompted, although she was wary of more gushy praise.

After a slight hesitation, Ruth carried on; eyes bright, voice full of enthusiasm and excitement. She started on a new subject, one that Crystal had never encouraged her to bring up.

"Well, I know you probably did some stuff in Afghanistan and Iraq that you can't ever talk about..."

She left her sentence unfinished, and Crystal was not about to complete it for her. It was true, and it was not just *some stuff,* but all of it. Classified, top-secret operations involving the Navy Seals, the CIA, and a bunch of other agencies. Black Ops, in other words, throughout her entire career and up until the very last mission, which had almost cost Captain Thor her own life. She was the only one of her crew to survive that particular accident.

Her teammates, her friends, the four guys that she considered her family... They had endured a terrifying, painful death, and there was nothing Crystal could do to save them. She was there when it happened. She had heard their screams. The memories kept her awake most nights. There was a reason she spent so much time in the gym, and a washboard stomach was definitely not it. Physical exhaustion was better than alcohol, drugs, or popping the pills that so many Army veterans became addicted to these days. She cleared her throat, and glanced at her stitches.

"All done?" she asked, impatient to move on.

"Almost, just hold on a sec." Ruth wrapped a tight bandage around her waist, and pulled back with a satisfied nod. "There. You're all set."

"Thanks for doing that, Ruth. I owe you one."

As Crystal got up, the young woman stood in front of her.

"Look, Crys," she said quickly, awkwardly. "Before I ship out to the Army, I just wanted to thank you for being such an amazing role model for me, and a wonderful friend, too. I think you're awesome, and I'll work hard to make you proud." She blushed again, as if suddenly embarrassed at her own emotional statement. "Uhm. Okay... Well, I guess that's it, then... Oh, and I dare you to break my stitches!"

Crystal could not help but smile at her obvious discomfort, and an even clumsier attempt at pretending that she was not that shy. The fact is, she really did like Ruth a lot.

"I'll be careful," she promised. "Now, I'm only going to say this once, so listen good, rookie."

Ruth leaned forward with an enthusiastic nod.

"Since we're being honest with each other, I just want to tell you that I think you're great too, kid," Crystal simply said to her. "Smart, caring, good with people, brilliant at your job... Pretty fit and strong when it comes to it too. Officer material, for sure."

"Oh... Thanks," Ruth exclaimed, blushing even harder.

She sounded equally bewildered and delighted at Crystal's words. She must not have expected this kind of response from the normally reserved and aloof Army Captain. Tears suddenly filled her eyes, and she paled in reaction.

"Oh, shit... Sorry, it's just those damn nerves..."

"Don't worry," Crystal said. "It's a myth that soldiers don't cry."

Ruth drew in a breath to speak but stopped suddenly.

"Yes, even me," Crystal chuckled. "Is that what you were about to say?"

"Yes..." Ruth giggled. "Soz, Crys."

Crystal passed a reassuring arm around her shoulders, and flashed her a gentle smile.

"I don't want to go too deep into the details, but when I got hurt in Afghan, a rescue unit took me to the closest FOB they could find. I was lucky that there was a British med team there on their way to someplace else. The lead surgeon was a woman, a Major in the Royal Artillery, as I later found out. I was in a bad way, in and out of consciousness. Apparently, at one point, she had her hands inside my chest, pumping my heart with her bare hands."

"Oh, my God," Ruth murmured. "Open-chest CPR. That's hardcore."

"I guess that's a good word to describe it," Crystal agreed. "Anyway, many hours later that day, or night, whatever it was, I woke up. She was there. She talked to me for a few minutes, told me I'd be okay, and knocked me out with some morphine. I can't even begin to describe to you how reassuring it felt to know that I wasn't alone, and to have a woman there, an officer, to tell me I had nothing to fear. I'll never forget her."

"Wow..."

"Wow, indeed," Crystal grinned. "Ruth, I know your family isn't keen on your choice of career, but as far as I'm concerned, it's a most meaningful and worthwhile decision. I'm sure they'll come round eventually. In the meantime, I'm with you."

Ruth pulled her into a tight hug.

"Thank you so much. It means a lot, you know."

"I know. Just watch the stitches," Crystal joked.

Ruth flashed her a piercing stare as she moved back.

"I'm sure you don't want to talk about this stuff, but do you miss it?"

"What? The Army?"

"Yeah. Do you wish that you could go back sometimes?"

Every damn day, Crystal almost blurted out. But she did not. What she missed about it was an illusion, or something that she could never get back anyway. Not her beloved crew, certainly; not the sense of genuine belonging that she had felt among the Armed Forces community; as for the conviction that her own sacrifice, and theirs, was for a just and honourable cause, this was the lie, the illusion. Hopefully, it would be a lot different for Ruth. Change was in the air; socially, culturally, and politically. Crystal did not want to share her disappointments with her, especially not right before the woman went off to Basic Training.

"Sometimes," she said with an ironic smirk. "But I don't miss the cold showers, nasty MREs, the drill sergeant yelling in my face, and…"

"All right, all right," Ruth interrupted, laughing now. "Stop it, please!"

Crystal squeezed her shoulder.

"Come on," she invited. "I'll buy you a beer if you want, and give you some good insider's tips to survive your first week of Basic."

"Awesome!" Ruth exclaimed. "Burger's on me!"

∞

It was just after nine thirty that night when Crystal arrived back at her apartment. Not too late, but Ruth had some packing to do, and neither of them were big drinkers. Still, they enjoyed a good few hours together, during which the soon-to-be Army recruit bombarded her with all sorts of interesting questions about her career. Crystal warmed up to the conversation eventually. She went home feeling restless, wondering how long she could stick it out at the women's shelter to make the money she needed. It was expensive living in New York, and she was not making any quick progress. Also, there was the big picture to consider. What was she doing, really? Ruth was on her way to Basic. It was the start of a new life for her, and an exciting adventure. With the medical skills that she already had, and her ambition to build on her existing knowledge to become a specialist military surgeon, no doubt she would do some good for the army, and humanity as a whole someday… Meanwhile, Crystal was saving up to buy a van so that she could go and hide in the mountains. It had seemed like a good idea once upon a time, but now, it hit her suddenly and without warning. *I'm only thirty-three years old… What the hell am I doing with my life?*

CHAPTER SIX

He was tall, well-built, dressed in expensive clothes. Standing in front of her door in the dimly-lit corridor. She liked it dark in that one spot, and she had purposely not fixed the bulb when it broke. Crystal stood quietly in the shadows, watching what he was doing for a while. He obviously had no idea that she was there, which told her something else about him. This guy had to be a civilian. Not military, certainly not CIA. He tried another knock, which of course, was not answered. The way that he sighed and cocked a disappointed hip after deciding that she really must not be home was endearing. Reassured that he must not be a threat, Crystal stepped up to him, as silent as a ghost.

"Hey," she said in a low, sharp voice.

"Oh, Jesus!"

He turned around, jumping in genuine surprise and a good dose of fright as he discovered her standing so close behind him. He looked straight into her eyes, and swallowed uncertainly. Abi had said that there was an interesting intensity about Thor, at least from the few pictures that he had provided in the file. Russell could well agree now that she looked intense, all right. *Damn scary, actually;* to be honest and blunt about it.

"Uh… Captain Thor," he stammered. "Hi. I'm glad you're here. I would have called, but I was unable to find a number for you…"

Not many people referred to her by her military rank these days, and Crystal felt a spike of what could only be excitement suddenly run down her spine. *Easy, soldier,* she told herself.

"There's no number," she said. "Who are you?"

He seemed more comfortable after she took a step back to give him a bit more space to breathe, and he quickly regained his composure. He stuck out his hand to her, and offered a warm, friendly smile at the same time.

"Captain, my name is Russell Stark; I am Candidate Abigail Christensen's Campaign Manager. Do you have a few minutes to talk?"

Crystal kept her eyes on him. She had heard of Christensen, of course. Despite a self-funded campaign, the woman seemed to be just about everywhere these days. On social media, TV, radio, in the streets, on car bumper stickers... If there was life on Mars, no doubt even those guys must have heard of the passionate, driven Congresswoman by now. Her message was controversial and different enough from all the other democratic hopefuls to have attracted Crystal's attention too. Now, she did wonder why in the world Christensen's campaign people were knocking on her door...

"Talk about what?" she asked.

"We need your help, Captain," he replied.

She stared at him for a few seconds. One thing was for sure, if Stark had shown up at her place like this at any other time, Crystal might have refused to even listen to what he had to say. She wanted to believe that she was done with her service with a capital *D*, no matter what new form it may try to take. She was aware that the belief may just be an attempt at fooling herself. *Nothing to lose, Crys,* she reflected. *Why not just hear him out, and see what you think after...?* She nodded briskly.

"Okay, you've got five minutes."

∞

The next afternoon, Crystal found herself in a room full of eager people, waiting for Abigail Christensen to make an appearance. Stark had shared just enough with her the previous night to make her curious. Crystal was fully aware that his calling her *'Captain'* every few seconds was a calculated move. And the words, *'We need your help'* had not come out of his mouth by accident either. The man knew which buttons to push. He was skilful, clever, charming... He seemed pretty genuine too, which matched the general vibe that came out of the Christensen camp. Crystal had never been attracted to make big bucks as a celebrity bodyguard in the past though, unlike some of her colleagues, and she told him so early on in the conversation.

"It won't be big bucks," he laughed. "Sorry."

"So, you need private security. Is there a specific threat?"

He seemed reluctant to get into the details of it.

"Why me?" Crystal insisted. "And why now?"

Again, he did not elaborate. Instead, he informed her that Christensen was due to hold an unscheduled Town Hall at the Firefighters Museum on 278 Spring Street the next day; inside the 9/11 Memorial Room, no less.

"Please, come to our meeting," Stark urged her. "Abi would be right here to see you now if she could, but she was scheduled to appear on Live TV tonight. You can have a private talk with her after the session. It'll be worth it, I promise."

Implied in the statement was the notion that Representative Christensen would be the one to answer her questions... Or not, for that matter. He wanted a definite answer about the town hall, but Crystal just gave him some evasiveness of her own.

"Maybe," was all she said.

Inside, she was cautiously interested. Spending the evening talking to Ruth about her old job had fuelled a sudden sense of dissatisfaction. After Stark was gone, Crystal pondered the pros and cons of his offer. Close-protection duty... Life on the road... Long hours; low pay. She snorted. *Yeah, sounds about right.* She had never been motivated by money or stability anyway. Feeling restless, as it dawned on her that she might want to accept the offer, she made herself a cup of coffee and sat on the couch with her laptop on her knees. She spent several studious hours online researching Christensen. In the end, way past midnight, Crystal decided that she had found enough material of interest to justify showing up at the town hall. Now, she stood at the back with a good solid wall behind her, and a view of the rest of the room and the attending crowd in front. It was diverse, to say the least. From Wall Street executives to young office or shop workers, tradespeople, pensioners, men and women, on their own or in twos and threes, and veterans, of course. Quite a few of those, actually. Crystal checked her watch. *Almost time for it to start...* Right on cue, all heads suddenly turned toward the door.

"A-BI! A-BI! A-BI!" the audience began to chant in unison.

Crystal spotted Stark walk briskly in, followed by a smiling camerawoman, and a bunch of staff all dressed in Christensen-branded gear. The rhythmic applause quickly grew in volume and intensity, and Crystal gave a faint smile as well. The crowd's enthusiasm and their excitement were contagious. Stark grabbed a microphone to introduce the star of the show.

"Good afternoon, everybody!" he announced. "It's great to see you all! Without further ado, please give it up for Colorado Representative, and the next President of the United States of America: ABIGAIL CHRISTENSEN!"

The audience roared in approval, and the woman that they were all waiting to meet finally walked out to take centre stage.

Crystal had been leaning easily against the wall, ankles crossed, hands in her pockets. Now she straightened up and almost stood at attention. Truth be told, she was unprepared for how seeing the candidate in real life would make her feel. She liked what she had read about her so far, but she did not really expect anything special from seeing the woman in person besides the usual. She was taken aback by her own reaction. In her career, she had met plenty of so-called important people; actual presidents, heads of state, foreign agency bosses, etc. It took a lot to impress Captain Thor, but all of a sudden, as she watched Christensen make her way forward, she actually felt it. *Wow… Talk about charisma, and presence as well…* The woman greeted each and every person that she encountered with a warm smile, a firm handshake, and some nice words.

"Hey, how are you? Hi, it's nice to meet you, guys. Thank you for coming… Hello, good to see you again…"

Microphone in hand, she stepped onto the stage and started with a few words of thanks for the museum and the supporters who had made the event possible.

"I want time for questions at the end and taking pictures if you want," she declared. "So, let's get right to it. I am so happy to be here in New York City! I love this place… Its energy, its vibe, its beautiful people. Yet, pollution is a big problem in New York; the city is one of the smoggiest in our nation. All over the country, our water is being poisoned; our air is being polluted; our soil is being depleted. The basic foundation of life on Earth is being eroded a little bit more every day. As your President, I will stand up to the big oil and fossil fuel companies to invest all in renewable energies, and bring about real change. Change for all of us… For our children, for theirs, and future generations to come. I am talking about the survival of our entire Human race here, nothing less. Let's do it together; right here, right now."

Christensen paused strategically to allow a generous round of applause.

"Damn right!" a man shouted from the front.

"We're all in this together!" someone else said.

Crystal kept quiet and her eyes fixed on Christensen. From all her research, she understood that the *'Humanity first'* theme was an important one for the Colorado Representative. All of her statements were so big-picture that it was hard to tell sometimes whether she was running only for US President, or a full-on representative of Planet Earth. The idea was subtle, but it was there all right if one paid attention; and Crystal certainly did.

"Now, let's talk about Healthcare," Christensen said.

She spoke eloquently in simple yet powerful terms. She was clear, to the point, and managed to make even the most complex subjects deceptively easy to understand. She knew her stuff, and she had plenty of common sense as well, which seemed to be a rare thing among politicians. After a captivating twenty minutes that just flew by, Christensen prepared to conclude.

"When I was growing up," she smiled, "I used to always try to protect other kids. I would go and speak to the bullies, reason with them, argue, debate, and work to bring everyone together. I got punched in the face a few times…"

"Still beautiful!" a man yelled, and people laughed.

Crystal smirked ironically. *Oh, please…* It was true, though. The woman really was striking. She reminded her vaguely of the actress, Mary McDonnell… Except with ash-blond hair styled in a long pixie cut, and luminous, smoky-grey eyes that sparkled with every smile. Crystal caught herself lingering on that smile, and getting unusually distracted, as Christensen gave an easy chuckle and continued.

"I guess there were clues early on that I was already on the path of service that has led me to stand in front of you today."

She swept her eyes over the audience, no longer joking now, but solemn and pretty sombre in her demeanour. The room quickly grew quiet and still. You could have heard a pin drop.

"I am asking you to put your trust in me, and to elect me as your President," Christensen declared. "Why? Because trust is at the core of everything I stand for. I cannot bear injustice of any kind; I detest lies and corruption; and I abhor the idea, which is true, sadly, that our government has been lying to our soldiers for decades and decades. No more lying! Let's be open about the human cost of war."

The room erupted into another round of applause and loud cheers, but Christensen carried right through this time. She had excellent timing. She sounded fierce. She used emotional words that were sure to strike a chord with her audience.

"My first job as President will be to bring our people home. I will not be sending anymore of our loyal troops to their deaths under false humanitarian pretences. Those that seek to control our government, the corporations that sacrifice the lives of our soldiers for money, oil, and power... And the dark hidden hand behind it all. You mark my words now: I'm coming for you."

"GO, ABI!" someone shouted.

Christensen nodded passionately.

"Help me get to the White House," she said, "and I promise that I will restore our values of integrity, honour, and respect to our government. I will disclose the..."

Everyone jumped when a furious voice suddenly rose from the far side of the room, interrupting her, and provoking a ripple of astonished gasps across the audience.

"What about all the immigrants and Muslim invaders?" the man shouted in a venomous tone. "What are you gonna do to stop those fucking terrorists, woman?"

CHAPTER SEVEN

Several people in the room immediately attempted to shut down the angry speaker, challenging him in the worst possible way. It was abundantly clear to Crystal that pointing out to him that he was out of line, urging him to calm down, and ordering him to show some respect, was never going to work.

"Fuck off!" the man snarled, as expected, and he just grew louder and more obnoxious.

Stark seemed a little concerned as he murmured something into Christensen's ear, but she gave a firm shake of the head, and Crystal read the words off her lips. *'No, I've got this'*. He winced in reluctance and looked like he might argue, but she ignored him. She stepped forward, microphone in hand, total confidence written all over her face. *Too much?* Crystal wondered. People were shouting at each other in that corner. Not getting physical just yet, but it was always a possibility. She moved forward in case someone made a stupid move... And someone did, all right; but incredibly, it was Christensen. With great aplomb and not an ounce of hesitation, the Congresswoman stepped off the stage and right into the middle of the rowdy group. Crystal stared at her in disbelief and amazement.

"Excuse me... Excuse me! Thank you. Let's calm it down," Christensen instructed. "Everybody's allowed to speak here, so let's make it happen. What's your name, my friend?"

She addressed the disrupter directly, looking him in the eye and projecting such strong energy outwards that he was lucky not to get blown off his feet. Everybody else grew respectfully quiet around her, and gave her some space. For the second time that day, Captain Thor was impressed with the politician.

"Name's Mike," the man sniggered. "I just want to say my piece, okay?"

"Mike; right," Christensen acknowledged with a curt nod. "I heard your question and I will answer it right now. First of all, let me address the issue of Muslim invaders. It is an easy one to settle, since the idea is a manipulative construct with no actual basis in reality."

People clapped, the atmosphere did settle, and Christensen finally returned to the stage. Stark, for one, looked like he might pass out in utter relief. Crystal was pleased as well. There was something off about the disrupter, and she did not like the way that he kept staring at Christensen. At first, she thought he may just be drunk. Then, she wondered if he might not suffer from mental illness. Now, she realised that this had the potential to be something else a lot more sinister. He was dressed in jeans, black boots, and a thick bomber jacket. Long black hair tied in a greasy ponytail. Probably in his early-thirties, fit and strong. Something about him just did not add up, and Crystal was not happy about it. She scanned the room for any sign that there might be at least some level of security around. A woman in a Museum uniform stood looking bored at the far end of the room. Definitely not it. Crystal remained fully alert. Meanwhile, Christensen finished outlining her plans for immigration reform, and she moved on to another questioner. Crystal noticed the man shuffle out of the room after one last snarky glance toward her. She followed him down the stairs, careful not to be noticed. She watched him go through the main doors and disappear outside.

∞

Abigail had finished her speech and was now meeting people one-to-one, posing for pictures and selfies, etc., by the time she spotted Thor walking into the room. Midnight-black eyes sought her out across the crowd. From what Russell had told her of his encounter with her the night before, Abigail was not convinced that she would turn up. But the woman was the only one on his list who had piqued her interest, and Abigail was not prepared to compromise. Even without Senator Birch's chilling warning, she was an increasingly polarising public figure, and certainly, one of the most controversial presidential candidates of recent times. Abigail knew that she needed to watch her own back, or have someone do it for her. She observed Thor as she made her way across the room, and again, something about her made her pay attention. The soldier was tall, lean, fluid and lithe in her movements. Her clothes; blue jeans, combat boots, and a winter jacket unzipped to reveal a simple black T-shirt underneath, only highlighted her athleticism. Abigail kept her eyes on her as Thor made her way through the crowd. People moved out of her line without prompting, as if sensing unconsciously that there must be something special about this woman, with the dark crew cut, purposeful stride, and youthful looks that did nothing to hide her true toughness.

"Captain Thor. I'm glad you could come."

Abigail stepped forward to greet her. Both her tone and her handshake were attuned to the moment, warm and intimate in a manner that she reserved for meaningful personal encounters. Thor held her gaze easily as she took her hand, a faint but polite smile floating on her lips.

"Representative," she nodded. "I enjoyed your talk. It's a pleasure to meet you."

Abigail had wrongly assumed that she had just walked in. She was pretty good at scanning crowds from the stage when she made a speech; picking out potential detractors, unhappy people who might challenge her later, like this more recent one; or simply influential members of the community she may want to mention by name. She liked the fact that Thor had managed to remain invisible up until now. It boded well for the future.

"We're almost done here," she declared. "Would you like to ride back to my hotel for a chat?"

"Okay," the officer agreed.

"Perfect. Walk with me."

Russell took charge, as he always did after an event of this kind, facilitating Abigail's exit. Some people always tried to stop her for a lengthy chat at this point, to pull her aside for a private rant which invariably focused on their inflexible neighbour, sick pet, or unruly children. Important topics fort them, but Abigail could hardly afford to dedicate this kind of one-to-one time to all who sought to steal it from her.

"Thank you for coming. I'll see you soon. All right, thanks. Bye, everybody!"

With Thor by her side, and armed with a friendly wave and an ever-ready, genuine smile, Abigail made her way to the door through a crowd of well-wishers, and across the hallway to the emergency stairwell. She turned to flash her campaign manager a grateful wink.

"Thanks, Russ. Nicely done."

"If you take the stairs all the way down, our car's just across from the back exit door," he said. "You can't miss it, it's the one with all the *Vote for Me* stickers over it. Don't be too dazzled. I'll be right with you; I just need to grab the camera off JoAnn."

"All right, got it," Abigail chuckled.

She noticed Russell glance toward Thor, looking for all the world like he was sizing up the competition. She was amused to witness her lack of reaction to his joke about the car. Russell's brand of humour was an acquired taste. The former soldier also did not seem like the kind to force herself to smile when she did not feel like it. *Good*, Abigail thought. She liked authenticity.

"Shall we?" she invited.

Thor fell into step with her, and at the bottom of the stairs, casually slipped in front of her to be the first one out. It was not lost on Abi that she checked both sides of the alleyway before stepping aside, and holding the door open for her to follow.

"Thanks," Abigail nodded.

"No problem."

Thor flashed a brief smile, allowing a tantalising glimpse of the woman behind the stern façade of the Army officer to appear for just a second. It was a side of her that Abigail was interested to discover more of... Whereas the files on the other guys who had made Russell's final list included an overview of what else might be a part of their lives besides their careers, the one on Thor had been strikingly devoid of personal information. Abigail saw her glance toward the flashy Ford Explorer parked a short distance away, and raise a thoughtful eyebrow. She did not have to say anything for Abigail to immediately react.

"Yes; I know, Captain," she said with a touch of impatience. "We're dead easy to spot, but that's the whole point. Throughout this campaign, I have to be visible. I must appear approachable and relatable to people. The car's a marketing tool; a good one."

Taller by a few inches, Thor looked down to rest her coal-black eyes on her, and Abigail went a little still inside. She was taken by the warmth in the woman's gaze. The captain looked amused at her irritation, and it forced a smile out of Abigail too.

"Let's hear it," she declared. "You think the car's a security issue; right?"

Thor shook her head just once as it began to snow.

"I have no problem with your vehicle," she said.

"Really? Well, okay..."

"Just with you travelling in it."

Abigail could recognise sound advice when she received it, and this was definitely one. It should have occurred to her to organise a second car for herself before, to be fair. But she had been so focused on her mission, and on the campaign... She had blissfully avoided spending too much time thinking of anything else. Denial? *For sure,* she admitted to herself.

"That's a good point, Captain."

"Do you always park at the back of a venue?"

"Yes... We tend to do that quite a bit."

Thor did not comment, and Abigail got the idea that she did not approve of the practice either. They headed toward the car at a fast pace, fighting a vicious wind and thickening snow. Abigail pulled her coat collar up for added protection. She glanced at her companion. Thor did not seem to have even noticed the weather. She walked with her head up, fully alert and switched on. Her attitude was reassuring to Abigail, yet sobering at the same time. *This is it,* she thought, *about to hit crunch time.* The good news was that it seemed as if Captain Thor was interested in joining her team; she would not be here now otherwise. Abigail hoped that Russell had done his research well, and that the officer would not just disappear once she explained to her everything that was at stake. On a personal level, the realisation that Abigail now required the services of an ex-Army Ranger to protect her really did bring home the fact of everything she had to lose. Or rather, one thing: her life. She gave a loud, heavy sigh at the thought, and Thor shot her a penetrating glance as they reached the car.

"Everything all right, uhm…?"

"Please, call me Abi," Abigail replied.

"Sure, and you can call me Crystal," Thor replied. "Crys, if you prefer. So; are you okay, Abi?"

Abigail sensed genuine kindness and sincerity in her voice, and her chest tightened. Russell had teased her about the woman of her dreams, and Abi was very well aware that Captain Thor, *Crys*, ticked many if not all of the boxes on her list. A handsome soldier with a beautiful smile, tough as nails, and just as fiercely protective… It was already clear to Abigail from her demeanour around her that Thor must be a natural at that. *To protect and to serve…* Abigail gave a quiet exhale. She did not consider herself weak by any standard, but it did occur to her that if she had to go into battle, this woman might make an ideal partner for her. She mused on the word, *'partner'*, and looked up into her eyes. Although she had hidden it really well from the rest of her team, Abigail's teeth had been on edge since that warning call from Birch. She had been feeling extremely tense for several days, and the way that Thor returned her gaze, so beautiful and sharp, did nothing to calm her nerves.

"I think I'll feel better once I've had a chance to fill you in," she admitted.

The captain just gave her a quietly reassuring nod.

"I'm here to listen," she promised. "And help if I can. I was thinking that we could…"

Her sentence ended with an involuntary gasp. The attack occurred so fast that Abigail had no time to think, or even realise what was happening. Let alone be scared…

CHAPTER EIGHT

It was many years since Crystal had felt excited or even moved by a politician's speech. From personal experience, she believed that a majority of them could not be trusted, and actually were dangerous. It was the same for journalists, with only a few rare exceptions. So-called independent reporters were mere repeaters of the corporate elite's lies. *'Corporate media'.* The label said it all, really... Since leaving military life behind, Crystal had grown steadily more irritated by, and dissatisfied with every aspect of mainstream society. She wanted out of this madness. And yet... There she was now, incredibly. Hanging out and getting friendly with one of those politicians she did not trust, and also keen to take a new job that would put her right back in the middle of a system that she did not want to be a part of. It was nuts, as was the fact that for the second time in just a few days, someone was coming at her with a lethal weapon.

"Move!" she yelled.

Crystal reacted with lightning-speed efficiency. She shoved Christensen aside, and raised her arm to block his strike. *Fuck!* It was a devastating blow. Anybody else but her, and he may have broken their forearm with that hit. In a flash, Crystal recognised the irate individual who had tried to disrupt the meeting earlier.

53

I knew it… She had followed him outside, and watched him walk away. She had lingered in front of the entrance for a good fifteen minutes afterward to make sure that he was really gone. She had sensed something odd about him besides the obvious, and now, it was all being confirmed. Crystal had to take a quick step back to avoid losing an eye. He carried a slim dagger, standard-issue in the Marines. When she slipped, her boot sliding to the side in the fresh snow, he crashed into her with alarming power. Crystal managed to stay on her feet and avoid another life-ending slash of his blade. She found new purchase in the snow, and delivered a blinding kick to the side of his head that put her right back in charge of the fight. Before he was able to recover, she launched a second strike to disarm him. There was a sharp, sickening snap as she smashed his wrist bone. He dropped the dagger.

"Hold it!" she yelled, as he attempted to retrieve it.

He looked up. Crystal reached behind her back for her gun. She was not licenced to carry a concealed weapon in NYC, but because of the nature of her appearance at Christensen's event, she figured that it would not hurt to bend the rules a little. Now, she was hoping not to have to fire, but she would if she had to. Her main goal was to keep him away from Christensen, and if it took shooting a bullet in his leg to achieve, she had no problem with that. She saw understanding flash across his eyes as she whipped the side of her jacket open. He snarled. It could have been due to the snowflakes swirling in the air, or the added lack of visibility in the glare of street lights, but for a brief moment as well, his face shifted in the most disturbing way… Of course, it would take more than an ugly grimace to scare Captain Thor. She wrapped her fingers around the handle of her Sig Sauer and brought it out in front of her in one swift move. Amazingly, he still took a step toward her. She pointed the gun straight at his head.

"Freeze!" she ordered.

He shot a predatory glance toward the car, and Crystal did not dare do the same. She had him in her sights, and yet, he still appeared primed and dangerous. Clearly, he had not given up.

"Try it, and you're dead," she warned him.

A door slammed in the background, and from the corner of her eye, Crystal spotted Stark walk out and immediately come to an abrupt stop as he took in the scene. All in all, they were not even three minutes into this situation, but Crystal decided that it had gone on for plenty long enough all the same. One way or another, she needed to put a stop to it.

"Get down on your knees," she ordered. "Down! Now!"

Three things happened next in rapid succession, not what she wanted. The man's eyes, hard and unblinking from the start, took on an unnaturally reddish glow; a hurricane-force gust of wind blew a cold flurry of snow into Crystal's face. She blinked to clear her vision, and that was all it took. In less than a second, the guy was gone. *What the hell happened?* Crystal whipped her head around. He was still there; she was sure of it...

"Stay where you are," she yelled toward Stark.

Finger light on the trigger, but not taking any chances now, Crystal quickly scanned the area. It was infuriating. She could no longer see him, but she could feel his presence, lingering in the air like a hard, oppressive weight across her chest. Heart racing in tension, she picked up his dagger and shoved it in her jacket pocket. She checked under the car, and up the fire escape ladder which the vehicle happened to be parked almost directly under. *What a damn stupid idea...* At least, the sense that they were not alone disappeared. It was sudden, which was just as strange as all the rest of it, but it allowed Crystal's heartrate to start to return to normal. She lowered her weapon, took a slow breath. Her respite was short-lived, as Stark's agonised cry reached her.

"Abigail!" he gasped. "Oh, my God!"

Crystal instantly rushed to their assistance, disturbed at the note of profound fear in his voice. She remembered grabbing hold of Christensen earlier, and pulling her out of danger's way. Roughly, admittedly; but not hard enough to cause her any harm. Yet, Stark sounded like something might be seriously wrong with her, and Crystal pursed her lips as she suddenly recalled seeing a dark stain on the attacker's dagger when she had picked it up. Her worries were soon confirmed. She found the Congresswoman on the ground, leaning against the car for support, her face whiter than snow. Testament to her strength of character was the fact that she seemed more intent on reassuring her campaign manager than putting herself first.

"No 911. No police, no press," she said firmly.

"But you're hurt!" he argued. "You are, aren't you?"

"It's nothing, Russ," Christensen insisted calmly. "I'm fine. Start the car, please. I want to get out of here quick; we can talk later."

He looked dumbfounded, but nodded as she gave him the keys. By some miracle, the alleyway was still empty of passers-by or selfie-takers. It was a good thing, probably due to the fact that a major snow storm was developing. Crystal caught Abigail shivering.

"Fast as you can," she instructed Stark.

As she knelt beside her, the Congresswoman automatically reached out for her hand. She seemed to know instinctively that there was no need to fake it with the ex-soldier, and her easy countenance slipped. She winced in pain.

"How bad is it?" Crystal murmured.

"I can move my arm. And my fingers too. So, probably not that bad…"

"Okay, good," Crystal said tersely.

She shared Christensen's desire to jump in the car and leave as quickly as possible. They could decide what to do and where to go once they were safe. Crystal did not feel it there at all.

"Hold on to me," she instructed.

Gritting her teeth, Christensen passed her good arm around her neck. Crystal registered the involuntary gasp of pain that escaped her lips as she pulled her upwards with her, in spite of the Congresswoman's best efforts to remain stoic. She was a real trooper, for sure, although when she swayed unsteadily on her feet and slumped against her, Crystal realised that she might be about to pass out. Good thing they did not have far to go. She instantly tightened her grip around her waist, taking up most of her weight.

"Stay with me, Abi," she urged.

Stark had the engine running, both hands on the wheel and ready to go. He shot an anxious glance over his shoulder as Crystal pulled the back door fully open, and helped a struggling Christensen to slide onto the seat.

"Damn... Damn. Goddammit!" he exclaimed.

Crystal did not bother asking what his problem was, since it was so obvious. She would have felt pissed off and frustrated in his place too. The whole exit procedure following the event had been an absolute shocker. Stark was the guy in charge of it all, and Christensen had paid the price of his inefficiency. Still, the man was no security expert, and it would be unfair to blame the incident solely on him.

"Drive," she ordered.

"Nearest hospital is Bellevue," he announced as he stepped on the accelerator. "Eleven minutes via 6th Avenue and W 23rd Street."

"Great, Stark," Crystal nodded. "Go for it, man."

"No," Abigail murmured. "Don't go there."

She was resting with her head back against the seat; still as pale as before, but at least her eyes were open, and clear. Russell shot her a bewildered look through the rear-view mirror.

"What do you mean, '*no*'?" he argued. "You were stabbed, for God's sake!"

"But the second we show up at a medical centre, the press will drop on us like a bunch of flies," Abigail reasoned. "I don't want that to happen."

She leaned forward, trying to shrug out of her coat.

"Let me help you," Crystal volunteered.

"Thanks. Hopefully, it won't be too much of a problem…"

It occurred to Crystal that she spoke as if she was trying to convince herself that nothing had actually happened, which was probably easier to deal with in the moment than acknowledging the truth that someone had just tried to kill her. Crystal noticed tiny droplets of sweat on her forehead, as well as the fact that she was still trembling. Shock was working its way through her system, and she wanted to make sure that this was all it was. If Crystal thought for even one second that the Congresswoman might be putting her life at risk by refusing to head straight to a hospital, she would not hesitate to override her instructions.

"Can I have a look?" she asked.

Christensen gave a quiet nod, and as Crystal moved closer, she fixed her with a burning stare.

"Thank you," she murmured. "Without you, Captain…"

"Crys," Crystal reminded her gently.

"Crys. You saved my life… Thank you."

Tears filled her eyes as she actually spoke the words, and it must all have started to really sink in then. Abigail blinked in reluctance, and she clenched her fists when she noticed herself shaking. She seemed both irritated and even embarrassed at her body's visceral reaction, and her own inability to regain control.

Strong leaders never like to show vulnerability... Crystal felt a rush of pure sympathy for the woman that came from deep within her heart. She seized on the first thing she could think of to help.

"I hope that means I get the job, uh?" she muttered. "After all that..."

The joke did the trick. Abigail seemed grateful to her for the shift in focus, and she relaxed, head rolling back against the seat. She touched Crystal's leg briefly, and managed a weak chuckle.

"You sure aced your interview..."

"I sure did, hey," Crystal grinned.

She undid the top buttons on her blouse and slipped it over her shoulder, aware that Christensen kept her eyes firmly fixed on her face the entire time. Hot and searching, slightly hazy from the pain, and Crystal wondered what might be on her mind. The stare was distracting, although not unpleasant. Finding blood on her white bra strap was more of an issue.

"Abi, can you lean forward a bit?"

As the woman did, Crystal narrowed her eyes at a spot just below her right shoulder. It was a nasty wound; the blade must have penetrated several inches deep. The skin on either side of the cut was swollen, dark, and the bruise was already spreading across her back.

"Is it okay?" Abigail murmured.

She leaned against her side, unable to maintain the position without support.

"You'll be alright," Crystal replied. "Just a sec."

She took the expensive silk scarf that the Congresswoman had been wearing earlier, which was still clean, fortunately, and pressed it carefully against the wound. She felt her stiffen.

"Sorry... Okay, you can lean back now."

Christensen looked even whiter, and weaker too. Without thinking about it, Crystal took her hand back in hers.

"Look; you really need that wound disinfected and closed up properly," she said. "And a tetanus shot as well, probably. You can't just ignore this one, and hope it heals on its own."

"We're almost there," Stark announced. "Bellevue."

He glanced in the mirror, as if he knew already that his boss would not set foot in the hospital even if a gun were pointed at her head. He knew why. If the media got wind of this, a storm of biblical proportion would be unleashed on the back of it; their campaign would be buried under lurid headlines. The people who pulled the strings behind the scenes would make sure of it, and *they* would win.

"You have to get that thing looked at," Crystal repeated.

Abigail gave her a soft glance, but she shook her head.

"Negative," she replied. "I'm not going to Bellevue."

CHAPTER NINE

Ruth's eyebrows shot up to the ceiling when Crystal greeted her with exactly the same sentence that she had used to ask for help the previous night.

"Hey. Can you do me a quick favour?"

"No way!" Ruth exclaimed. "You broke your stitches again? I mean, the ones that *I* put in? I can't believe it! It's like the worst case of déjà vu; just like a glitch in the Matrix!"

Things got weirder, and she did a sharp double take at the sight of a woman that she had only ever seen on YouTube up until that night, slowly approaching her door with the help of a tall blond guy that Ruth thought she recognised as well.

"Uh..." she frowned. "Are you..."

"Questions later; let's go inside," Crystal instructed.

Eyes wide, Ruth stood aside to allow the small group in. Her puzzled expression turned to delight as she confirmed that she was not hallucinating; the great Abigail Christensen, another one of her favourite heroes, indeed had just entered her home.

"I'm such a big fan of your work, ma'am... Such a fan!" she beamed.

"Thank you," Abigail replied in a strained voice, but with a genuinely grateful smile. "May I sit down?"

"Of course! Please." Ruth frowned again in deep wonder, and she glanced toward Crystal. "So... You guys want a beer?"

"Water would be great, if you don't mind," Russell replied. He quickly held out his hand to her, along with a gentle smile. "I'm Russ. Nice to meet you. And thanks for your help."

"Uhm…" Ruth was still none the wiser. "Sure. What help?"

She turned in time to see Crystal grab a spare Ziploc bag off the table, leftover from her packing in prep for Basic Training, and drop a bloody dagger into it. The young woman blinked in amazement at that, and as her Special Forces friend then held it up to the light, and stared at it with such intense focus that it looked as if she was trying to burn a hole through the plastic.

"Uhm, Crys?" she said.

Stark went to sit next to the Congresswoman, his attention only focused on her. It suddenly occurred to Ruth that she did not look very well at all. What the hell was going on…?

"Crystal," she repeated.

"Yeah. What?"

"What's happening?"

Christensen opened her eyes long enough to fix her with a penetrating glance, as if assuring herself that she really wanted to go ahead with this. She looked toward Crystal, thoughtful and grave, and eventually gave her a small nod of approval.

"All right, Ruth," Crystal said. "Look, the less I tell you, the less you'll have to keep quiet about. What happens here tonight needs to stay strictly in between us. Are we clear?"

Ruth squared her shoulders back, as it dawned on her that the reason Christensen was here had to be serious, and not just motivated by the urge to meet a Brooklyn resident for a nice chat and a cold beer; no matter how cool that would have been.

"Okay, Crys," she answered instantly. "I've got you."

Crystal summarised the situation in a few brief sentences, leaving out most of the details about the attack, focusing only on what Christensen really needed from the young medic.

"Sure," Ruth nodded confidently in reply. "I can help with that, and the tetanus shot as well. And as for keeping it quiet, you were never here, my friends."

Crystal squeezed her shoulder.

"Thanks, girl. You're awesome."

She sat in the lounge with Stark, as Ruth disappeared into the bathroom with Abigail and closed the door behind them. The man was dead silent. He looked preoccupied and glum. Crystal nudged his shoulder.

"Hey," she said. "What's wrong with you?"

He sighed, and gave a frustrated shake of the head.

"This whole thing," he replied. "Ambush in an alleyway in the middle of a snow storm; getting patched up in somebody's bathroom... Feels like scenes from a Hollywood movie. *Minority Report*, or something like that."

"Great movie," Crystal remarked.

"I know. And damn scary as well, uh?"

"That, too." She shrugged casually. "Oh, well."

He chuckled this time, and flashed her an approving grin.

"Yeah, that's the attitude. Feel the heat and keep going."

She spotted fierce intelligence in his gaze and a huge dose of resolve and determination as well. Crystal returned his smile. She was beginning to like the guy. He was clearly dedicated to Christensen and the campaign, and he had proved himself to be dependable, flexible, and a quick thinker during times of trouble. Now, he leaned his forearms over his thighs, and looked at her intently.

"So; you're with us now," he stated. "Right?"

Crystal detected hope, eagerness, and something else in his voice as well that she was not so sure that she liked to hear; it was pure tension... And a hint of fear? She leaned forward, matching his position, and held his gaze.

"What are you not telling me, Russ?" she asked.

He pursed his lips and glanced toward the bathroom door, where his powerful boss and Ruth were still busy taking care of her shoulder.

"I find it strange," Crystal carried on, "that you come to me with a job offer one day, all nice and matter-of-fact about it, like it's just a formality; and then, some lunatic makes an attempt on your candidate's life the very next day. Something doesn't add up here. You know what I'm saying?"

"Mmm," he muttered with a frown. "Yeah."

"If you guys want me on your team," Crystal concluded in a much sharper tone, "you'd better tell me the truth. Level with me, and do it quick, or I'm out."

"We're not lying to you, Captain," he protested.

"You're holding back; same thing. And call me Crys."

She spoke in a firm yet not unfriendly tone; just letting him know that she had no personal stake in this game, and that she could simply walk away any time she felt like it.

"Crys," he grumbled. "Look, I know that Abigail will want to handle this conversation with you, but..."

A car backfired in the street down below. Nothing unusual in New York, to say the least, but he was startled all the same. He shot a suspicious glance behind his back, as if to check that no one was standing there. Crystal frowned in renewed wonder at his behaviour. No one had a clue that they were here. She was armed and dangerous. Why was he still acting so scared?

"But... What, Russell?" she pushed him impatiently. "Has someone been stalking her in recent times? Has this been going on for a while?"

He threw her a dark and gloomy look.

"They're always watching," he murmured. "Always."

"*They?*" Crystal almost screamed. "Who?"

"Did you notice anything weird or unusual about that guy earlier?" he asked.

Again, avoiding the question. Crystal was not amused, and quickly losing patience with his politician's games.

"Yeah," she snorted darkly. "Most people don't try so hard to gauge my eyes out upon first encounter. That was unusual, all right."

"I mean, about his body; his physical appearance," Russell insisted. "Did you notice anything different about that?"

Crystal took a few seconds to review the fight in her mind's eye. The man had been strong, for sure, perhaps unusually so. A professional hitman hired to get rid of Christensen? *Unlikely*, she mused. In order to dispatch someone with a dagger, you had to get up close and personal, and Crystal did not wish to linger on the memory of how she knew that fact. Then, if he was there to kill the candidate, why attract attention to himself when he was in the room? It made absolutely no professional sense. And as for the other stuff... Well; Crystal knew that it was only due to poor weather conditions, and the unsteady glare from a broken street light. It had looked to her as if the guy's face had slipped at some point, and his eyes turned red, but this was just a trick of the light. Then again, Russell was asking strange questions about his appearance, and acting bloody weird himself.

"What are you talking about?" she asked.

"Now it's your turn to hold back on me," he remarked.

"It was dark; windy. I had snow in my eyes. He didn't look weird when I saw him in the room, just shifty. Same thing when we were outside, I guess..."

Russell locked eyes with her.

"What?" she repeated. "Don't get all spooky on me, Russ."

"The people we're up against," he murmured, as if she had not said anything. "They're not like us, you know."

∞

Ruth and Abigail both reappeared before Crystal could get to the bottom of this enigma. The two were all smiles, and high-fiving each other. Christensen appeared high as a kite.

"Russell, would you mind taking the *Vote-for-Me* car back to the hotel, please," she instructed. "I'm going home with Captain Thor."

Crystal pulled Ruth aside.

"Give me a Sitrep," she demanded.

"Sure, I'd love to," the young woman replied, looking like this was all good fun for her. "The knife went through a layer of muscle in her shoulder, and she'll be pretty sore for a few days. Other than that, no serious or long-term damage to speak of. I disinfected the wound, gave her a Tetanus shot, and some fast-acting painkillers as well. All she needs now is a nice warm bed and some shut-eye time."

"Okay. Thanks for all your help once again."

"No problem, I'm happy to do it. She calls you *'my gorgeous bodyguard'*, by the way."

"She calls me what?" Crystal frowned.

"Just happy drugs in her system," Ruth chuckled, looking amused at her reaction. "It won't last for very long. But is it true? You're on her security detail now?"

"I don't know yet. Maybe."

A grinning, swaying, drunk-looking presidential candidate came over to grab hold of Ruth, enfold her in a grateful hug, and kiss her on the cheek.

"Thank you for patching me up, sweetie," she said. "All the best of luck with your Basic Training. You've got this thing, trust me."

Ruth pulled back with a goofy smile on her face, blushing hard. Crystal suppressed a smile at her obvious pleasure.

"I'll vote for you," Ruth promised.

"Me too," Christensen replied, nicely confused. She turned toward Crystal and looked her up and down in a decidedly non-PC correct manner that made her campaign manager cough in sudden embarrassment. "Shall I call us an Uber, my dear?" she enquired.

It was hard for Crystal to make an informed decision when she was still unclear about the nature of the threat that they were facing. She glanced at Russell, and raised a quizzical eyebrow.

"What do you think? Should we do that?"

The look on his face told her that he was not keen to drive their campaign car on his own, and she could not blame him. Crystal reflected that it might be a good thing to keep the small team together for the time being anyway. It had been a traumatic end to their day. Travelling in an unmarked vehicle also made sense.

"Can you get us a car, Russ?" she asked.

"You got it," he nodded, relieved. "Sure thing."

Outside the window, the wind was howling, and it was still snowing hard.

"At this rate, we'll need a team of huskies and a sleigh!" Abigail announced with great enthusiasm. "Let's do it Colorado-style. Who's with me?"

The magic drugs stopped making her so giddy at about the same time that their Uber showed up. Russell jumped in the front next to the driver. He kept him engaged, entertained, and his attention off the back seat for the whole thirty-minute drive back to their hotel on the edge of Central Park. Ruth had offered Christensen one of her baseball caps to wear. It kept her face nicely hidden, and the driver never gave her a second glance.

Twenty minutes into the journey, she winced as the car went over a series of speed bumps. Crystal automatically laid an arm around her shoulders.

"You can lean on me if it helps," she murmured.

"Yes. Thanks… I am so sorry about this."

"Don't worry about it, Abi. Just rest."

Christensen slumped against her shoulder with a weakened sigh. She sounded bone-tired, and Crystal glanced down to see her face better.

"Are you in a lot of pain?"

"Not really… Just beyond tired."

"All right, then. We'll be there soon."

Christensen was quiet for a few seconds, resting against her shoulder, breathing slowly, and then Crystal felt her looking at her. She met her gaze, trying not to reflect on how intimate their embrace felt. It was a long time since she had held a woman in her arms like this, in such a close and protective grip. The last time that she had, the woman was wearing a US Army uniform, and she ended up dying in her arms…

"Things aren't normally this chaotic around me."

Crystal pushed the memory away, and the horror of what had happened on this day in that godforsaken piece of lawless desert, before the emotional charge could get under her skin and really hurt her. Every once in a while, it still could. For now, she focused all her attention on Christensen, and kept it there. Those smoky grey eyes looked right back at her, and Crystal nodded.

"Good to know," she said. "Although I'm used to it."

Christensen flashed her a groggy smile.

"The thing is… It might get worse before it gets better," she murmured. "Look, I know that I still haven't had a chance to talk to you properly. I want to. I will, I promise… Thank you for not bailing out on us, Crystal."

CHAPTER TEN

It was dark when Abigail woke up a few hours later, with a start, her shoulder on fire. The painkillers had done a good job for her at the beginning, but now their soothing effect was wearing off. For a moment, her mind was totally blank. She lay on her side, staring at the darkened window, until the memories started to trickle through slowly. The Town Hall, the disrupter, and the attack. A delightful young woman named Ruth; driving through the snow in the back of an Uber; resting in the arms of Captain Thor. *Crystal.* Abigail grew instantly alert at the thought of her. When they had arrived back at the hotel the night before, Sam and JoAnn were both waiting anxiously for news of their leader. Abigail rallied long enough to reassure her troops, then went up to her room. She remembered riding in the elevator with Thor, leaning against her side, barely able to walk in a straight line... Abigail sighed. *Did she put me to bed?* She was in her underwear, her clothes folded neatly on the back of a nearby chair. *Oh, well; who cares?* The woman had not only saved her life, but found her a reliable doctor, and stuck around to make sure that she and Russell were safe afterwards. She had gone above and beyond all expectations... Where was she now? *And is she okay?* One thing Abigail remembered clearly was how brutal that fight had been. She wondered if Crystal might have just gone home, or if Russell had got her a room at the hotel... She checked her phone.

It was five in the morning, her usual time to wake up and get to work. No missed calls or messages, always a good way to start the day. Abigail got up, pulled on some sweats, and rolled her injured shoulder carefully a few times. It was tight, but nothing worse. The young medic, Ruth, had done a really excellent job. Abigail walked into the front room, intent on going to find Russ, and froze in surprise as she was about to switch on the lights. *Oh... So, she's not gone home, then.* Crystal lay asleep on the couch, stretched out onto her stomach, with her boots still on and her weapon within easy reach. Abigail remained in place, watching her in silence. It was pure relief to find that she was still there, and in more ways than one... Abigail was a natural leader, it was true. She was the one who often provided encouragement, help, support, and reassurance for others, not the other way around. She gave of herself fully, rarely received back in return, and it was fine with her. She lived a life of service which was its own best reward. To claim that her fierce independence and self-sufficiency were only based on this desire to help others would have been a lie, though. There had been disappointments along the way, cutting betrayals, inadequate relationships, and hurt. A few of these events had contributed to developing what Russell called her *lone wolf* mindset. She did not mind that. It made her efficient and successful. But Abigail was not made of stone either. It had been wonderful to have Thor with her the previous night, a strong woman to lean on for a change. She sighed, and shook her head. *Dangerous thoughts, Abi.* She stopped staring at the sleeping soldier, and made a quiet move toward the door.

"Where are you going?"

The question, issued in a soft yet firm tone of voice, stopped Abigail in her tracks again. She glanced back over her shoulder, and spotted Crystal watching her intently. Still lying down, but definitely awake now, and fiercely alert.

"Hi. Didn't want to wake you," she said.

"No?" Thor gave an ironic, impatient shake of the head. She sat up, rubbing sleep from her eyes. "I wish you would. Give me half a chance to keep you alive, at least."

Well, duh, Abigail reflected in irritation. *Get with it, Abi.*

"Sorry," she apologised. "You're right, of course."

"'Course," the officer muttered unhappily.

Okay, so maybe she was not a morning person.

"Mind if I turn the lights on?"

"Mmm..."

Abigail assumed that this meant yes, and she flipped on the switch. Once able to see better, she noticed the takeaway pizza box on the low table in front of the couch, and an empty sports drink bottle. She lingered over other items that she was not so used to seeing lying around; the Sig Sauer, a spare magazine, and what looked like a combat knife tucked inside a slim leather holster. Her eyes drifted to Thor herself. *Yep; still as appealing as yesterday.* Abigail winced as she noticed herself having that thought, and she suppressed a smile at the sullen sneer that her companion gave when she checked her watch. *Definitely not a morning person.* Only then did Abigail finally notice the state of her right arm, and she frowned in sudden concern.

"Whoa! Why didn't you say something before?"

Crystal looked up, seemingly puzzled at the question.

"About what?" she asked.

"Oh, come on," Abigail snapped in disbelief. "This!"

She hurried to sit on the couch next to her, carefully took hold of her wrist, and lifted her forearm to take a better look. It was swollen just below the elbow, vivid purple and darker blue, almost black in some places. Thor just shrugged.

"It's just a bruise," she said. "Doesn't affect my grip; I can still shoot. No problem."

Abigail sighed inwardly at the lack of emotion in her voice when she referred to her own body like this, detached and cold. To her, it was probably just a tool to be evaluated in terms of its performance, nothing else. Russell would have teased her about it: *'These efficiency-driven people and their annoying lack of common emotions... What a bummer, hey!'* Abigail shook her head, irritated. Come to think if it, she was cut from the same ilk, really. She sought the woman's eyes, such a clean-cut and startling shade of black. Thor just more or less repeated what she had already said.

"It's no big deal," she stated. "Won't hold me back."

"I understand that," Abigail nodded softly. "But... Does it hurt?"

Now the soldier flashed her a crooked grin, and started to laugh.

"Oh, yeah," she agreed, amused. "It hurts like..."

"Like what?"

"Can you swear in front of the next POTUS?"

"You can, a hundred percent," Abigail chuckled.

"Well, then. It hurts like fuck," Crystal concluded.

Said next POTUS laughed even harder at that. It was great to be able to relax, in what was actually her first opportunity to do so since she had met the captain the previous day. A lot had happened since, most of it traumatic. It felt really good to laugh, and Thor looked like she was probably thinking the exact same thing.

"How's your shoulder this morning?" she enquired.

"Feels much better than your arm looks," Abigail shot back in a confident voice. "I can still work. It won't hold me back."

They exchanged a smile and a friendly glance.

"Roger that, Abigail. Now, what?"

"We need to talk, Crys."

"Yes, we do."

∞

Crystal was pleased when Christensen decided to make them both some coffee first; strong, black, no sugar. Meanwhile, she threw the leftover pizza to warm up in the microwave.

"It's still stormy out," Abigail announced. "And snowing."

"Please, don't stand in front of the windows," Crystal said instantly. She went over to draw all the curtains shut. "We don't know who may be out there watching. Safety 101, hey?"

"Sorry. It might just take me a little time to adjust to that."

The candidate looked crestfallen at the sudden realisation that even windows might be off limits to her now, and Crystal gave her a quick, encouraging smile.

"Won't be forever," she promised.

"I sure hope not," Abigail murmured.

She went back to the couch, and Crystal sat directly on the table, facing her. She took a sip of coffee, and leaned forward in anticipation.

"Okay," she said. "I'm listening."

She really hoped that the Congresswoman would not dance around the issue the same way that her campaign manager had done the night before. So far, Crystal liked her; both the woman and the politician. She had not spent much time around her yet, sure, but she was an excellent judge of character. Christensen was the real deal; she was sure of it.

"Let me cut straight to the chase," Abigail said, as if she was reading her thoughts. "Last week, I received a warning call from a senator I serve with in Congress. He's an ally; I trust him. He confirmed that I have come to the attention of some powerful and dangerous people who will stop at nothing to take me out if I become too much of a risk to their alliance."

Crystal bit into a slice of pizza. If Christensen had not been stabbed the day before, this would not have constituted such an earth-shattering statement. All candidates on the campaign trail had to expect to receive threats these days. There were a lot of loonies out there. For the most part, thankfully, they kept their violent comments and promises to do harm confined to the even more insane world of social media forums. Not so in the case of the woman in front of her, who boldly reached for a piece of her pizza as well, and cocked an ironic eyebrow.

"Pineapple, Captain Thor?"

"Oh, it's the only way," Crystal assured her.

Abigail smiled but she seemed tense despite her joking, and it was no surprise, really. Crystal appreciated her toughness, and her choice of humour in the face of adversity.

"Powerful and dangerous people," she prompted. "As in..."

"I don't have specific names. But just to give you an idea of the nature of this business; to drive his point home the other day when the senator called me, he did mention JFK as an example of what could happen to me."

Crystal kept her gaze on her, her pizza forgotten.

"What do you think happened to Kennedy?" she enquired.

"Not what they want us to believe, that's for sure."

"Who are 'They' that you keep referring to?"

Abigail stared laser-like into her eyes.

"I assume you have a Top-Secret Security Clearance; right?" she asked.

"I used to," Crystal nodded slowly. "Not anymore."

"Still; you understand how the system works. And if you've done your research about me, which I'm sure you have," Abigail carried on, "then you must know that I favour an open book and total transparency in ninety-nine percent of all governmental issues."

"I've read your record on issues," Crystal confirmed. "And your election charter. I know what you stand for and your vision for the country going forward."

"Good. So, you know I firmly believe that our government must be of, by, and for the people; therefore, open to scrutiny by anyone who wants to know how it's being run, what we do with people's taxes, why, and how... The whole thing."

"But you do have a one percent reservation?"

"I do." Abigail lowered her voice slightly. "It will come as no surprise to you that my exception is in matters of National Security. To protect our people at home; when the lives of our soldiers are on the line; or when it comes to the continued safety of our Intelligence officers around the world... A reasonable level of secrecy is required, and must be maintained at all times. Sure. I have zero problem with that."

"Then I don't get it," Crystal said, shrugging lightly. "As far as I'm concerned, every single one of your ideas for reform and improvement of our current administration is a breath of fresh air. Your suggestions make a lot of sense. And according to the latest polls, I'm not the only one thinking that either."

"Thank you," Abigail nodded with a soft smile.

"Of course, I understand that the likes of Google, Facebook, Amazon, and all the rest of the big corporations must despise you for wanting to break them up, crack down on them about taxes, and take away all their power, essentially."

"Oh, yes. Actually, that's putting it mildly."

Crystal raised a thoughtful eyebrow.

"And so, you think that these people are pissed-off enough to want to give you the JFK treatment?"

"It's more complicated than that," Abigail replied, her tone rising in passion and a touch of anger. "Most people believe that corporations pull all the strings. But they don't."

"No?" Crystal was surprised at her answer. "I thought that was your point…"

"Only partly. Don't get me wrong, these guys are powerful all right; but we're not talking only about economics and market domination here. This is about the control and manipulation of events, people, opinion, elections, both at home and abroad…"

"Like I said, it sounds like the usual suspects to me."

Christensen gave a weary shake of the head this time.

"Trust me, the corporations are only a front," she repeated. "Ultimately, the goal is much bigger. This is about the complete hijacking of human perception. If you can control what people perceive about who they are and what the world is, then you will be in control of the reality that they believe is real too. I'm just giving you the headlines here, Crystal; okay? It goes way deeper. Suffice to say for now, whoever can do that will be in total control of the entire human race."

"To what end?"

"Exploitation," Abigail said grimly. "Enslavement."

Crystal let out a sharp exhale. She was no stranger to this kind of crazy wild talk, for which large amounts of tin foil were usually required… But to hear it from a presidential candidate, and a woman who seemed so centred, grounded, and reasonable was definitely a first for her.

"Do you have proof of this?" she pushed.

"Not yet. At least, not completely, just bits and pieces for now. But I'm working on it, and actively investigating. I've been doing it for years… Only this time, I'm on my way to the White House, and they're getting pretty nervous." She gave a brief, tight smile. "Now, I really need the sort of help that only you can provide, Captain."

CHAPTER ELEVEN

For once, Crystal did not correct her about using an old title that held little meaning for her now. She was feeling both captivated and wary. This was extraordinary stuff; some might even have called it insane. *Just the headlines?* she thought. *Wow!* For all the weirdness and tension of this conversation, she could have been back in one of those black ops briefings she used to attend when she was still active in the Special Forces. A shiver ran down her spine, reluctance and excitement hitting her in a 20/80 split. *Not just a regular security job then, uh...* It was true that Crystal would not have known what *'regular'* was even if it smacked her in the face, but still... Part of her wanted to walk away now. Just ignore it all. Buy the campervan with the money that she had in the bank, never mind if she could not afford the exact model that she had hoped for, and just go. Vanish, disappear; escape this crazy world while she still could. She rubbed her forehead, as a single memory managed to snake its way inside her mind. *A sinking tank; Her crew screaming; An IED blowing up; Excruciating pain, as a piece of burning shrapnel ripped her chest open...* Crystal shook her head in irritation. She realised that she was on a dangerous slide, and took a nice deep breath to regain control of her wandering thoughts. When she looked up, she found Abigail watching her intently, with perhaps a slight hint of concern. Thankfully, the candidate did not ask. Instead, she repeated her own question.

"Will you help me, Crys? I need the best security officer I can find. You're my first choice…" Abigail smiled again, warmly this time. "My only choice. Please; I need your help."

Crystal suppressed a sigh as dreams of Montana faded into nothingness. Or rather, into a pair of luminous grey eyes and the most attractive, heart-melting smile that she had seen in a long time. *No fair, Representative,* she reflected. It occurred to her that taking on a job simply because she liked the person could be the best and fastest way to disaster. At the same time, perhaps it was too late to turn around. She had already saved the woman's life once; they were connected. Something about the things that Christensen talked about also resonated deeply with her. Crystal had always sensed that the world was not like everyone told her it was. It felt a little fake to her, a little forced and unnatural. She did believe that most people just walked around in a state of unconsciousness, unaware of their true nature, driven by an outside perception of reality that Abigail rightly described as manufactured and put in front of their eyes by others. The result was a population disconnected and driven to distraction, surfing on anxiety pills, and drowning in a sea of consumerism. *Maybe I've been drowning as well,* Crystal reflected unhappily; *in my own way…* How different would their years of service be for soldiers like Ruth with a woman of Christensen's calibre as Commander-in-Chief? Crystal could find out for herself right now, she did not have to wait. She felt another sizzle of excitement at the thought. Not only did she miss duty, but she was also fascinated to learn more about what drove Christensen. *Control of the entire human race? Enslavement?* It sounded like science fiction, and the stuff of heroes. Did Crystal want to be a part of it? She reached for more coffee, and grabbed herself another slice of pizza. She did not have to think about it for much longer. The answer was a big fat YES. *You can rest while you're dead, soldier…*

"All right," she nodded. "You've got your security officer, Abi. Now tell me who we're up against."

∞

Abigail was eager to do so, to get into the details of what she knew, and this for at least two main reasons. One, it was the only way that Thor would be able to protect her. She had to know what they were facing in order to do her job properly, and make sure that Abigail did not end up as a tragic casualty of her own crusade. There was also the fact that although she could not have explained why, Abigail had a strong intuition that underneath her cool and dutiful exterior, Thor might be a true kindred spirit. At least, she would be open-minded and solid enough in her own mind, Abigail believed, to handle the terrifying truth that she was about to reveal.

"So, you may have heard of that thing called the Military Industrial Complex," she said, which caused Crystal to smirk. "I thought so. What I am talking about is bigger, darker, and a lot scarier than anything you may have heard before."

Thor was watching her intently, with great focus, interest, and the usual touch of careful reserve mixed in as well. Abigail would have been worried not to observe it in her. This was fine. She took a deep breath to steady herself, looked her in the eye, and finally revealed who 'They' were.

"I am talking about a secret and fully independent group; a rogue Global Intelligence Network built on a series of secret and undercover projects. To use your army lingo, Crys, this would be similar to Black Ops, essentially. But on a gigantic scale."

"And I assume it is nothing that's in line with the reason for your one percent rule," Crystal commented.

"That's right. The work that you were involved in may have been confidential, but it was not SIP; Special Interest Projects. Nowhere near, in fact."

"Are those programmes you talk about classified at a higher level of clearance?"

"Yes and no," Abigail replied in a dark tone. "What I mean is that they're off the charts in terms of clearance. Unsupervised, unacknowledged… And they run independently of Congress approval. Even top-ranking military officers are kept in the dark about the SIPs. They have no idea that they exist. In fact, the President himself doesn't know about this stuff either. Even his own security clearance does not reach that high."

Now, Crystal shook her head in disbelief.

"No," she declared. "That's impossible."

"You really think so?" Abigail challenged.

"Look, I've been involved in enough covert operations of this kind over the years to know. Some in which my team and I were told beforehand that if we were captured, or messed up in any other way, our government would refuse to acknowledge their involvement. Deniable operations, in other words; always high-risk, high-stakes, and high-reward. I'm well aware of the level of confidentiality that goes on around these things…"

Abigail gave her a polite, conciliatory nod.

"Indeed, I do not doubt you are. Or your level of experience either."

She could have added that it was the main reason she had chosen Thor from Russell's list of potential candidates… But it would not have been entirely true.

"I'm not worried about street creds," the soldier shrugged. "But to suggest that there is a global network in place that runs parallel to our government, essentially, and controls everything without even the President's knowledge… Abi, that's insane."

Abigail caught the sliver of resignation in her voice though, even as she said that. Thor sounded sad, as if part of her already knew. For Abigail, her reaction came as the perfect confirmation. Now she was pretty sure that her instincts had been spot-on, and that she was indeed speaking to the right woman to support her cause, help her to expose the lies... And keep her alive, of course.

"You're right," she admitted softly. "It is insane."

"But it doesn't make it any less true?" Crystal suggested in a weary voice. "Is that what you're going to tell me next?"

"Correct," Abigail agreed. "Sorry about that."

It went a lot deeper too, as she had said before. There was more to explain, discuss, and understand. Some of it would be hard to stomach, extremely difficult, and this really must be the understatement of the millennium; but Abigail had complete faith in Captain Thor. For whatever reason, she felt familiar and safe. In truth, Abigail knew next to nothing about her, and she abruptly changed the subject to this now.

"Your file is surprisingly vague about your background, and lacking in detail in pretty much everything else."

Thor was sharp, a quick thinker; she did not miss a beat.

"It is so," she agreed. "Although your comment makes me wonder how come I was your first and only choice, then."

Touché... Abigail lifted one shoulder in a matter-of-fact half-shrug, and she opted for the truth.

"Reason number one," she started to explain; "All the other candidates were male, and I..."

"Ouch," Crystal interrupted, faking consternation, but with an amused smile back on her lips. "Are you sure you should say sexist things like that, Candidate?"

"If you let me finish, you'll see it's not sexist."

"Yes, ma'am," Thor said wryly, and she flashed her a brief, irreverent salute.

"What I was going to say is that I wasn't keen on having a guy follow me around 24/7. So, when Russell showed me your file, that was one point already in your favour."

"May not be 24/7. But close enough. And by the way, this is definitely a sexist comment. Biased and discriminatory as hell. Just saying."

"What are you?" Abigail queried, somewhat puzzled. "My CPO? Or a damn employment lawyer?"

"What's a CPO?"

"Close Protection Officer. What do you call a bodyguard?"

"Oh, I don't know," Crystal grinned. "The muscle?"

Abigail rolled her eyes, but she could not help herself from glancing at the woman's tight upper body, her strong shoulders, and the well-defined muscles in her arms. She was tempted to keep staring, to be honest, but she did manage to tear her eyes away.

"Anyway, you get my drift," she concluded. "I wanted a person I could relate to, and trust. The other guys did not have your Special Forces experience. I got the sense that they might be more interested in social media ratings and chasing a lucrative book deal than anything else. So, there you go."

"Is there a Reason number three?" Crystal enquired.

"There is. You looked good in the photo," Abigail informed her with a bold and full-on shrug this time. "My apologies for another controversial statement if you think it is... But I'm a gut-feel kind of person. You'll just have to get used to it."

Thor fixed her with a faint smile, looking both amused still, and nicely thoughtful.

"You really are very good at evading personal questions; you know that," Abigail added.

"Mmm. It might be because you haven't asked me anything yet," Crystal remarked.

She was correct about that; all Abigail had done so far was comment on the lack of general information in her personnel file. The woman would make a great negotiator, she reflected. Or a brilliant lawyer, indeed. She sat still seeping her coffee, quiet and focused; open, it seemed, to having a conversation and sharing more of herself.

"I'd like to know what prompted you to leave the Army," Abigail said.

"The same thing that prompted my interest in you and your campaign," Crystal replied instantly. "I joined right after 9/11, you know? Like so many others who did then, I wanted to serve and help to protect our people. I wanted to fight for our country and our way of life. I really believed that what the government was saying about Bin Laden and Al Qaeda terrorists at the time was true."

"Until...?" Abigail prompted.

"Until some of the missions that I was involved in started to jar with the official narrative; it was the worst kind of cognitive dissonance, and I wasn't the only one experiencing it either. A lot of soldiers grew disillusioned and unhappy at the realisation that we weren't fighting for what we thought we were."

Abigail gave a quiet nod of approval.

"Soldiers aren't encouraged to voice their opinions out loud or ask questions," Crystal continued in a bitter tone. "Some quit, others chose to ignore the truth. Personally, I also did not want to believe it. My preferred version of reality, one in which I was making a positive difference to the world, may have been naïve, but it was much nicer than the alternative. I carried on. I tried to ignore all this other stuff for a few years, but eventually, I had no real choice left but to face it. I realised the enormity of the lie that we were being told about what really happened on and after 9/11, for instance."

"That's right," Abigail said. "If only just the problem of two planes, three buildings…"

"Yes," Crystal agreed. "And a ton of undisputable evidence that contradicts the official story of what happened on that day. I finally accepted the fact that there had never been any weapons of mass destruction; 9/11 was an inside job; we weren't in Iraq and the Middle East to protect anybody. I was being used, along with everybody else, and our soldiers' sacrifice was for nothing. Then, there was that last mission…"

Abigail leaned forward in anticipation. She was fascinated to hear the rest of this story. But then, the front door flew open. Thor reacted quicker than she could even see. She dived for her weapon, and leaped over the table on a mad scramble toward the door at the far end of the entrance hallway. *Oh, dear God; not again…* It was the only thing that Abigail had time to think.

"Stay there!" Crystal yelled at her. "Get to cover!"

CHAPTER TWELVE

Two minutes later, Russell sat wincing on the couch, rubbing the painful spot on his throat that came from Crystal's death grip. She had grabbed him violently around the neck and smashed his face into the wall. She could and probably would have done a lot worse… Fortunately, she recognised him in time.

"Okay, Russ?" Abigail enquired.

"Yeah," he nodded sheepishly. "Yes, I'm good."

"Sorry about that, Stark," Crystal said, although she looked thoroughly pissed off.

"I think we need to set some rules," Abigail decided with a calming glance toward her.

"Sure," Crystal replied. She tried to hold off on the sarcasm. "I didn't think I needed to say this, really, but please, Russell: don't ever come bursting into a room like that again. I was ready to put a hole through your head, man."

"I won't," he promised. "Sorry, Captain…"

"Crys," she reminded him. *Damn!*

"Yeah, Crys. I just didn't think."

Crystal raised a dangerous eyebrow, but managed to refrain from further comment. Being distracted led to stupid mistakes. It could get people killed. In her world, *'I just didn't think'* was the sort of excuse that would earn you a rightful punch in the face. Crystal was fuming at Stark's response, and Abigail did notice.

She circled soothing fingers around her wrist, gave her a smile, and a gentle squeeze.

"Thanks for reacting so fast and efficiently, by the way."

The gesture took Crystal by surprise. It was unexpected, for sure, although kind of nice too, and it definitely took her mind off her anger.

"Yeah," she sighed. "Okay... That's what I do, hey."

Satisfied, Abigail turned back to her right-hand man.

"Russ, what made you run in here like that, anyway?"

"Fake news about you all over the Internet," he replied. He handed her his phone. "Have a look."

Crystal watched Abigail's face darken as she stared at the screen for a few intense seconds. Then she passed her the phone without a single word. The lurid title was everything they had been trying to avoid by not going into a hospital the previous night. It read: *'Congresswoman in lethal assassination plot – Abigail Christensen: DEAD!'* Crystal snapped her head up.

"That's click-bait," she exclaimed in disgust.

"Oh, absolutely," Abigail agreed. "And illegal too." Before Crystal could even say it, she added; "Don't worry. I know that your friend Ruth had nothing to do with this."

"Of course not," Russell sneered. "This is not a leak. It had to be planned. I'll get our lawyers on the case."

Calm and collected, Abigail grabbed her own cell phone.

"Give me just a sec," she announced. "I'm going Live."

Crystal watched her head toward the window, frown as she remembered that she was not supposed to, and divert straight back to the couch with the briefest of glances toward her. Crystal nodded in approval. She watched her, as Presidential Candidate Christensen, still dressed in her pyjamas and without makeup on, hit the Live button on her Facebook page, and launched into an improvised speech. It was brief and to the point.

"Hey, good morning, Guys," she greeted her audience with a dazzling smile. "In case you've already seen some questionable news this morning, I wanted to put your mind at rest: there is no lethal plot to kill me, and as you can see, I am alive and kicking. Just getting ready to rock and roll here in snowy New York City. If you're local, please come and see me tonight at the Town Hall in Soho. All the details are on my website. As always, thank you so much for your support and your donations; I'm excited about meeting some of you later on today. Hope you all have a great day, and remember the three rules: Focus on what you want; Be grateful; Remember you are always more than you think you are. Okay. Bye for now."

Crystal was impressed with her delivery, but her heart sank at the thought of the crazy challenge ahead of her. Christensen's campaign currently was all about putting her centre stage. Hugs, handshakes, and close interactions with her potential voters had to be allowed in the name of this game. It made her vulnerable.

"Okay, what's the plan today, Russ?" Abigail enquired.

"You have a live CBS interview at twelve o'clock," Russell reeled off the top of this head. "Then, recording a radio podcast with Matt Nellis from NPR, followed by a talk at a vocational college in Harlem, and one at a local hospital nearby. And in the evening, there's the Town Hall in Soho you already mentioned."

"Right. Let's do it," Abigail nodded.

"Hold on," Crystal interrupted. "Is your schedule always so packed?"

"Pretty much, yes."

"Well. I need a team."

"Really?" Abigail enquired. "Why?"

She sounded puzzled, and it became even more obvious to Crystal how much she must have ignored her own safety until this very moment. That sure was insane too.

"I'll be your CPO, Abi," she explained patiently, using her own words. "I'll travel with you, ensure your personal safety at all times, and basically stick to you like glue, as agreed."

She spied a spark of interest in Abigail's gaze, amusement, and perhaps something else, but it was gone almost instantly, and the woman only gave a sharp nod in response.

"What else do you need?" she asked.

"Backup. At least two guys I can send to your venues ahead of time, and who can help me keep an eye on audiences as well; provide extra bulk when you're on the streets greeting people… And relief for me when I'm sleeping, or whatever else."

"Agreed," Abigail nodded. "Makes sense."

"I know who to call. Ex-colleagues of mine."

"Perfect; do it, Crys. Russell? I'll just have a quick shower and then we can hit the road." Abigail flashed a wry grin. "That CBS interview comes with perfect timing in light of my dramatic *death*," she added, using air quotes with her fingers.

On that comment, she disappeared in the bathroom. Russell lingered behind. When Crystal looked at him, he held her gaze intently.

"Anything I can do to help?"

"Not really. I'll just call my guys now; Matthew Scott and Tommy Greer, both Jersey-based. They're good at what they do, trust me. The best you can get."

"Okay. Uhm, Crys?"

"Yeah," Crystal replied a touch impatiently. "What?"

"I know you can't be very impressed with my performance so far," Russell said, standing firm in front of her. "But this work we do to expose the lies, it's my whole life. I'd put it on the line for Abigail in a heartbeat, and for anyone else on our team too. That includes you now. Just so you know, I never make the same mistake twice. If you need me, use me. Okay?"

That's more like it, Crystal reflected; definitely much more in line with her first impressions of the man, and she immediately stood up to shake his hand.

"Thanks, Russ. Will do. Sorry I almost strangled you, man."

"Don't flatter yourself," he joked. "I wouldn't have let you."

Crystal gave him a playful shove.

"Yeah, right! Love your confidence."

"Welcome to our team, Crystal," he grinned.

"It's an honour, Russ," she replied, and she meant it.

∞

Once he had left, Crystal got in touch with her trusted contacts, two long-time friends who were both available and eager to get involved.

"Whenever you need any help, Thor, it's always a yes from me," Scott said. "Just tell me where you are, and I'll be on my way."

"I've been keeping a close eye on Christensen and the work that she does," Greer informed her when she got through to him next. "Yeah, she's all right. Sure thing, Crys; I'm in."

By lunchtime on that same day, Crystal's security crew was fully briefed and active. She had worked with the two men on a few critical missions, both in and out of the military. She knew they were made of the right stuff. Both had long since left their Army careers behind, but always maintained a low profile and an efficient lifestyle. In other words, they were as switched on now as they were then, perhaps even more so. Scott and Greer were not the kind to sit around looking pretty, just waiting for a flashy book deal, as Christensen had pointed out ironically. They were the sort of men who could make all the difference between life and death for the presidential candidate if things heated up...

And from the dark topics that Abigail had begun to share about the ultimate goal of her campaign, it was likely that they would, probably sooner than later. On this point, Crystal was still not satisfied that she knew the full story. On their way to the CBS building that morning, in the back of a freezing taxi, she made sure to tell Christensen that there was a lot more she wanted to know.

"Of course, and I fully intend to finish briefing you later," the woman promised. She followed that up with a loaded glance toward her. "We were interrupted before you could tell me what happened to you during your last mission, Crys. I'd like to know that as well.

"No problem," Crystal agreed. "We'll talk."

It was a fact that she did not often share her personal story with anybody. Still, she found herself surprisingly eager to open up to Christensen. She supposed that it was no big mystery as to why; the woman was incredibly charismatic, for a start. She oozed that attractive mix of power, quiet strength, and genuine authority. Underneath this formidable appearance also ran a gentle streak, compassion, and warmth. She was a combination of so many traits of character that Crystal appreciated and which made her feel safe and settled. *You're the one who has to keep her safe, soldier...* Not that she needed the reminder.

"So, my guys are in place," she said, low enough that only Christensen could hear. "You don't need to look for them or pay attention to them; just know that they're around, and fully alert. The same goes for me. I'll be close to you at all times, but feel free to concentrate on your work and just ignore me."

The woman flashed her another dubious look.

"Problem?" Crystal enquired.

"Not at all."

"What, then?"

"At the risk of sounding inappropriate again, you are not an easy one to ignore, Ms Thor," Abigail replied in a laughing tone. "But I shall do my best to forget your delicious presence in the background, and focus only on the business at hand."

Crystal suppressed a grin. *At least, she's remembered to drop the 'Captain' bit this time...*

"Do you flirt with all your staff, Representative?" she asked.

"I don't have staff," Abigail corrected. "I have partners who share my passion for truth, justice, and freedom. The work that we do is crucial. It can be dangerous, but that doesn't mean that we can't have fun with each other. In fact, it's essential that we do, especially in light of these dark reasons."

Crystal smiled in approval. Having spent most of her career working as part of a small team of trusted friends, in high-risk environments, she knew exactly where Christensen was coming from on this one. She felt instantly even more at home with her.

"This reminds me, actually; do you know what the first step to enlightenment is, Abi?" she enquired.

"Not sure... You tell me."

"To lighten up on oneself."

"Ha!" Abigail exclaimed in an easy laugh this time. "True! So, I take it you understand. I knew you would."

"Sure, I do," Crystal shrugged. "Life's too short to take it so seriously."

At the same time, she could not help but wonder... Was this really all innocent banter on the part of Christensen? Or was the teasing comment motivated by genuine appreciation? As they approached the TV network's building, and their driver looked for a free space to pull up in front, Crystal saw her companion straighten up, and unconsciously rest a hand over her injured shoulder.

"Okay, Abi?" she murmured. "You all right?"

This time, there was no mistaking the hint of nervousness in her eyes when Abigail turned to face her, although it was gone almost as soon as Crystal spotted it. Abigail gave a firm nod.

"All right, Crys," she said. "Let's go."

She grabbed the door handle and leaned forward to get out, but Crystal held her back.

"I'll go first, and hold the door," she explained. "You follow on my side. As soon as you're out, I'll put my arm around your shoulders, and we'll walk inside together. No flirting, just safety 101. Okay?"

Abigail did crack a brief smile at that.

"Yeah. Got it. You go first."

"Take a deep breath," Crystal invited.

Abigail obeyed, and she also gave a flustered smile.

"I don't usually get this nervous," she groaned. "Sorry."

"Don't be." Crystal smiled in both reassurance and genuine appreciation. "I admire you for having the courage to get back out there so quickly after what happened to you last night. It's normal to feel a bit nervous."

"Thank you for your understanding. I'm good to go now."

"Great. And just remember: I'm here to protect you, and I'm awfully good at my job. No one gets past me when I'm on duty. I'll keep you safe; I promise."

CHAPTER THIRTEEN

After that first morning, and a detour via her apartment to settle the lease, and pack everything she owned into a single rucksack, Crystal just allowed herself to be swept along by the Christensen campaign machine. Life on the road was fast-paced, intense, just as she had expected that it would be. It was rewarding as well to once more be part of a team with such a strong sense of purpose. Proof of Christensen's relentless work schedule was that despite spending such a lot of time in close proximity together, Crystal did not get another opportunity to talk to her properly again until just over a week later, on a stormy night in Dubuque, Iowa. She was on an evening break in the hotel gym, loosening up after several long hours sitting in the back of a car, when Abigail walked in too, escorted by a stony-faced Tom Greer. Curious, Crystal looked up at them from the weights bench. Christensen was dressed in workout clothes, with wireless earbuds draped around her neck, and carrying a big bottle of water. Two things immediately crossed Crystal's mind at the sight of her: one, how fit and attractive the woman looked in her black Nike gear; and two, that she appeared pretty wound up for some reason.

"Hey, Crys," Greer said to her.

"Hey, Tommy. Everything okay?"

"Yep. Just handing back over to you."

Crystal nodded, and he looked toward his charge.

"Ms Christensen; have a good evening, ma'am."

"Thanks. And sorry about earlier," she replied.

"No problem." He grinned. "I enjoyed the challenge."

As he left, Abigail headed straight for the treadmill with only the briefest of glances toward her bodyguard. *Only a week into it, and she sure is getting pretty good at ignoring me,* Crystal reflected. She held back an ironic smile at the realisation, got up from the bench, and grabbed her towel. She wiped the sweat from her face, and walked over to join Christensen on the other side of the small room.

"So, what's going on with you and Tom?" she asked.

Abigail looked at her and just gave an impatient shrug.

"I nearly gave your sidekick a heart attack, I'm afraid," she declared. "I left my room and headed down here without letting him know. Wasn't my intention to give him the slip at all, I just completely forgot. He caught up with me on the stairs. That's it. Anyway… Is this thing plugged in, or what?"

Crystal watched her get off the machine and go around it to check the connections. Christensen was in a bad mood, clearly, and not happy to find that there must be some kind of fault with the treadmill. It was indeed plugged in, but it remained just as dead, no matter how many times she banged over the controls. Now unable to get on with her preferred method of exercise, she stood surveying the rest of the room with a critical frown on her face.

"Ugh," she muttered. "They call that a gym?"

Crystal gave her an encouraging nod. The gym was tiny, for sure, but something else was going on here.

"Would you like to train with me?" she offered. "There is plenty we can do with just this one bench here; I have a short but useful routine that includes some cardio, and that is guaranteed to make you sleep well tonight."

She caught the woman's eyes on her, not exactly lingering over her bare legs, her training shorts, or the grey T-shirt that she wore, but definitely taking note all the same, assessing, and she raised a quizzical eyebrow.

"Aren't you done here?" Abigail asked in response.

Crystal just concluded from the question that she must look appropriately hot and sweaty. She was done with her workout, indeed, and had been about to leave, but now she was back on duty, apparently.

"If I'm going to be in the room with you, I may as well carry on a bit," she pointed out politely. "That's okay though, there's no obligation to do what I do."

Abigail stared hard at her, frowning still.

"Yeah, I suppose you need to stay put now that I'm down here too, uh," she reflected eventually, as if it had only dawned on her.

"Correct. Stick to you like glue, remember?"

A brief, unhappy smile appeared over the woman's lips.

"All right, then," she conceded. "That's fine, I guess."

Crystal kept her eyes on her, curious as to what may be the cause of Christensen's angry mood. It was pretty unusual, to say the least.

"Hey, Abi. Are you okay, really?" she repeated.

"Well…" Abigail sighed in irritation. "I've just wrapped up an interview with the most obtuse and misguided so-called *'journalist'* I've ever spoken to, which is saying a lot given how many I interact with on a daily basis. Gosh, these people are so brainwashed…! They have no idea they are being controlled, and not a shred of awareness of the damage that they create by attacking me and spreading the lies of the establishment. So, to answer your question, I'm feeling angry and frustrated as hell tonight."

"Sorry to hear that… But a workout should definitely help."

"I also keep forgetting to tell one of you people every single time I want to move around," Abigail snapped, as if she had not heard. "I guess this whole security process thing must be getting on my nerves on some level. No offense, just stating the facts."

She flashed another furious look toward the treadmill, and Crystal chuckled.

"Wow. You really are having a tough one, aren't you?" she remarked.

"Told you," Abigail shot back. "How was your day?"

"Pretty boring," Crystal shrugged, matching her tone. "But you're still alive. So, frustrated or not, that's still a success for '*us people*'."

The softly sarcastic vibe of that comment earned her a more focused glance from Abigail this time, and Crystal even caught her struggling not to smile. The woman must be enjoying this bit of sparring in the conversation between them. *Good…*

"So, are you up for training with me?" she asked.

Abigail rolled her shoulders in reply, and she came to stand in front of her. She looked confident and serious; Crystal noticed. Effortlessly in the zone, as with everything else she ever did. It was an attitude that Crystal appreciated in people, especially the ones that she worked for.

"Yeah, okay; let's do this thing," Abigail decided. "What sort of workout did you have in mind?"

"Like I said; the sort that will make you forget all about the stresses of today."

Abigail once again allowed her gaze to roam.

"Sure, you're not too tired to take me on?" she challenged.

Crystal flashed a brilliant smile, chuckled, and made sure to give her the sort of flippant answer that she knew Christensen was bound to like.

"I wasn't aware this was a competition," she said, "but do I look like I would struggle?"

Abigail laughed out loud this time, indeed, delighted at the spirited reply. She reached out to squeeze her arm, which was a friendly gesture that Crystal had noticed her use before with all her team.

"Thank you for this, Crys," she said. "I feel better already."

"Oh, so you do remember my name," Crystal remarked.

She spotted a touch of tiredness in Abigail's gaze this time, and the woman lingered with her touch for perhaps longer than she did with everybody else. Crystal felt the sudden change in her, from easy banter and confident ribbing to a flash of genuine emotion. It may have been sadness, or a hint of vulnerability... Crystal did not ask; her intention was not to make the moment uncomfortable. She just allowed her smile to turn warmer and softer instead of mischievous, and her gaze to reflect the same.

"Just be mindful of your shoulder, okay?" she said.

Abigail was also no longer teasing either.

"I will," she replied. "Thanks."

Crystal led her through a series of easy stretches, then into the workout. She was inventive with the one bench in the middle of the room, using it for leg exercises and jumps, as a support for push-ups, triceps dips, leg raises, abs work, and variations on those, which included burpees thrown in at regular intervals. Forty minutes later, Abigail lay on a mat at the back of the room, covered in sweat and wheezing. Crystal gave her a gentle nudge.

"Hey, we're not done, partner. Sit up," she advised.

Abigail did so reluctantly, and with an exhausted groan.

"Actually, I am done," she nodded. "Like, over-toasted."

"You look a bit red in the face," Crystal laughed. "But you'll enjoy this next bit, I promise."

"I'll hold you to that, you know."

"No worries. Okay, sit with your legs crossed; back straight. Good. Touch the tips of your thumb and index fingers together, and keep your other fingers straight. Excellent. Close your eyes, and just focus on my voice."

Crystal paced the previously stressed-out politician through a deep calming meditation, beginning with a simple breathing exercise, then directing her focus onto a series of specific power words that she used as mantras, to finish with a nice five-minute stretch of no-mind meditation.

"And... Open your eyes," she murmured eventually.

Abigail did, blinked, looked at her, and did not say a word.

"Okay?" Crystal asked, amused. "You enjoyed that?"

"I loved it... Gosh. I feel so relaxed!"

"Wonderful."

Crystal was genuinely pleased to have been able to help.

"So," Abigail mused, fixing her with an interested stare. "A meditating soldier, uh?"

"Yeah, I have many talents," Crystal joked. She got up and offered her a helping hand. "Now, I am dreaming of mountains of food."

"I was going to ask you one last thing," Abigail said.

"Sure. What is it?"

"Russ says that I should learn self-defence."

Crystal gave a light shrug at the obvious statement.

"That kind of goes without saying."

"Will you teach me?"

"What, now?"

"Yes, now," Abigail chuckled. "I promise you mountains of food will follow."

"In that case," Crystal grinned. "I can show you a few tools every woman in the world should have in their arsenal. It takes six seconds to choke someone unconscious; did you know that?"

Abigail's smile faded.

"No, I sure did not know that."

"Once you're in that state, your attacker can do to you what they like, including raping or killing you. That's why you need to avoid giving them that first advantage at all cost. Right?"

"Right. Makes sense."

"Okay, so what would you do if I grabbed you like this?"

Before Abigail could react, Crystal reached forward and she circled her hands around her neck in a perfect choke hold. Grip just tight enough to make this demo count, and Abigail reacted instinctively by grabbing hold of her wrists and trying to pull her hands apart. Crystal tightened her fingers a little, and kept her hands in place.

"Dammit!" Abigail exclaimed, struggling.

"This would only work with someone who is much weaker than you," Crystal said. "Remember, you only have six seconds here."

"Okay, then how about I kick him in the groin?"

"That's assuming your attacker is male. And also, that you won't miss, and that you'll cause the right amount of pain for him to let go. Say, you miss? You're down to three seconds. And what if it's a woman who's got hold of you?"

Abigail gave an ironic snort.

"I don't know. Lean forward and kiss her?" she ventured.

Crystal did laugh at that, but she still did not relax her grip.

"Snog your attacker into submission, uh?" she said. "Is that your best strategy?"

"Would it work?" Abigail asked, watching her intently.

Probably, Crystal reflected, although she was not about to admit to that, not even jokingly.

"You won't flirt your way out of this one, Ms Christensen," she declared instead.

"All right, then," Abigail replied, and she stopped trying. "I give up, Ms Thor. What should I do?"

Smiling, Crystal let go of her and pointed to her own self.

"Your turn," she invited. "Hold my neck tightly."

Abigail reached for her with all the enthusiasm of a newbie intent on not losing a dare. Crystal slapped the sides of her arms in challenge.

"I said tight. Come on, Abi," she pushed her.

At the same time, she easily broke the woman's grip with the most fluid of all moves, and quickly stepped away from her, chuckling at the look of disappointment on her face.

"Ah!" Abigail exclaimed. "What? Just like that?"

"Yep, just like that," Crystal laughed. "Did you see what I did?"

"Uhm… Step back? And bow down?"

"Yes. Target your thumbs with my whole body. Try it."

They resumed their earlier position, and this time, Abigail had no problem escaping her instructor's hold.

"So simple," she marvelled.

"It is when you know how. Right. Can I go eat, now?"

"Wait, wait," Abigail insisted. "What if someone's holding me from behind? Like this."

She stepped behind Crystal and stood on tip toes to wrap her arm around her neck. Crystal bent her knees a little to allow her to do it. She did not focus on how comfortable the position might have been under different circumstances, and just quickly, with minimum effort, once again slipped out of the woman's hold.

"Did you see that move?" she said.

"I think so," Abigail frowned. "Uhm…"

They swapped places, and Crystal ran her quickly through the technique for this one.

"I've got my right arm around your neck, so what you do is step forward with your left foot, where the opening in my body is; then cross behind with your right leg, and then when you're more or less facing me, push off me with both hands, and away quickly."

Abigail was perfect at this once again.

"This is fun," she declared. "What now?"

"Okay, I'll show you one last trick," Crystal decided. "Let's say your attacker has managed to get you pinned down on the floor. You're lying on your back, and he or she is right on top of you, holding you in place."

Abigail allowed her to get into the position, straddling her body with her hands resting softly around her neck; but then, instead of trying to free herself, she just lay there grinning her head off. She started to laugh.

"What now?" Crystal smiled.

She expected another dubious joke, a wiseass comment, or some kind of teasing, and she was not disappointed. Abigail was right on cue, but no longer laughing anymore, not really, when she delivered her next line.

"This is when I kiss her, right?" she said.

CHAPTER FOURTEEN

Crystal could not help but hesitate slightly, at least internally, at what really could have been some serious flirting going on. She was a little confused. But then Abigail poked her in the ribs to regain her attention, and revealed the reason for her seriousness.

"Hurry up with this, instructor," she said. "I don't like lying down on dusty hotel gym mats. This thing stinks."

Crystal quickly re-focused. She took hold of her wrist, and raised her arm up.

"Try to touch my face," she instructed.

Abigail extended her fingers and attempted to do it.

"I can't," she said. "Not from this position."

"Meanwhile," Crystal replied. "I can do this."

She made a fist and pressed it delicately against the side of Abigail's cheek, so as to drive her point home. She encountered warm, soft skin under her folded knuckles. She got to stare into that pair of sparkling grey eyes looking up, and boldly back at her. In this position, Crystal was the one who could have easily initiated a kiss. Not that she necessarily wanted to, but Abigail's banter had got her mind wandering. She chased the thought out of her mind, and did her best to remain on topic.

"If you try to fight someone who's sitting on top of you like this, you're just going to get punched in the face until you pass out," she predicted. "So, here's what I want you to do instead;

Put your hand on my wrist, no thumb, and grab onto the back of my arm at the same time."

"Okay," Abigail nodded, and instantly did so.

"Good. Keep your elbow close to your body. Your left foot goes outside my leg, and the other one right in between. Now, raise your hips..."

Abigail naturally followed through on the movement before she needed to be told. She was strong, and quick with it too, and Crystal soon found herself on her back, a grinning presidential candidate resting on top of her.

"Well done," she approved. "That was really good."

"It's nice to learn from the best. Thanks for teaching me."

With a satisfied look on her face, and no added teasing, Abigail rolled off her and got to her feet. Crystal did the same. She picked up the small bum bag that she always carried with her when she was in the gym, which contained her weapon and her cell phone, and clipped it safely around her waist.

"I'll walk you back to your room," she offered. "What are your plans for tonight?"

"I gave my crew the night off," Abigail replied. "And I'll be staying in."

They walked into the elevator and she pushed the button for the very top floor, where her suite was situated, sandwiched in between Crystal's room and the one that her two additional security officers occupied. Russ, JoAnn, and Samantha were all in different rooms on the floor below.

"What will you do for food?" Crystal enquired.

Abigail drew in a breath to reply, but right at this time, the elevator lurched abruptly and came to a sudden stop. All three overhead fluorescent lights went out.

"Damn," she muttered. "Are we stuck?"

"Mmm..." Crystal replied in the sudden darkness.

This could be nothing, and she was not overly worried, but all the same, she quietly unzipped her pouch and pulled out her weapon. Abigail turned on her phone for some light, and flashed it at the control panel. She pressed the emergency button, twice. When nothing happened, she shook her head impatiently, and only then did she notice the gun in Crystal's hand. She raised a single eyebrow.

"Just ignore me; you're good at it," Crystal said.

Abigail rolled her eyes, and she cracked a wry smile.

"Right, I'm calling Russ," she announced. "I am not going to spend my first evening off in a number of months stuck inside this thing…"

Thankfully, even as she said those words, the lights came back on, and the elevator started on its way up again. Matt Scott was waiting for them in front of the doors when they reached the top floor. The corridor was plunged into darkness, with only a series of green emergency exit signs glowing on the walls at regular intervals.

"Half the town's gone dark, Crys, it's not just the hotel," he informed her, before Crystal could even ask. "There's a nasty ice storm going on out there that's affecting the whole electricity network. Crews are working on it, but it could be a while before the lights are fully back on. I went in and put some candles in your room, ma'am."

"Thank you, that's very kind," Abigail replied.

"Oh, and there's no hot water either, I'm afraid."

"Okay, thanks for your help, Matt," Crystal replied.

She escorted Abigail to her suite and walked in ahead of her as she always did. She performed a quick check of the room, even though her teammate had been in recently, and just made double-sure that everything was in order, before stepping aside with an amused grin.

"All clear," she announced. "Your cold shower awaits."

"How delightful," Abigail groaned. "If you hear screaming, just ignore me. By the way, I'm going to order in. The Tex-Mex across the street should do the trick. What do you think?"

"Okay; well, if you have your order delivered to Reception, I'll bring it up for you when it arrives," Crystal instructed. "Put it under my name, and don't give out your room number."

She was about to leave when Abigail called her back softly. Crystal turned around, and spotted a rare flash of hesitation in her eyes as she met her gaze.

"Everything okay?" she asked. "Is there anything else you need?"

"No, I'm fine." Abigail smiled, all signs of hesitation gone, as if Crystal had just dreamt it. "I meant to say, if you want to order yourself some food as well, perhaps we could eat together tonight, Crys?"

∞

Crystal stopped by her room for a brief shower, which reminded her of those challenging swims in icy mountain lakes she used to practice when she was in the Forces. It was fun then, surrounded by beautiful scenery and her Army buddies, but not so much now, inside of a dark hotel room. She rinsed the sweat off her body and washed her hair in record time, dressed back in her usual jeans, boots, and a thick shirt, and headed down to collect their food. The invite to dinner had surprised her... Although why, she was not sure. She knew that Abigail was the type of hands-on leader who liked to know her troops on a deeper level, and they had only just started. Having a friendly chat over some food made sense, and there were still some things that Crystal needed to know about the campaign, and Abigail's motivation.

At the same time, the woman had pointed out that this was her first night off in months, and Crystal could not help but wonder; Again... Abigail Christensen had her wondering a hell of a lot. If this was not work for her, then what? *And why do I even care?* Crystal told herself to forget it. She was a soldier, and here to do a crucial job. No matter how attractive or alluring her client may be, and regardless of the amount of flirting that she did with her, which was enjoyable, to say the least, Crystal knew that she had to keep her mind clear and her priorities straight. *No problem.* Downstairs, she exchanged a few words with the receptionist on duty about the power cut.

"I'm sure it won't be long," he assured her.

"I hope not. Good thing the heating's still on."

"Yep." With a grin, he offered her some more candles. "Just in case, hey..."

"Yeah, all right," Crystal chuckled. "Thanks."

She grabbed their food, which smelled heavenly and made her mouth water in anticipation, and quickly jogged her way back up the stairs to Abigail's room. She knocked once on the door, and announced herself.

"Abi, it's me. All clear," she said.

There was no response, and the door remained firmly shut. Crystal frowned and she knocked again.

"Abi?"

Without waiting this time, Crystal dropped the bag of food and she reached for her Sig. She used her own key card to get in the room. It was not as dark as before, since Abigail had lit some candles... *But where the hell is she?*

"Abigail?" she called.

She went through the rooms, checking one after the other. Everything looked in order, no sign of an attack or struggle. All good... Apart from the fact that the main woman was missing.

"Oh, come on, Abi..." Crystal muttered impatiently under her breath. *Damn, we've just had this conversation!* She raced out the door and straight to her crew's quarters. "Guys; have you seen Abi since we got back?" she fired at them.

The answer was negative, and they instantly shot to their feet.

"The woman is slippery as hell," Scott remarked.

"I know," Crystal groaned. "Matt, you keep an eye on her floor. Tom, let's go check with Russ."

They flew down the stairs and almost broke right through the man's door. At least, he was inside to open it. Crystal did not give him a chance to say anything. She burst through the room as if she was on fire, gun in hand, her backup hot on her heels. Both came to an abrupt stop at the sight of Christensen sitting on the couch, safe and sound.

"Oh, man!" Crystal exclaimed in equal parts frustration and relief.

She was seething, but she had enough sense not to explode at her client right here and then. They would just have a private conversation, and Crystal would deliver a few hard truths to her. This was not okay. She had no problem with having a sense of humour, but she certainly was not going to tolerate the sort of behaviour that could lead to the candidate getting hurt, or much worse. *Not on my watch!* Crystal was about to demand a quiet word when Abigail stood up and walked straight toward her.

"I'm sorry, Crys," she murmured. "Stupid move, I know."

Crystal was taken aback when she spotted hot tears shining in her eyes, and all her anger evaporated in a single second. She glanced toward Russ, and noticed how pale and worried the guy looked as well.

"What's wrong?" she asked.

Tom Greer gave her a brief nod.

"I'll leave you to it, Crys; all right."

"Wait, Tom, I'm going too," Russell announced, as if he did not want to walk out alone. "Abi, I'll prep a statement for you and handle all the press requests. I know that you don't want to comment just yet, so I'll work something out with Jo and Sam."

"Thanks," Abigail murmured. "Thank you…"

She seemed miles away, and Crystal started to worry. She was aware that there might be more to it than just professional concern… Russell grabbed hold of her arm on his way out the door, and he glanced briefly over his shoulder toward his boss, who was paying them no attention at all.

"Whatever you do tonight, don't let her out of your sight," he hissed.

Puzzled at the sharpness of the request, Crystal gave him a steady nod in response.

"I won't," she promised. "Don't worry."

She locked the door after him and returned her attention to Abigail, who was back on the couch now, leaning forward with her face buried into her hands. Crystal hesitated. Her job was to keep the woman safe, she reasoned, not to offer her a shoulder to cry on. She did not get the sense that Abigail would appreciate that if she were to try it anyway. *She's not on happy pills this time…* Crystal bit on her lower lip, unsure of how to proceed. The thought that she should have trusted her instincts and cut loose in favour of a campervan and the open road did cross her mind, even as her feet took her resolutely toward the sofa. She sat down next to Abigail, close, but she did not touch her.

"Hey… Abi? Is there anything I can do?" she murmured.

Abigail gave a heavy sigh, but she still shook her head no. She was not crying anymore, but Crystal was once again taken aback by the sheer intensity of the sadness and the hurt in her eyes when the woman looked at her.

"I never finished briefing you about the reason behind my campaign the other night," she said tightly, clearly working hard to stay on top of her emotions. "But I need to tell you the rest of it now. All of it, right now."

A secret global network; Enslavement of the entire human race... A powerful, icy shiver ran down the length of Crystal's spine. She had filed all that crazy stuff at the back of her mind, unsure that she believed it, or that she even wanted to. Now though, it looked as if she was going to get an opportunity to make up her mind once and for all.

"Okay," she replied. "I'm ready to hear it."

Abigail took a deep breath and she seemed to brace herself. She grabbed hold of her hand. All reservations forgotten, Crystal instinctively held on tight.

"I just got off the phone with a colleague in Washington," Abigail said. "You remember that I told you it was my friend Senator James Birch who warned me to be careful?"

"Yes." Crystal nodded, her chest tightening in anticipation of some unpleasant stuff. "You said he was an ally, and that you trusted him immensely."

A single tear rolled down the side of Abigail's cheek.

"Birch is dead," she murmured. "They took him out."

CHAPTER FIFTEEN

Abigail was still shaking from the awful news, and she could not suppress anger and bitterness from heavily affecting her tone as she continued.

"They're trying to pass it off as a tragic accident, of course. No surprise there, I knew they would. But this was no goddamn accident. Senator Birch was murdered! I am sure of it."

"How did he die?" Crystal asked.

She sounded calm and in control, Abigail noticed. She drew comfort and reassurance from that, and reflected once again that it was awfully nice to have a woman like Captain Thor on her side. The first person that Abigail had wanted to tell about Birch was Russ, hence her mad dash to his room upon finding out about his death. The senator had been a friend and a mentor to Russell too... He had shared her deep shock, instant grief, and the horror of the discovery, but now Crystal provided the solid layer of strength that Abigail needed. The soldier's understated yet powerful energy helped her to speak out the words that she struggled to even contemplate.

"They found his body floating in the Potomac river. A small boat and fishing gear were also recovered. His car was parked in a popular spot nearby. The official line is that he fell off his boat, couldn't get back on, and drowned. The perfect crime."

Abigail had never expected Thor to simply nod and agree with her on that, not with her experience as an Army Ranger and Special Forces operator. Even though there was a hell of a lot she did not know about Crystal personally, and wanted to find out, she did not expect someone with her background to be naïve or uninformed about the darker side of some of the things that they were dealing with. Sure enough, Crystal asked her the question.

"How do you know it was murder?" she enquired.

"Because I know James," Abigail snapped angrily.

She instantly caught herself. *Damn. And here I thought I was handling this...* Before she could apologise, she felt the slight but firm pressure of Crystal's fingers around her own, squeezing gently. Abigail had forgotten that they were still holding hands, and that she was the one who had initiated the contact. Part of her cringed inside at her lack of self-control... Another part did not want to let go. Thor did not seem to mind either way.

"I'm sorry about your friend," she said.

Abigail felt hot and painful tears rise in her eyes, and she averted her gaze. She did not want to cry, here... As for the rest, she held on to the soldier's hand, and to hell with it.

"I'm just trying to understand," Crystal added.

Abigail nodded, and she took a deep breath.

"I know," she said intently. "And I appreciate it more than you know. Crys, the thing with James is this: he could not swim. He had a phobia of water that came from almost drowning in a swimming pool when he was just a kid. He never even went for a walk along the river... He didn't like boats, and he certainly was not into fishing. Hell, the man was a vegan!"

"I see."

Crystal's face darkened. Abigail spotted a muscle in her jaw tighten too. She let go of her hand, and went to get them both a glass of water. On second thought, she opened the fridge.

"Whiskey?" she asked. "Something else?"

"No, thanks," Crystal replied with a brief smile.

Abigail had not expected her to say yes. She grabbed herself a mini-bottle and returned to the couch. A fierce blizzard was raging on outside. The electricity was still off, but the soft light from a few lit candles warmed up their circle, inviting closeness, intimacy, and secrets to be shared.

"I must say," Abigail reflected sadly, "James was playing a dangerous game."

"How so?" Crystal enquired.

"He was fully aware of what was going on, and open about the fact that he wanted to blow the lid on the whole thing. He had contacts deep inside the machine; people in the military, and contractors who were involved in those Special Projects I told you about, but who wanted to expose the lies. James was building a strong case, but you have to understand the risks of swimming in such shark-infested waters. He sure did, but…"

Abigail winced. She tried not to dwell on the fear and terror that her trusted friend would have felt as he was put on a boat, taken out on the river, and thrown overboard. *Maybe they killed him first…* She shivered. She knew that mercy was not their style.

"I'm not asking you to take my word for it, Crys," she said. "But from what I just told you about James and his fear of water, does it make sense that there may be more to his sudden death than we are told?"

Crystal looked straight at her, deep-black eyes shining with warmth, easy understanding, and just as much toughness in the flickering candlelight.

"Yes," she simply said. "I think you may have a point."

Abigail let out a quiet sigh, and she swallowed back some fresh tears as well, except that this time she felt more relief than anything else. Crystal kept her eyes on her, unwavering and hot.

"Do you think they killed him as a warning to you, Abi?" she asked.

"I'm sure it must be part of it… James must also have been close to discovering or revealing some crucial information for them to suddenly have to take such drastic action."

"Like what sort of info?" Crystal enquired.

"I'm not sure yet. But I'll find out."

Abigail noticed a flash of impatience cross her eyes, and a touch of frustration as well, which she shared, of course.

"Let me explain a bit more," she said. "The global network that is behind all this, and that we are up against today, did not start out as a breakaway group. It was always secret, yes, but under the rightful control of both the UK and US governments. During WWII, it was a task force made up of military personnel, Air Force pilots, some civilian engineers and scientists, formed to investigate troubling reports of unidentified flying objects over the fields of France and Germany."

Crystal blinked just once, and a tiny line appeared on her forehead, but she did not comment, or interrupt. Abigail carried on with her story, determined to share with her the full picture this time.

"It was assumed at first that the objects must be enemy jets, and that the Nazis must have somehow managed to develop secret technology we knew nothing about. A worrying enough prospect in times of war, right?"

"Sure," Crystal nodded, her face still impassive.

"Well, it turned out to be unfounded. A report issued by the task force in 1946 concluded that the objects in question were not German, but might be interplanetary craft of unknown origin."

Crystal did react this time, by running both hands through her hair, giving a sharp shake of the head, and flashing a longing glance toward the mini-bottle that Abigail had not opened yet.

"There's more, you know."

"What? Whiskey?"

"That. And to the story," Abigail nodded.

"Of course, there is," Crystal muttered. "Is this for real?"

"Everything I'm telling you is backed up and supported by official documentation. Most of it still classified, of course, but like I said, I have sources and informants on the inside. I've seen enough official CIA and Pentagon memos, MI6 reports, as well as a bunch of original letters exchanged between the UK Prime Minister and the White House to believe that this is all true."

Crystal stared at her intently, her eyes flashing.

"We are not alone," she said. And then, again; "We are not alone? That's what you're telling me? Officially?"

"Did you think that there was a chance we were the only intelligent species around?" Abigail challenged. "In this gigantic universe teaming with life?"

Crystal gave a slow exhale, and she shrugged.

"Probably not," she admitted. "But... You really have proof of this?"

"Like I said. The stuff I've seen is absolutely undeniable."

"I see. So, is disclosure your campaign's ultimate goal?"

"Yes... And to expose the Global Network that was borne out of the task force I just mentioned. From 1947 to 1956, it took on a complete life of its own. A handful of corporations, mainly American, began to assume control of all the research projects. Little by little, our own government lost oversight of what they were doing. And on that note; Crys, do you remember President Eisenhower's last speech before he left Office?"

"Uhm... No, I don't think I do..."

"The entire speech was a stark warning. *'Beware the Military Industrial Complex'*, is what he said."

"He knew?" Crystal frowned.

"Oh, yes. Indeed. And he could see where it was all going. Sadly, his words fell on deaf ears, and the entire operation went underground. By 1961, when Kennedy was elected to office, the takeover was complete."

"So, a bunch of big US corporations really is behind it all," Crystal commented. "I thought you said it wasn't them?"

"The Global Network controls the corporations," Abigail replied. "Let me tell you something about Kennedy too: in June of '63, on his way to the famous speech that he made in Berlin, a Lieutenant-Colonel who had flown combat missions over France during the war asked him about the UFO issue. You know what Kennedy's response was?"

Crystal shook her head, eyes still riveted onto her face.

"He said that he had been briefed, albeit only superficially. His exact words were: *'It's out of my hands, and I don't know why.'* He said that, and then he just started to cry."

When Crystal opened her mouth to speak, Abigail pre-empted her question.

"Before you ask me if I have proof," she said, "the answer is yes, I do. I listened to the original recording, and I can tell you it was absolutely not tempered with. It was John F. Kennedy, one hundred percent sure, and that is what he said. It was the most shocking conversation I ever heard in my life. It made me cry, too."

With that, Abigail picked up the miniature whiskey bottle, unscrewed the top, and downed half of it in a single confident swallow. She caught the thirsty expression on Crystal's face as she watched her do it, and it made a shiver run down her spine. This one was not due to fear or reluctance. Abigail looked away, ashamed at the instant spark of desire that sizzled through her. *What the hell, Abi?* Now was hardly the moment for this sort of reaction. Come to think of it, the candles probably did not help...

Abigail set the bottle down in front of her. Crystal did not reach for it.

"You may already know that Kennedy planned to dissolve the CIA, get us the hell out of Vietnam, and make peace with Russia," she added. "He was also going to reveal to the world that we were not alone in the universe. That was in June of 1963. By November of that same year, he was dead. You think it was a coincidence?"

"Jesus!" Crystal exclaimed. Her fists were tightly clenched; she looked like she would be grateful for something to punch. "Now your friend's warning really does hit home in a big way... Fuck!"

Abigail kept her eyes on her, as for the first time since she had met the soldier, she started to show signs of stress. *Or at the very least, massive irritation...* Abigail sensed absolutely no fear in her. She gave a light shrug.

"I know," she said. "Good thing I've got you, uh?"

Crystal fixed her with a single dark, disbelieving stare.

"You think I alone can keep you safe from these people?" she snapped. "This Global Network that you speak of?"

"I think you are supremely qualified to give it a good go," Abigail replied. She passed her the open bottle. "It's pretty weak stuff, it won't take your edge off. Go on, Crys."

Crystal grabbed it without a single word, and she tipped the remaining liquid into her mouth. She went to check the door. Abigail watched her pace in front of her, looking quite furious indeed. She had only one fear; that Crystal might decide she was crazy, and walk out on her. Of course, Abigail would be able to find someone else, probably just as qualified, at least on paper. But it probably would not be a woman... And certainly not one that made the back of her neck tingle every time that she caught sight of her at an event, alert and focused in the background...

Armed and dangerous, and watching fiercely over her. Abigail remembered pulling Crystal's file out of Russell's bag. She could not explain why, but she had felt a certain connection with the woman even before they met in person. If she had been aware of the fact that Crystal thought that she was ignoring her, or even that she wanted to, she would have laughed at such a ludicrous notion. Not paying attention to her, and treating her the same as anybody else on her team, really was becoming the hardest thing in the world to do lately... Abigail did not want her to leave.

"Are you okay?" she asked. "And are we?"

Crystal did not reply straight away. She remained standing in the middle of the room, staring at the floor, completely lost in thought and frowning hard. Abigail felt another pang of anxiety hit her in the chest.

"Crys?" she repeated. "Please, talk to me."

CHAPTER SIXTEEN

Crystal wanted to stay furious. She told herself that she would have liked to know all this stuff before she signed up for the job. If she had, she would not have agreed to work for Christensen. *You know that's not true...* Crystal blew an impatient exhale. In truth, she had been drawn to her from the word go. Knowing that there was a lot more to her campaign than Abigail let on officially also made her curious. She looked at her, aware that leaving had never even been an option.

"Yes," she nodded. "I'm okay. We're fine."

"And you're happy to stay on as my CPO?"

Abigail looked worried, incredibly anxious. Crystal flashed her a reassuring smile, just the right side of cocky.

"Despite the enormity of the challenge, and the insanity of your mission," she replied. "The answer is yes, Ms Christensen. I'll have one hell of a good crack at it."

Abigail touched her hand.

"Thank you," she murmured.

They both jumped as the lights suddenly came back on, and someone knocked softly on the door.

"It's me, and Tom," Russell announced.

Crystal opened the door. He glanced at her as he came in.

"See," he remarked with a knowing grin. "I'm learning."

"Good man," Crystal approved, smiling back.

He went straight to the couch and started to brief Abigail on the latest press updates regarding Birch's death, how they were handling requests for reactions, and her upcoming schedule. He looked sad and properly exhausted, just like his boss did. While they were catching up, Crystal also took the opportunity to share a quiet word with Greer.

"Everything okay with you and Matt?" she asked.

"All good, Crys, no worries. I'm on watch until midnight, then he'll be on." He cracked a wry smile. "It's all kicking off, uh? Should have known this job would be fun, since you were involved."

"Yeah," Crystal shrugged. "I guess so, hey."

"Jokes aside," Greer added in a lower tone. "We realise the seriousness of the mission, and everything that is truly at stake here. We've got their backs. And yours as well, Thor."

"Roger that," Crystal approved. "Thanks, as always."

"Sure thing. See you later."

As Greer left, Abigail beckoned her over.

"Crys? Do you have a minute?"

She looked solemn and determined, her face grave yet calm. *Now this,* Crystal reflected, *is what a Commander-in-Chief should look like...* Her mind was still reeling from Abigail's revelations. She had questions, lots of them, and one in particular had her tongue on fire. But Abigail spoke first, in a clear and decisive voice.

"Here's the schedule for tomorrow," she announced.

Crystal swallowed back her impatience.

"I'm listening," she nodded.

"I'll be doing a series of interviews at the local News station in the morning. We've got two town halls in the afternoon, and a meet-and-greet at a Farmers' Market to follow. Once we're done with that, we'll be driving on to Waterloo in the evening."

Crystal suppressed a frustrated sigh. Abigail already knew what she thought of those open and close interactions with the public. *It would be so easy for a killer to infiltrate the crowd and try something...* Christensen was aware of all those risks, and clearly intent on carrying on. The only other alternative for her would be to drop out of the public eye, say goodbye to her campaign, and give up on her real purpose. It was never going to happen, Crystal knew, and so, there was no need to rehash the same old stuff. Just up to her to do her job and keep the woman safe.

"Okay," she replied. "I'm ready, and so is my team."

"I can guess what you're thinking," Abigail conceded. "It's on my mind too, as you well know. But the show must go on, and it's time to pick up the pace. "

"What do you mean?"

"The best defence for us now is offence."

"How?" Crystal frowned. "What will you do?"

Abigail rolled her shoulders back a couple of times before answering.

"I will use the interviews tomorrow to challenge the official version of Birch's death, and I will also talk about the Network. I have built enough trust with my audience now that I think it will be a beneficial move. Time to let everyone know that this is not just about the next US presidency, but a global issue. It's about the future of our entire world."

Russell took over from her.

"Once the truth is fully out in the open," he declared in a fierce, vehement tone, "it will also make it much harder for those people to take Abi out. Right now, a sniper's bullet is all that it would take. They could get rid of her easily in this way, and just spin whatever bullshit story they want on the back of it." He glanced toward his friend. "Sorry, Abs."

"No need. It's the truth."

Crystal reflected that she had never seen him look so fired-up or passionate. She knew that he was committed, but this was something else. He had her full, undivided attention, and now he sure was not blushing, as he continued.

"If Abi were to disappear, like Birch, no one would question it at the moment. People would swallow all the lies they're being fed, and those who are in this fight with us would sink further into obscurity and fear of consequences. We need to be bold with our actions at this stage, and go public. This is our one chance to make it work. We must take it and run with it."

"So, that's the plan in a nutshell," Abigail concluded. "What do you think, Crys."

Crystal shrugged in uncharacteristic reluctance.

"What's wrong?" Abigail prompted immediately.

"Nothing, but why ask me? I'm just the muscle here."

"Don't be ridiculous. We are a team now. There is no *'just'* this or that between us. No divisions. I trust your experience, and your soldier's instincts. So, please; tell me what you think."

Crystal relaxed. This was a nice confirmation of where she stood with this crew. Not that she needed another one, to be fair.

"I think it makes perfect sense," she agreed. "Be All-In, or get off the field. The more open and transparent you can be, and the more visible you can make yourself, not just to voters but to the entire world, the harder it will be for them to get rid of you. Russ is absolutely right about that."

"Okay. Glad you think so. Any questions before we call it a night?"

"Yes," Crystal replied instantly.

"Go right ahead," Abigail nodded in turn.

As she stood in front of her, Crystal truly felt as if she were on the edge of a huge abyss. Part of her still struggled to accept the information that she had been given so far. *Such crazy stuff...*

So unbelievable, in fact, that she would not have been surprised to discover that she had been dreaming this entire conversation; or even the last few days on the road with Christensen. *Maybe that bullet from Darlene's husband did a bit more than just graze me,* she reflected. *Maybe I'm in a hospital back in New York, in a coma, hallucinating...* It was a measure of how disturbing the whole thing was for her that Crystal might have chosen the shot-and-wounded option as a better alternative to the one that she was in now. Then again, she did rather like a world that had Abigail Christensen in it. *Stop that, soldier,* she told herself; *And just ask the damn question.*

"Abi, you mentioned a secret joint military and civilian task force charged with investigating UFOs during WWII," she said, focusing back on the matter at hand. "And you also told me that disclosure of everything around that subject is one of the goals of your campaign."

Abigail gave another quiet nod of assent.

"And Russ," Crystal continued, "the other night, you were asking about the guy in the alleyway, and if I'd noticed anything different about him. You said that the people we're up against, they are not like us. I thought you meant sociopaths..."

Russell also did not reply. They were probably just waiting for the real question behind the string of aimless statements. *Stop hesitating, for God's sake!* Crystal took a deep breath, and she went for it.

"Have we made contact with extra-terrestrials?" she asked.

Abigail exchanged a brief look with Russell, and then she returned her gaze to her, her eyes intent and steadfast. She went on to drop the sort of bombshell that made Crystal's legs grow weak in reaction.

"Yes," she said. "Absolutely, we have."

∞

Crystal needed to sit down first, then she had to remind herself to keep breathing once again, as Abigail just went on with more revelations that made everything that she had told her up until then seem pretty insignificant in comparison.

"First contact was achieved in 1955 with a peaceful extra-terrestrial civilisation," she announced. "There is proof of this, before you ask. Photos of the craft hovering over a secret base in New Mexico; witness testimonies. Letters and diary entries from President Eisenhower, who met with these beings. Of course, it's all classified."

"Why, 'of course'?" Crystal muttered.

"I was being sarcastic," Abigail replied. "That's my point. It should not be. This record of evidence belongs to Humanity as a whole."

"Why then? Why all the secrecy?"

"At first, they just wanted to avoid a complete panic. Being honest about what was really going on at the time would have meant admitting that our United States government could not ever truly guarantee the security and safety of our people."

"Really?" Crystal said with a dark frown over her face.

"Yes, really. I know it's not a nice thought for a soldier, but let's face it: if anyone can pop over here from the other side of the universe, using technology that is so far in advance of our own, then what if their intentions are not peaceful? Just imagine what people's reaction would be to that very real possibility."

Crystal rubbed her forehead, as a nasty headache started to take hold.

"Still, I would always prefer to know the truth," she said.

"I'm with you on that," Abigail replied. "That's what we're fighting for."

"So, anyway. That first encounter was peaceful; right?"

"That is correct. There was an exchange of knowledge and technology between our civilisation and theirs; it was mutually beneficial at the time, but a one-time only event. Pretty much, it was a case of *'Hello, 'Nice to meet you guys'*, and *'See ya later'*."

"All right." Crystal braced herself. "Now give me the bad news about this whole thing."

"The bad news," Abigail nodded, "is that we have reason to believe that another contact took place in 1964, in Scotland this time. Unfortunately, the Global Network was fully in control by then. Our officially elected government was out of the loop for good, and so was the UK's. This time, the deep secrecy that surrounded the encounter was no longer about avoiding a public panic, but to hide their true purpose."

"Let me guess," Crystal muttered. "It's not a nice one."

"We think not. Now, you have to keep in mind that this field of special projects is so secret and compartmentalised that it is hard to get a sense of the big picture behind it. But enough has emerged over the years to make us believe that the Global Network has struck an alliance with an ET civilisation that is not friendly, not peaceful, only after a single thing: the exploitation of the human race."

Crystal glanced toward Russ. Her head was spinning, her heart racing. She was kind of hoping that he would just burst out laughing, slap her on the back, and yell *'Gotcha!'*. But he looked grim.

"I'm afraid that's all true," he confirmed. "And it gets even worse, my friend."

"Are you kidding me?" Crystal grunted.

"I wish. But look, the guy in the alleyway the other night; did he seem to you like he had bright glowing red eyes and a liquid face, by any chance?"

Crystal swallowed hard at the memory.

"Yes..." she murmured. "Like that exactly."

Abigail rested her earnest, passionate grey eyes on her.

"Then that's your proof, Crys," she said. "These beings are already here. Walking among us on our planet, hiding in plain sight. Just biding their time."

CHAPTER SEVENTEEN

Abigail carried on working well into the night. She rehearsed her statements for the News interviews the following day: short and impactful. She prepared her Town Hall speeches. When she did go to bed eventually, she felt ready, aware that they were about to pass a crucial point of No-Return. *Nothing will ever be the same after this...* It all amounted to a declaration of war on the very people who had murdered Birch, not only to get him out of the way, but also to deliver their sinister message to her. Well, now Abigail was going to send her own response. She tossed and turned for a long while, unable to settle fully, as a furious wind screamed outside the windows. She was nervous but also full of resolve as she contemplated the journey ahead. She had always known that it would come to this eventually. This next move might cost her the presidency, but it had never been only about that for her, not really. Her mission was global; planetary in its scope. Now she had reached the right audience. She had the perfect platform, and it was time to step it up. She stared at the ceiling. Eyes wide open, her mind racing. Her thoughts kept drifting back to the handsome soldier with the legendary name. Captain Thor... *No coincidence, I'm sure.* The full significance of Crystal's involvement was only just beginning to take form and sink in for Abigail. It almost felt cosmically-ordered, in a way; *She's a solid ally; A true friend; A lot more than a simple bodyguard...*

Now, Abigail just hoped that she was okay. The soldier had left her room looking pale and preoccupied. She had hardly eaten a thing. No wonder; and yet, it was just the beginning. Abigail did not think that the full scope and implications of everything that she had revealed to her had hit fully just yet, but when it did, it would be even worse. Every belief and conviction that she had ever held about the world, her own place in it, and the nature of reality itself would be shaken to its absolute core. Her world would literally shift on its axis, if it had not already. Russell had described the process of realisation as akin to being stuck on a bad DMT trip, and unable to wake up from it. *It's just the sort of thing that could drive people mad,* he concluded. Crystal seemed plenty strong enough to handle whatever was thrown at her, and yet, Abigail did not know for sure. Something kept nagging at the back of her mind. She never ignored her intuition, and right now, it was telling her to check on her. Without trying to rationalise it any further, she reached for the phone, and dialled her CPO's number. Crystal answered before the dial tone had a chance to kick in.

"What?" was her first, tense word. "Problem?"

"No, I'm fine. Just making sure you are as well."

There was a slight pause on the line. Abigail waited.

"Me?" Crystal sounded surprised. "Yeah. Sure."

"Did I wake you up?"

"Uhm... No."

Abigail pursed her lips. *Such reluctance and resistance...* As if Thor could not wait to get her off the line. *Something's wrong.*

"I'm coming over," she declared. "See you in a sec."

She ended the call before Crystal had a chance to reply, or tell her not to. She quickly threw on some clothes and hurried to the door. Surely, she could walk over to the next room on her own without needing to check in with the bodyguard on duty...

She peered down the corridor. Empty on the right; *Yeah, all good.* And...

"Good evening, Ms Christensen."

Startled, Abigail glanced sharply to her left to find Matthew Scott standing there, fully alert, and watching her intently. Kind of like he expected her to make a run for it, or something of the sort. She gave a quiet exhale, and flashed him a sheepish smile.

"Hey. Not pulling a fast one on you, I swear."

"Can I help you with anything, ma'am?"

"That's okay. Just going to see the boss."

He did not ask why she might need to do that in the middle of the night. His expression did not change, and he just stepped aside to let her through.

"Sure thing. You go right ahead."

Thor kept her door unlocked to allow her to respond faster to any emergency, and Abigail only gave a perfunctory knock before going right in ahead, as encouraged. The room was fully dark, but the light was on in the bathroom. She went to stand behind that door.

"Crystal?" she called.

There was no response, only the sound of running water, and a muted cough in the background.

"Crys? Are you okay in there?" Abigail repeated.

She was about to push on through when Crystal suddenly appeared in front of her, now only dressed in her jeans, a black sports bra, and shoeless. She was pale; dark shadows showed under her eyes that had definitely not been there previously. Abigail blinked in shocked surprise at the sight of the thick scar that ran across her chest. *Jesus...* She dreaded to think what might have caused this sort of injury. She noticed the thin line of stitches on her side, a more recent one. Finally, her eyes drifted over the set of perfectly-sculpted, hard muscles in her stomach.

It would have been tempting to linger over that spot, but Abigail did not, and she looked up to meet her gaze.

"What's wrong, Crys?" she demanded. "Have you just been sick?"

Crystal managed a wan smile. She leaned against the door frame as if it really was the only thing keeping her upright, and delivered a lame, half-hearted lie.

"Yeah… Must be that takeaway, uh."

"Don't give me that, I know you barely touched your food," Abigail shot back. "Talk to me, Crys. Is this about tomorrow? Or the job?"

"No," Crystal replied in a firmer tone. "I'm fi—"

Before she could say it again, Abigail reached up to cup her cheeks in both her hands. It was a totally impulsive gesture, only motivated by genuine concern for the struggling soldier in front of her. She felt Crystal stiffen instinctively in reaction, but grow still again almost immediately. She looked like she fought not to close her eyes. As for her, Abigail had to resist the urge to caress her face.

"You're burning up," she murmured in dismay.

"It's under control," Crystal grunted.

Still, she did not move.

∞

If Christensen had to come bursting in on her like that, with only minimum warning, Crystal was pretty glad of the fact that at least, it was not while she was on her hands and knees with her head above the toilet, throwing up everything she had. Or even worse, earlier; when she had been fighting not to lose control, as a severe panic attack the likes of which she had not experienced in many years threatened to overwhelm her and take her down.

When Abigail took her face in her hands, Crystal's first instinct was to pull away from her, but then, something else quickly took over. Whether it was meant that way or not, there was genuine tenderness in Abigail's touch. It was hard for Crystal not to lean in for more... Especially after the anxiety attack that she had just suffered. She tried to hide her reaction, and probably did not manage it very well. Abigail stood staring into her eyes for what felt at once like an eternity and nowhere near long enough. Crystal stared back. She did not dare ask what the woman was thinking. She suspected that it would only lead to more trouble of some kind. Abigail did not volunteer anything either.

"Come with me," she invited.

Crystal did not know where, or what for, but Abigail took her by the hand, and all she could do was follow meekly along. *Damn, I'm so tired...* Technically, she was off duty, which was a pretty good thing since she could barely put one foot in front of the other. Still, this was not all right, and come to think of it, she was never really off duty...

"I'm okay," she insisted.

"I know you are," Abigail just said.

She led her to the couch, made her sit down, and wrapped a warm blanket around her shoulders. She gave her a fresh bottle of water, and raised an enquiring eyebrow.

"Would you prefer something stronger?"

"I would... But I don't think it's a good idea right now."

"I agree. Some other time, hey?"

Crystal felt her hesitate, as she sat down next to her.

"Abi, you should go to bed," she said. "It's late. You have a big day tomorrow."

"You too."

"Yeah," Crystal sighed. "Me too. All of us."

Abigail made absolutely no move to leave.

"It's a hell of a lot to take in, I know."

"Well," Crystal shrugged. "It might take a bit longer to sink in, actually. This is such a fantastic story..."

"But you believe it? You believe me?"

"Yes, of course I do. The story makes sense, and it's not like I haven't heard this sort of thing before, both in the alternative media and when I was still in the Forces."

"Anything specific?"

"I spoke to fighter pilots who swear they encountered craft that are not of this world, and which were capable of the most incredible manoeuvres at even more unbelievable speeds. I've seen things too, when I was out in the mountains, or in isolated desert areas at night. The kind of stuff that I could not explain either. If I'm really honest, all this is not such a giant leap for me, Abi. I would just prefer not to have to think about it, that's all."

"I understand. Me too."

"Really?"

"Oh, yes," Abigail replied intently. "I am passionate about this fight, and I will not rest until the truth is known, and the Global Network dismantled. Still doesn't mean I wouldn't prefer an easier life. A safer one too, that's for sure. Unfortunately, you know that it's only going to accelerate from this point on."

"Yes, I guess you're right."

"And you are okay with that."

Abigail seemed to need to confirm this, even though Crystal had already told her that she was.

"I'm okay," she confirmed. "I just feel like I've been on hold since leaving the Army, to be honest. Waiting for the next call of duty that somehow, I knew was sure to come. Like you, I would rather be happy and safe... But I'm a soldier, and I think it's time for me to get on with the job at hand. I do trust you, Abi. I am one hundred percent behind you and your mission."

"All right. Thank you for saying so." Abigail edged closer, and she touched the back of her hand over her forehead. "What caused this fever, then?"

Crystal fought her instant reluctance to talk about it.

"Even though it's a relief to finally be at this stage, thinking of going back to duty brought back some memories that I wasn't expecting," she conceded. "Or ready for."

"Of your last mission?"

"Yeah. The last mission..."

Now Abigail seemed to finally get over her hesitation, and she slipped a bold arm around her shoulders. Before she could think or stop herself, Crystal flashed her an open, heartfelt smile.

"Thanks," she murmured.

Abigail gave her a gentle squeeze.

"So, what happened, Captain? How did you get that scar on your chest?"

Crystal rubbed her hand over it. Only a handful of people knew the full story of what had happened to her in Afghanistan. She did not enjoy telling it, but now she knew that she had to, and in actual fact, she also wanted to. This was no longer just a bodyguard job for her, and Abigail was no longer only a client either. What she truly felt about her, Crystal shelved at the back of her mind for now. Suffice to say that the close protection part was still relevant, with the emphasis on *close*...

"My team and I were on a mission around the Hindu Kush area, a high mountain range that lies across parts of Afghanistan and Pakistan," she started. "Insurgents used the Wakhan line to come and go between the two countries. We knew that one of the Taliban higher-ups would come through on a particular day; our job was to stop and detain him. But at the last minute, our Command pulled the plug on the op. No explanation. We were just ordered to hike fifty miles due West for extraction."

As she spoke, Crystal was also acutely aware of the fact that Abigail had started to rub her hand over her shoulder in a soft circle, in a soothing gesture that was pretty out of this world in terms of how good it made her feel. The urge to curl up against her side and close her eyes was there for Crystal. She did not give in to it, and resolutely carried on instead.

"We were dropped off at a Canadian base, spent the night with the Marines stationed there, then joined a US-led convoy that was headed back to Sangin. I was riding in an armoured vehicle at the front. My guys were together in a troop carrier at the back of the column. I knew the Lieutenant in charge of the convoy from training courses we'd been on together. Lt. Emily Cassidy… She was one hell of a good soldier."

Abigail obviously picked up on the word, and the wistful look in her eyes when she paused.

"Was?" she prompted gently.

"Yeah…" Crystal glanced at her, and gave a stiff nod. "We came under attack as we were crossing a low stone bridge over the river. The carrier that my team were in was hit by a rocket and burst into flames. It fell right off the side of the bridge, and landed in the water. Not completely submerged, but almost."

Abigail's hand on her shoulder went still. She sat listening intently, frowning in reluctant anticipation of what was to be revealed next.

"Uhm…" Crystal had to clear her throat before she could carry on. "After that, it's all a bit of a blur, but I think we must have returned fire for the next twenty minutes or so. Not sure. We were completely surrounded; enemy fighters were throwing grenades and shooting at us from every position. My vehicle had overturned as well, and a bunch of us were hunkered down behind the cab, shooting back at the enemy to try to regain the upper hand. My crew…"

Crystal swallowed hard again, almost choking on the words that always hurt like a knife through the heart. Abigail was even more still, and deathly quiet.

"My guys were trapped inside the destroyed carrier. I could hear them yell for help over the noise of the firefight, but bullets were flying, and I was pinned down in that one spot. I couldn't make a run for it. Meanwhile, the vehicle was sinking fast, filling up with more and more water. They started to scream in pure terror..."

CHAPTER EIGHTEEN

Abigail could not take her eyes off her, as Crystal had to take another break in her story. She noticed her chest rising up and down a little too fast. Thor was staring straight ahead with a flat and empty gaze, as if she had fallen into a deep trance and was no longer fully in the room with her, but back on the battlefield, fighting for her life. Concerned, Abigail grabbed hold of her arm.

"Crys. Crystal? Hey!"

She had to shake her again before Crystal even blinked, and slowly glanced her way. Still breathing too hard; black eyes hazy and unfocused... It took another few seconds before that far-away expression faded from her gaze, and her breathing found its normal rate.

"Are you still with me?" Abigail enquired sharply.

"Yeah." Crystal gave a soft nod. "Sorry. I, uh... I get lost."

Abigail tightened her grip around her shoulders. This time, she noticed how Crystal did allow herself to sink a bit lower against her side. Or maybe she was not even aware of doing it. *Certainly not*, Abigail decided. She could easily tell that she was fighting something, and that it was probably just her own self; the urge to let go, the need to drop her shield of invincibility for just a few restful moments, maybe even the impulse to cry...

"Crys, you don't have to carry on with this," she said.

"It's okay. I'm fine," Crystal repeated stubbornly.

"I don't think you are… And you really don't have to."

"I want to," Crystal insisted. "It's fine, don't worry."

She still looked pale and tired, but her voice was definitely stronger now.

"All right," Abigail sighed. "But take your time."

Crystal nodded and carried on. She did not get lost again, even as she related the rest of her awful tale.

"Lieutenant Cassidy was able to request air support. The fight intensified. I managed to move from behind our vehicle to help a wounded soldier. His Kevlar vest had been torn in half by the force of the explosion, and it was still melting. I stripped it off him, and gave him mine in replacement."

"Did he make it?" Abigail exclaimed. "Did he survive?"

This time, Crystal flashed her an instant, brilliant smile that lit up her entire face.

"Yes," she replied. "Now he's back home in Utah, running his parents' farm, and planning to get married to his long-term girlfriend."

"Wonderful. I'm so glad to hear it."

"He was one of the lucky ones, for sure. We lost several brilliant soldiers on that day," Crystal added, her smile fading. "My friend Cassidy was one of them. She was shot trying to carry one of her men back to the truck. By the time I got to them, he was gone, and she was barely breathing. She died in my arms. We were… close. You know what I mean."

'I'm sorry' would not even begin to express the magnitude of Abigail's sorrow at the true horror of this tragedy. Her chest tightened as she tried to put herself inside Crystal's mind, and feel what she would have as she listened to her people drown; And when she held her dying friend, her lover, by the sound of it, in her arms. *All that, and she's not even got to her own injury…* Abigail resisted the urge to put her arms around her more fully.

"Just as two coalition jets finally got on scene to help us, an IED was triggered only yards from my position. I was hit in the chest by debris," Crystal announced. "I wasn't wearing armour anymore by that stage."

Abigail winced in reluctance, but Crystal simply shrugged now. It seemed as if her own case and injuries were much easier for her to discuss, and even though Abigail kind of understood why, in a way, she certainly did not like it. She did not want to imagine the now subdued but usually vibrant woman wounded, hurt, or in pain. Of course, she knew that Thor was the selfless heroic kind who would always put her own life on the line to protect others. *To protect me...* Abigail pursed her lips in dismay. *But that's her job; what you hired her for,* she reminded herself, only to flinch in repugnance. *Still doesn't make her expendable... It's not okay.*

"From the look of that scar, it must have been a devastating hit," she remarked, not allowing her turmoil or her emotions to show.

"Oh, yeah; you can say that," Crystal agreed, unconsciously rubbing her hand over her chest again. "I was almost sliced in half by a piece of burning shrapnel. I don't remember much after that."

"I'm not surprised," Abigail muttered, shaking her head.

"I only found out later that I couldn't be evacuated straight away because the whole area was crawling with Taliban. What an Intel failure this whole thing turned out to be in the end... Our convoy should never have been sent out through that zone, and not even anywhere near, I'd say."

"Why was it, then? What do you think happened?"

Crystal shot a furious look across the empty bedroom.

"I don't know. Someone fucked up. It happens. Anyway; I was taken to another FOB, and looked after by a British surgeon.

That officer, she saved my life... Then, it's just all fade to black until I woke up in one piece almost a week later, at a German military hospital in Berlin."

Abigail did let out a brief sigh of relief at that point.

"Good. And did you recover quickly after that?"

"Physically, yes," Crystal replied, only to catch herself and immediately attempt to take it back. "I mean, uhm... There was no issue, really, other than that deep sense of betrayal I already mentioned to you."

Abigail just gave a thoughtful nod in response.

"Yes. I understand," she murmured. "I think, anyway..."

She was not naïve enough to believe that statement, not for a second. No one who had gone through the sort of ordeal that Crystal had just described to her would emerge from it mentally unscathed. There would be deep invisible scars beneath the one that everyone could see. There may not be an ongoing 'issue', but there would be trauma, for sure.

"What I mean is," Crystal insisted, "is that it was hard for me not to dwell on the fact that Cassidy and my team had paid the ultimate price for nothing. There was no just cause, and no meaningful purpose behind their sacrifice; just a bunch of lies and manipulation. Knowing what I know now, Abi, everything that you just shared with me... It makes it feel a hundred times worse, their deaths even more hurtful, and incomprehensible."

Now, Abigail understood. It did start to make sense.

"Hence the fever?" she said gently. "And the sickness?"

"Yes," Crystal admitted. "But it won't happen again."

"Even if it did, Crys..."

"No," Crystal interrupted firmly. "Don't make excuses for me, please. Today was a massive trigger. I reacted. End of story. Compared to how bad these panic attacks used to be, throwing up and feeling a bit warm is nothing to worry about anyway."

Abigail suppressed an exasperated roll of the eyes at the overly casual way she talked about it. What Crystal described as *'a bit warm'* had felt like volcanic heat to her.

"If you say so," she conceded. "But you..."

"And there won't be a repeat of this sort of thing," Crystal insisted. "I am fit to do my job, Abi. I will stand by your side in this fight, and keep you safe."

Now more than at any point before, Abigail wanted to grab hold of her and give her a hug. There was such sadness shining in her gaze... And such powerful resolve and toughness as well. *She's a true warrior,* she reflected. *Tried and tested in the fire, risen from the ashes, worthy of her name. And gosh; so damn beautiful as well...* She kept that opinion to herself, held back from the hug, but still went ahead regarding some of her other thoughts.

"For the record, Captain Thor," she declared. "I have never doubted you, your physical or mental fitness, your dedication to me and my team, or anything else related to your ability to do your job. Not for an instant."

Crystal held her gaze for a few seconds, looking thoughtful and tense still, as if unsure that she really could relax. But then, after what felt like an eternity, a faint smile appeared on her lips.

"Are you sure?" she said.

"What do you mean?" Abigail frowned.

"I thought you just chose me because I looked good in the picture, Representative Christensen."

She was joking, quite obviously, and Abigail relaxed. This was a huge relief. She was glad for an opportunity to lighten up the mood between them at last. It had been a tough evening, and she was keen to move on.

"At ease, Captain," she laughed. "I shall forever deny that I made such a sexist controversial statement. And you can just call me Madam President from now on."

Crystal flashed her an easy grin.

"Roger that, Ms POTUS," she replied. "You got it."

∞

Crystal was up at the break of dawn the next morning. The night had been short but surprisingly restful for her; the usual dark nightmares did not come to intrude, and she woke up feeling refreshed. She decided to go for a quick run around the block, in the snow, performed a set of push-ups and squats, and forced herself to have another ice-cold shower; this time voluntarily, since the hot water was back on. But it was good for the blood. After sharing a cup of coffee with her team, Crystal felt settled again, grounded, and ready for action. Breakfast took place in Abigail's suite, and it felt just like a war meeting with Russell, Scott, and Greer in attendance. Crystal noticed that the other two members of Abigail's core team were absent though.

"Where are JoAnn and Samantha?" she enquired.

"On their way to the airport, flying back to campaign HQ this morning," Abigail replied.

Crystal held her gaze. She understood what Abigail was not saying; it would be much safer for the two women back in DC., and Crystal knew that her team's wellbeing and security was a prime concern for the candidate. Crystal gave her a quiet nod of approval. She had no idea just yet that the time was near when their team would be reduced even further... For now, they all simply got on with a well-rehearsed routine; get in the car, drive to the News station, stay alert, safe, and just crack on with the mission. Abigail did manage to grab a private word with her before they left the hotel.

"Crys. How are you doing?" she asked.

"All good," Crystal simply said. "I'm ready."

She was in the zone, and Abigail also appeared fully back in her campaign mode. She was dressed simply but effectively in an all-white tailored suit that highlighted her slender figure. The small US-flag pin clipped to her lapel was a nice addition. Her hair was impeccably-styled. Along with a touch of makeup that she certainly did not need, she also wore an air of power and authority that would leave no one in any doubt as to who the most important person in the room had to be. Congresswoman Christensen was a rare jewel in this game of politics that so many other people seemed to play for personal gains. It would be quite obvious to anyone who paid attention that this woman did not; she was a hundred percent committed to service above self. She possessed all the attributes of a genuine world leader, and she acted like one. Well, most of the times, anyway... After her initial question, and Crystal's confident answer, Abigail did allow her gaze to linger over her, and she arched a playful eyebrow.

"Mmm. You do look pretty good, soldier," she said.

"I know," Crystal shot straight back. "Keep up, okay?"

Abigail snorted in a most un-world-leaderly-like manner. This was pretty typical of the sort of pre-News interview banter that she liked to have with her team, and Crystal was a useful partner in the exercise.

"I'll try not to let the side down."

"Don't try; just do it, Ms POTUS."

Abigail was laughing as they stepped inside the elevator. Russell and Greer had both gone to collect the car, and Matthew Scott was already downstairs, making sure that the lobby and main entrance of the hotel were clear. This was probably the last opportunity the two women would have to be alone that day. It should not have mattered or made a jot of difference to Crystal.

Still, as they stood facing each other, she found it difficult not to grow wistful, suddenly.

"So, this is it," she reflected. "Zero hour."

"Yep," Abigail nodded. "Do or die time."

She, too, was serious once again. Crystal stared intently into her eyes. She sensed that she may mean something else besides the obvious, but it was hard to be completely sure with Abigail, who could flirt so outrageously one minute, and act all cool and presidential the next. Unsure that she was reading her right, Crystal hesitated. Abigail did not. She boldly closed the distance between them, and took her face in both her hands.

"Now or never, Crys," she murmured.

Her heart racing, but with all doubt removed now, Crystal pulled her against her in a tight embrace.

"Oh, now," she said.

CHAPTER NINETEEN

Russell spent the morning either on his laptop or with his head buried in his phone, monitoring responses and online reactions to Abigail's hard-hitting interviews. By mid-morning, after only the first one, she was already trending all over Twitter.

"People are reacting to her comments about Birch's death," he whispered, as he and Crystal both stood at the back of a live-recording studio. "He was an extremely popular guy, you know; and so is our Abigail. She sure is pulling no punches, and this interview is already causing a hell of a stir out there."

"Great," Crystal replied, her eyes fixed on Abigail behind the glass. "That's what she wanted."

Her lips still burned from that first kiss they had exchanged in the elevator. *First kiss...* she reflected. She was not sure what would happen now, but she certainly hoped that it would not be the last. The contact had been brief but electrifying. Abigail had wrapped both arms around her neck. She had leaned into her with such joyful abandon and passion that Crystal suspected they might still be at the hotel if the elevator had not suddenly stopped, and the doors opened. Scott was waiting in the lobby. There was no time to even exchange a word after their intimate embrace. Crystal suppressed a smile as she remembered how, as they sat in the car on their way to the TV station, Abigail had reached out to touch her hand, and flashed her a gentle smile.

No other words were needed, to be sure. Crystal was slightly disturbed to realise that even in the midst of such threatening revelations about the murder of an innocent congressman, the existence of a nasty global network of sociopaths, and the notion that these people might be in league with hostile aliens, one kiss was all it took to melt her head. Oh, she was still as alert and focused as ever, but now a wildly enticing narrative also floated at the back of her mind. The thought of exchanging more kisses and a lingering embrace with the woman that she was in charge of protecting made her heart swell. *So damn unprofessional, soldier...* Then again, Abigail might have told her that it was not so bad, or even strange, after all. Perhaps it was just a natural expression of her precious humanity. *And in the light of everything that is at stake here, definitely worth fighting for...*

"All right," Russell declared. "I think we're going to break Google!"

He was not far wrong. By lunchtime, an excited call came in from their D.C. headquarters to inform them that the campaign website had crashed due to too much traffic. Twitter was going nuts with a series of wild hashtags, and by the time they arrived at the location of the first Town Hall, what looked like at least a couple of hundred people were queueing around the block for a chance to get in.

"Keep going," Crystal advised Scott, who was driving.

"You want me to do another drive-by?"

"Yeah, but let me off, first."

"Where are you going?" Abigail enquired.

She sounded impatient, business-like, certainly not focused on stealing kisses anymore... Crystal knew that she hated delays of any kind, but she had a good reason for wanting this one.

"I'll just go check out this crowd," she declared; and then, to Scott. "Meet you back here in ten."

He nodded; Abigail muttered an irritated *'All right, then'*. Crystal shot her a brief smile, got herself a reluctant one in reply, and jumped out of the car. She jogged across the street to join the people there. This was definitely a crowd, no longer an orderly line. Hands deep in the pockets of her jeans, the peak of her baseball cap pulled down low over her eyes, Crystal began to wander through the lines. She wanted to get a better sense of who had shown up there for this latest Town Hall, and ten minutes was more than enough to realise what was going on. She ran back to the car and the rest of the team.

"It's not looking good," she announced.

"Why? What's the problem?" Abigail exclaimed.

"This is a much different crowd to your normal ones, Abi," Crystal replied. "Lots of young guys seemingly on their own, but dressed the same and with significant markers that they're not here to hear you speak, but to start a fight. Most are wearing gloves; carrying heavy backpacks that might contain weapons; and bandanas around their neck that they can quickly pull over their face if they need to. I spotted a few with real masks on."

"Sounds like your typical pre-riot crowd," Greer said.

"It's nothing we didn't expect," Abigail declared.

Crystal raised an unconvinced eyebrow.

"Isn't it?" she challenged.

"Nope... When a long-term respected member of Congress, who also happens to be leading the race for the presidency, goes on the news to spill the beans about what most would consider insane conspiracy theories, all kinds of people take notice."

Abigail glanced toward Russell.

"That's right," he nodded. "We knew this would happen, but of course, our safety and that of our followers is always a big concern. That's why I have arranged to have a police presence at the event today..."

"Oh, really?" Crystal shot him an irritated look. "It's nice of you to let your chief security officer know about it, uh?"

He blushed.

"Uhm... Sorry. I only just got confirmation."

Scott had found a space to park across the street, far enough from the venue to not attract unwanted attention, but still within good visual distance of it. Now, he let out a low whistle.

"Hey, look who's just arrived. The local police sure aren't messing about with your request, Russ."

Crystal stared toward the two unmarked vans that had just pulled up in front of the building. A full contingent of officers all dressed in riot gear, as if they were expecting the worst, indeed, and carrying assault rifles, emerged from the back of the vehicles and went to congregate near the entrance.

"Man," Greer muttered. "These guys look more and more like military assault troops every day..."

"That's not a coincidence," Abigail groaned. "And today, they're on our side... But I wouldn't be surprised if it wasn't the case for very much longer."

The three military people in the car exchanged a heavy and silent glance. Not a single one felt like speaking in contradiction of that statement. Meanwhile, Abigail squirmed on her seat, and she gave another impatient sigh.

"We're running late," she announced. "Captain Thor; are we doing this thing, or what?"

Crystal looked at her. She was fully aware that Abigail was not asking, but just basically instructing her to get a move on, and get this show on the road. No matter how risky it might be for her out there, Crystal's job was not to argue with her about it, or the way that she went about her mission. She ignored the tiny flutter of emotion that crossed her chest when Abigail allowed her gaze to soften, only for a moment, and only for her to see it.

Crystal gave a brisk nod in response. She checked her weapon. *Showtime, soldier; and maybe a kiss later if you're lucky...*

"Let's do this thing," she said.

∞

Abigail had a bunch of reasons for insisting they go ahead with their original schedule, and one of them was because she wanted to gauge the impact that her morning interviews would have on the ground, with real people, where she could experience it. She had always expected a pretty significant reaction, but the speed at which her statements went around the country and the world surprised her. Perhaps it should not have... Russell himself sure did not seem to think that there was anything unusual about it. *And I did not even mention the word extra-terrestrial...* Abigail had simply made a solid statement regarding the murder of her friend Senator Birch, and repeated what she had been saying all along: that some powerful people were pulling a lot of nasty strings behind the scenes, and that it was time to put a stop to all their illegal activities. She did mention the name and existence of the Global Network in painfully clear terms, and also sent out a heartfelt message to *'anyone out there who knows what's going on, is involved in any way, and would like to break your silence now'*. She picked up on that theme in her first Town Hall as well.

"They can stop one person, but they can't stop us all. They may believe that killing Senator Birch will put an end to all the brave work that he has been doing... But guess what?" Abigail announced. "Last night, my lawyers received electronic copies of everything he had. Thirty-plus years of dedicated investigation into this Global Network and their activities. Every file, account, and witness testimony! You must understand: this is real. Now, we must fight for the truth. For our rights, and our freedom!"

Abigail did not reveal the fact that it looked as if Birch had been ready to self-publish a book, and blow the whistle on some very important people... Her speech already had the entire room on their feet, yelling and cheering as they applauded too. Abigail could tell that Crystal was correct in her initial assessment; these people were not like her usual audience. The police had done a good job of identifying the ones who were only there to disrupt; those who most likely would be armed with metal clubs, knives, or illegal guns. Even leaving aside this specific segment of the population, the people in front of her now looked much tougher and harder than her usual crowd.

"Are you starting your own militia, Congresswoman?" one guy yelled at her from the back. "Because I'm in if you are!"

Some people laughed, but most were serious.

"Let me be clear about one thing," Abigail replied, showing some toughness of her own. "I do not advocate violence of any kind. Not in any way, shape or form. Never."

"Sometimes, there's no choice," someone shouted.

Abigail was going to struggle not to agree with that one; she knew enough to realise that there may come a time soon when people had no other option. She was pretty sure that every one of her audience today must be a staunch supporter of the Second Amendment, originally drafted to protect people from their own government, and to stop the British who were there at the time from invading their homes. Abigail was convinced that a new kind of invader was waiting to pounce on humanity, but she needed to play her cards right, because right now, she had no solid proof. Birch had been close to a breakthrough; she was sure of it. He had told her as much. Was it irrefutable evidence that the Global Alliance was in league with a hostile group of aliens intent on enslaving humanity? Without proof, Abigail had nothing but an opinion; she could not go public with just that...

"Go to my website," she encouraged her eager audience, as she brought the Town Hall to a slightly earlier finish. "Review the information available, and please, please, remember: Senator Birch paid the highest price for us to have this knowledge. The struggle is real, dark, and dangerous; make no mistake about it. But we have the power to stop these people from stealing our future and our children's future, if only we rise together in peace and friendship. Join me on this journey. Thank you."

Abigail spotted the soldier who definitely deserved her title of *'Gorgeous Bodyguard'* stepping forward before the last word had even left her lips, looking like a heat-seeking missile zeroing in on her target. Abigail had done her level best to ignore her distracting presence during her speech, and to put the tantalising kiss that they had exchanged at the back of her mind for the time being. Now though, she was literally transfixed at the sight of her, and shaken to realise exactly how much she was looking forward to sinking into her embrace again.

"Hey, Crys," she murmured.

"Hey," Crystal replied, without once taking her eyes off the crowd. She linked her arm through hers and led her briskly off the stage. "You're not doing selfies this time, are you?"

Abigail leaned briefly against her side, grateful for her solid presence. The tension of the morning's interviews added to the pressure of this one event, and the raw emotional charge of her last appeal, when she was talking about Birch's sacrifice, had left her feeling drained.

"No selfies," she confirmed. "We're leaving."

Crystal nodded and kept walking fast on their way to the door. Greer was there too, slightly ahead of them and to the side, keeping an eye out for any surprises.

"According to the police, it's been lively outside while we were in here, Abi," Crystal informed her.

"As in, people fighting?" Abigail enquired.

"Trying to, as expected, but the police were quick to react and they even made a few arrests. There's still a sizeable crowd out in front, but they've calmed down. Anyway, we have a few officers to give us extra cover, and we're just racing straight to the car. Okay?"

"Okay. I'll just hold on to you."

Crystal finally broke her concentration long enough to flash her a confident smile.

"Do that. And I won't let go," she promised. "Hey, are you alright?"

"I'm glad you're here, Crys," Abigail replied huskily. Not really answering the question, but definitely speaking from the heart. "I can't tell you how grateful I am to have you with me, as a friend more than anything else."

Crystal squeezed her hand and flashed her a quick wink.

"Me too," she said. "I'm glad to be with you; *friend*."

CHAPTER TWENTY

Abigail kept it going on the road for another three days; it took a few more chaotic Town Halls, some challenging and sometimes violent crowds, a bunch of downright hostile interviews with the mainstream media, and one frazzled campaign manager, before she could finally be convinced to take a break. Of course, Abigail never called it that.

"Let's retreat and reassess before we go again, and hit them hard," she declared.

"Spoken like a true general," Crystal replied in approval.

The best place for her team to do this, the Congresswoman decided, would be at her own house in Colorado. Crystal had no issue with the location, so long as the rest of her security crew could come along as well.

"Of course, no problem," Abigail agreed.

"All right, then. Let's do it."

They flew back to Denver the very next morning, on the eve of what was predicted to be the snowstorm of the century.

"Sounds like a bad one, hey," Russell commented.

"They always say that," Abigail remarked, unconcerned.

That afternoon, she turned her living room into a campaign hub from which she could liaise with her office in D.C., conduct interviews, keep an eye on the TV, and work on strategy with Russell. Later on, that day, she came up with some bad news.

"My God…" she murmured.

Russell looked up from his computer screen.

"You okay, Abs?" he enquired. "Something wrong?"

Crystal immediately turned away from the window to look at her. Abigail sat on the couch surrounded by two open laptops, three phones, and a whole bunch of files. She looked pale all of a sudden, and Crystal grew still and attentive.

"I started to call up some of Birch's own contacts," Abigail announced. "You know the private list of names that his lawyer passed on to me? Engineers and scientists who were willing to testify about some of the secret projects they had taken part in?"

Russell nodded. Crystal kept listening intently.

"Well, I just tried to get in touch with the first three, only to find out that these people all died during the last week."

"What!" Russell exclaimed. "All of them?"

Abigail looked grim and sombre as she nodded.

"I'm afraid so. One guy lost his life in a car accident, driving at night in thick fog and snowy conditions; he lost control on a nasty bend, apparently. Another was a keen amateur pilot who encountered engine problems at ten thousand feet, and crashed his plane as he was attempting an emergency landing. The third one was run over by a truck while he was out on his morning run…"

Crystal pursed her lips, and she watched the colour slowly drain from Russell's face.

"Abigail," he murmured. "This is no mere coincidence, you realise that, right? They're cleaning up… And taking people out just like they did Birch…"

"I know." Abigail gave a heavy exhale and she shot a brief glance toward Crystal. "There's only seven names on Birch's list. I tried the other four and left them a message to call me back. I hope these people are too busy to pick up, and nothing worse…"

She sounded worried and discouraged. Crystal resisted the urge to go and sit down next to her, to put her arms around her, and offer any comfort she could. Russell was still in the room.

"You're doing all you can," she pointed out instead.

"Yeah," Abigail muttered. "Although it feels like the faster I go, the slower I get... Russ, can you give me an update on your side of things?"

"It's not a happy one either, I'm afraid," he replied. "Sorry. Our Google account has been off-line for the last seven hours. Facebook and Twitter have been patchy as hell too, coming and going like crazy. At least, YouTube is upfront about it: they've just sent me an email to confirm that they have suspended us, pending investigation."

"Of what?" Abigail enquired in a fierce growl.

"Our conduct both online and off, which according to them, is in violation of lots of things that could get us de-platformed." He gave a sullen shrug. "That's their end goal, as we know, and they're pulling all kinds of dirty tricks to make it happen. Our lawyers are on the case. More worrying is the fact that you are free-falling in all the polls."

Abigail waved an irritated hand in the air.

"But the polls do not reflect reality; now, you know that."

"Oh, for sure. I'm just concerned about the effect that these figures will have on the campaign overall."

"It'll be okay," Abigail assured with more confidence than Crystal suspected she really felt. "For now, let's not worry about the polls, and focus everything we have on finding the proof we need. There must be some key informant out there who can help us to shift the balance in our favour. The Global Network would not suddenly be taking people out of circulation if they weren't nervous about what we're doing. I know it's awful, but we must keep going."

"You're right," Russell agreed, and he sounded much more energised this time. "So, do you want to make the information that you uncovered about Birch's contacts and their untimely deaths available on the website?"

"Absolutely, I do," Abigail said fiercely. "Don't reveal their names or give leading details, though; simply state that all three lost their lives in a series of unrelated accidents, and all within the time of a single week. That should be enough to make people think a bit deeper."

"No problem; you just leave it with me."

A blizzard was just starting outside, and as he returned his attention to his screen, Abigail stood up. She made her way to where Crystal was standing in front of the window, which was safe for her as well since it directly overlooked the annexe where her security team were staying. She allowed her fingers to brush lightly against hers.

"I know you probably won't think it's a good idea, Captain, but I need some fresh air," she declared. "Like, right now."

Crystal held her hand, playfully, refusing to let go.

"Oh, I'm always in favour of some fresh air," she replied.

"Good. Because the house is pretty empty, and it looks like we're going to get a ton of snow. I'm going to the store to stock up on some food before the roads become impassable."

"Ugh," Russell groaned in the background. "You need me to come with you?"

"That's okay, Russ," Crystal shot back with an ironic roll of the eyes. How clueless could he be? "I'll go."

"Cool. Thanks, Crys."

"My pleasure," Crystal replied, her eyes fixed on Abigail.

They hurried to the Range Rover in the garage, but before Crystal could jump behind the wheel, Abigail laid a demanding hand over her shoulder.

"Wait, Crys."

"Oh, sorry; you want to drive? Might be best, anyway."

"No; I want a hug," Abigail replied, and she threw her arms around her neck.

Crystal was still getting used to the dizzying speed at which she could make the switch from her sharp, commanding political persona, and the much more private, gentler side of herself; the woman who loved to snuggle up in her arms for a quick cuddle whenever they could... It was a while since they had been alone together. Crystal wrapped her arms around her, closed her eyes, and allowed herself a rare moment of complete relaxation inside the embrace.

"I missed you," she murmured.

"Me too," Abigail mumbled against her shoulder.

They stood holding each other for a long time, oblivious to the freezing cold inside the unheated garage. So long as it was just the two of them in there, nothing else truly mattered. Abigail shifted after a while, but just so that she could rest better against her partner's chest. She sighed in pleasure as Crystal laid a warm hand over the back of her neck, gently kneading the exhausted muscles there.

"Sometimes, I wish we could just leave..." she whispered.

Crystal pulled back just enough to look into her eyes.

"Are you serious?"

Abigail flashed her a thoughtful smile, and locked her arms tighter around her neck.

"About the wishing; definitely," she said. "About the notion that I would just drop everything and get out if given the chance to quit...? No way. I couldn't. Wouldn't."

"Same here," Crystal reflected. "Although when I showed up at your Town Hall in New York, I was almost ready to hit the road, you know?"

"Really?" Abigail exclaimed. "You never told me that."

"Yes… I was planning to buy a campervan, and head out to Montana; I wanted to find an isolated spot in the mountains, and just…"

"Just what?" Abigail prompted when she did not finish.

"Good question," Crystal chuckled. "Sit on a rock and stare at the trees, I guess… I realise that I was just looking to run away from it all. It didn't feel right, somehow, even though part of me really wished that I could do it. And then, I met you…"

"Mmm… Tell me about that," Abigail invited.

"Are you fishing for compliments, Ms POTUS?"

"You think I need to, Captain?"

Crystal smiled, amused at the question.

"No, you certainly don't," she replied.

"Maybe you're wrong," Abigail remarked in a quiet voice. "It wouldn't work too well for a presidential candidate to act all shy and hesitant, but it doesn't mean the woman underneath is bulletproof."

Crystal did not react visibly at her choice of words, but her heart tightened. *As long as I'm with you,* she promised herself; *I'll make damn sure that you are…*

"Did you like me when you first met me, then?" Abigail insisted with a hint of teasing in her voice now. "Even though I ruined all your escape plans? I'll be honest with you, Crys; I couldn't take my eyes off you when I saw you walk across that room in New York. You were gorgeous, for a start; and you had such an awesome vibe about you."

"Oh really?" Crystal smirked. "What awesome vibe?"

"Well; you looked tough and dangerous, but because you're one of the good guys, you were safe to me. Sizzling good looks and a bad attitude…" Abigail blushed hard. "I have to say that's a pretty irresistible combination, Ms Thor."

"Bad attitude?" Crystal laughed. "What?"

"You know what I mean. Sexy and dark. Mmm..."

"Stop getting all mushy on me, Ms Christensen."

"And stop being so serious," Abigail instructed.

Smiling softly, Crystal raised her hand to caress her cheek.

"I was impressed when I first saw you as well, if you must know," she replied. "You were the brightest light in the room. Later, I got a glimpse of the real woman behind the presidential candidate, and a hint of your vulnerability..."

Abigail winced at that, but Crystal shook her head.

"Don't," she said. "It only highlighted your own toughness. I didn't take this CPO job because of any sense of commitment to a political ideal, or even a particular cause, you know? I took it because I liked you. I like you now, Ms Christensen; a hell of a lot."

"I like you too," Abigail replied, a dreamy smile floating on her lips.

"Good. And by the way, despite what you told me when I first asked, I know that you don't flirt with all your people quite as aggressively as you did with me in the beginning," Crystal pointed out with a satisfied grin. "I like that as well."

"I'll do it more often, then."

"Roger that, Abigail..."

They shared a gentle, smiling kiss that did not remain quite so tame for very long. Soon, Abigail leaned into her impatiently, a touch aggressively. She was bold and purposeful as she raked her fingers through Crystal's hair. Even though it was so short, she still managed to grab onto a handful to better lead the kiss. Crystal had zero problem with this kind of rough, and she was happy to let her partner take charge if she wanted to. She allowed her fingers to wander up beneath Abigail's thick winter shirt. The kiss became hungrier and deeper, seriously heated.

Impatiently as well, Crystal clasped her partner's right breast in the palm of her hand. No bra... Crystal was delighted to be able to feel hot, smooth, naked skin under her fingertips. She brushed her thumb over the tip of her nipple, and started to rub gentle circles around it. The gesture elicited a deep alluring moan from Abigail. She slipped one leg in between Crystal's, and pressed harder against her thigh. She broke the kiss to utter just a single word.

"More," she breathed.

"Mmm, yeah," Crystal replied.

She was eager to comply, and recapture that sizzling kiss, but a not-so-polite cough coming from behind made her glance sharply over her shoulder. Crystal frowned in pure irritation at the sight of Tom Greer hovering at the entrance to the garage, looking like he was trying not to laugh.

"Uhm; sorry, Thor." He gave Abigail a respectful nod. "Ms Christensen."

"What's up, Tom?" Crystal enquired in a sharper tone than perhaps she would have used if he had not interrupted such a precious moment.

"Nothing, just doing the rounds," he replied. "Thought I'd come to check in here too, since the lights were on... Didn't mean to interrupt."

"Yeah," Crystal muttered. "Well; we're fine."

"Obviously, uh?" he grinned.

She flashed him a dark warning look. Abigail was laughing as she grabbed her hand.

"Come on, soldier," she invited. "Let's go get some supplies before this snow makes it impossible. I want to make tonight a special occasion for all of us."

CHAPTER TWENTY-ONE

"You may still not agree that it's the worst winter storm of the century," Russell declared later on that day, "but I think it's fair to say that it's the worst one we've had in about ten years..."

Abigail did not argue with that one. The snow began to fall when she and Crystal were about to leave the store and head back to the house, thick and heavy from whitish-grey skies laden with a lot more.

"No snow tyres?" Crystal remarked.

"Not been home a lot, lately; forgot to get it done. But hey," Abigail added with a knowing smile, "I'm sure someone with your credentials can handle a few flakes, right?"

"I can, just not sure about your car... If not, you can always push," Crystal joked in reply.

The 4x4 struggled quite a bit to get up the steep hill that led to Abigail's property, but Crystal got it there eventually after a few entertaining slides.

"Great weather," she declared in satisfaction. "It'll make it pretty damn hard for anyone to sneak up on us tonight."

Abigail would have loved to be alone with her at home that evening, as she put on an old favourite compilation of soothing classical music to play, cooked her specialty lasagne, and sipped a red wine in front of the fire... But it also gave her a brilliant opportunity to treat her entourage to a well-earned night off.

"Oh, look! A blue moon has risen!" Russell exclaimed when Abigail told him to come off his laptop, put his phone away, and have a glass of wine. He laughed when she glared at him. "Only kidding, Abs. Hey, this wine is absolutely de-lish!"

Her security detail never completely powered down for the evening, which did not surprise Abigail at all, since Crystal was in charge. She did manage to convince them to enjoy a few sips of wine each though, and Crystal went on to demolish two large portions of lasagne.

"Forget about all that POTUS business, Abi," she declared afterwards. "You should open your own restaurant. Man! This is amazing food!"

Abigail smiled, amused at her enthusiasm. She stood up to rest both hands over her shoulders from behind her chair, and bent to brush a soft kiss over her cheek.

"Thanks, darling," she replied. "Kind of you to say."

She was oblivious to everyone else around. As Russell had confirmed to her earlier, they had not been fooling anyone for a long time, anyway.

'Not that we were trying, to be honest,' Abigail pointed out to him.

'I guess not,' he laughed. *'Not with the way you guys always look at each other. Damn! I'm surprised neither of you has burst into flames yet!'*

At around nine-thirty, Scott retreated to the annexe to catch a few hours of sleep before his next round of duty; Greer went out to check the property; and Russell decided to go watch a movie in bed. Abigail propped up a few comfortable pillows on the couch in front of the fire, and shot a hopeful glance toward Crystal.

"Alone, at last," she said, smiling softly. "Will you keep me company for a bit?"

She was well aware that her trusted CPO would probably want to go out at some point, as she usually did, to catch up with her team and take her turn on watch outside. Captain Thor was no slacker when it came to duty, but tonight, Abigail was hoping to keep her in with her for as long as she possibly could.

"I'd love to keep you company," Crystal said.

She dropped onto the sofa; Abigail stretched out against her side, all tucked in under her arm with her face resting lightly on her chest. Crystal began to stroke her hair.

"Thanks for a lovely evening, Abi," she murmured.

"That's okay... I think everyone was in need of a bit of rest and normality."

"Yep. That's for sure."

Abigail looked up to meet her eyes.

"Even you?" she enquired. "How are you doing?"

Crystal returned her gaze, black eyes glinting beautifully in the light of the fire.

"I'm a bit on edge," she admitted.

"I thought you were. Talk to me, Crys."

"Ah... It's nothing new under the sun," Crystal replied with a light shrug. "Crucial informants who could help you to prove the truth about Birch and all the rest of it are being taken out; your means of communicating with your audience, social media and your website, are all under serious threat; the mainstream media have turned viciously against you..."

"Toeing the line of the Global Network," Abigail said.

"No doubt about that... And it's working. Your ratings are down, and I don't care whether it's real or not; if it's real for the people who see it, they won't question the information."

Abigail nodded quietly. This was true, of course; all part of the war on perception being waged from the highest levels of the network.

"Now," Crystal continued in mounting irritation, "instead of the trustworthy, intelligent, and grounded congresswoman that you are, public opinion is being manipulated to make them switch over to believing that you are just a furious, unstable, and insane conspiracy theorist. You know what that means, right? If people start to think that about you, who is going to care, then, if you suddenly get taken out as well? No one, that's who!"

She ran out of breath on that last frustrated sentence, and just went on to stare at her partner intently, as emotion made her eyes sparkle like ice in the sunshine, and a deep rush of colour suffused her cheeks. Abigail reached out to rest a cool, soothing hand against the side of her neck. She felt real heat under her fingertips, and a racing heart as well.

"A bit on edge, hey, Captain?" she murmured.

She watched Crystal swallow back her emotion. It seemed to take quite an effort for her to calm down. She did not look happy at all, for sure.

"Well; you did ask," she muttered.

"Yes..." Abigail smiled. "I did, indeed."

"That's what you get for making me drink."

Crystal flashed her a rueful glance at the same time. Abigail knew that she was not serious about it. All in all, she had not even consumed one half-glass of wine. But she could tell that Crystal was keen to get over her nervous outburst. She must not enjoy having her emotions creep up on her like that without warning. Abigail understood. She was not going to insult her by issuing empty reassurances. They all knew exactly what was at stake here, and what they had to lose; but they also knew how good and committed they were as well. At war with a worthy opponent, it might just take a bit longer to win, that was all.

"We'll be okay," she just declared. "Trust me on that."

"Yes, ma'am," Crystal replied in a firmer tone.

Abigail moved to rest a heavy kiss over her lips, probing deeper inside her mouth, lingering just long enough to make her gaze go unfocused. She could feel her heart still beating fast, but probably not for the same reason as before. It was just as well, really, given what Abigail was about to ask her now…

"One more question, Crys," she said. "If that's all right?"

"Sure; go ahead," the soldier replied, stern and serious.

"Is it okay to fall in love with one's CPO?"

∞

Crystal opened her eyes a few hours later. She was unsure of the time; it was still pitch-black outside Abigail's bedroom windows. As she began to remember the events of the previous night, and one burning question in particular, a sleepy but brilliant smile blossomed over her lips.

'Is it okay to fall in love with one's CPO?'

The answer had rolled off her tongue without a split second of reflexion needed.

'I don't care if it isn't… I'm in love with you too, Abi.'

Crystal recalled how Abigail had just simply got up from the couch then, taken her hand in hers, and led her upstairs. She had lit candles around the room, put on some more soothing music to play, and stepped right back into her arms.

"Dance with me," she whispered.

What ensued was the most wonderful, unhurried, intimate, thrilling and passionate sexual encounter of Crystal's entire life. They undressed each other, slow-dancing to the tune of *Georgia On My Mind*. They kissed deeply, caressed boldly, and embraced with total abandon. Items of clothing landed and just remained wherever they did. A couple pieces of equipment required a bit more care, of course…

"Weapons down, soldier," Abigail instructed her softly. "I'll be the one to keep you safe tonight."

Crystal could not get rid of her gear fast enough. That night, she was experiencing the kind of pure authentic love that drove her to want to be totally present and naked for Abigail; not just physically, but in mind and spirit as well. She let her push her down onto the thick, sweet-smelling sheets. She wrapped her arms around her body, and she returned each one of her kisses with ardent fervour. She surrendered to her lover's every wish and desire, just because she knew that Abigail wanted her to. She made love to her without an ounce of restraint, bringing her to the edge and beyond, more than once. In turn, Abigail made her lose all track of time, space, and boundaries... They became lost in each other for several precious hours, and Crystal was sorry to have to wake up on the other side of it all. Now it was early morning, probably. She lay all wrapped up in her lover's arms, unable to tell where her body ended and Abigail's began. She could still taste her on her lips... Another delighted smile broke across her face.

"Mmm..." Abigail sighed. "Crys?"

"Yeah, right here," Crystal whispered.

Abigail turned into her, tightened the embrace even though Crystal did not think that it was possible. She nuzzled against her chest and kissed the side of her neck, right underneath her jaw, making Crystal shiver.

"Not time to get up, is it?" she mumbled.

"Not yet, I don't think."

"What time is it?"

"No idea."

Abigail gave a soft chuckle as she found her lips.

"Forget about time," Crystal murmured.

"Roger that, my darling."

They dozed for a while, on and off, until Abigail became a little more still, her body a little less pliant, and soon, the tension in her was impossible to ignore.

"Abi; what's wrong?" Crystal enquired.

"I don't know. I just feel worried all of a sudden."

The slamming of the front door downstairs made them both jump, confirming Abigail's keen intuitive sense; something was happening. Crystal flew out of bed. She reached for her weapon first, wondering where on earth her underwear might be found only second. There was a sudden, loud knock on the door.

"Abi!" Russell yelled. "Come downstairs!"

Abigail turned on the lights and she jumped out of bed too.

"Everything okay?" she enquired, her voice under control.

"Just come down!" he replied frantically. "Hurry up!"

Crystal finally located her boxers, threw on her T-shirt, and jumped into her jeans and boots. Weapon in hand, she yanked the door open.

"Hold on."

Abigail came to stand in front of her. She was dressed now, too, and as she laid both hands flat over her chest and looked up into her eyes, deeply and intently, time seemed to slow down to a crawl for Crystal once again.

"Before all hell breaks loose, a reminder for you, Ms Thor."

"Yes?"

"I love you, Crys."

"I love you too, Abi," Crystal murmured.

They exchanged a grounding kiss, a smile, and then raced downstairs. Crystal was not too sure what she expected, but it seemed rather tame at first glance. Russell and her two buddies just sat on the couch in front of the TV, in studious silence. It was only when they did not acknowledge their presence that Crystal noticed the look of consternation on all their faces.

"What's happening, Russ?" Abigail enquired.

He looked up at her, eyes wide in shock and a good dose of disbelief as well.

"It's breaking news," he replied. "There's been a series of explosions; it could be attacks, maybe. All we know is the White House is going up in flames…"

Crystal stepped forward to take a better look at the screen.

"That's not the White House, Russ," she frowned. "It's the Russian Kremlin."

Greer threw her a sombre look.

"Yeah, that's burning too," he informed her. "And there's been similar blasts at other significant places around the world: the French Elysée Palace, the Kremlin, as you can see here, the Houses of Parliament in Britain, the Vatican, even in China…"

"Look!" Russell exclaimed. "This is happening now!"

The CNN News report shifted back to live images of the White House. This time, Crystal froze in pure astonishment, and Abigail let out a sharp gasp at the sight of the burning building. This was not just a small fire; not even a serious one…

"It's an absolute roaring furnace," she murmured.

"There will be nothing left of the structure by the time this blaze is over," Russell concurred. "It'll just be a black hole in the ground."

"Same kind of thing happening all around the world, Crys," Scott repeated through gritted teeth. "Can't explain what's going on here, but I know it's like, uh… It doesn't feel…"

"What?" she prompted when he hesitated.

He struggled with his answer, and Crystal did not like the nervous look on his face as he thought to figure it out. A scared Matthew Scott was not something that she had ever experienced, or even wanted to.

"Doesn't feel natural," he finally muttered.

Disconcerted, Crystal turned to Abigail.

"What do you think?" she asked.

Her lover appeared every inch the Commander-in-Chief as she stood in the middle of the room, erect and firm. There was a trace of sorrow in her eyes from the dismal events taking place, sure... But on the whole, she radiated deep resolve and crushing strength.

"I think Matt's on to something," she replied. "Whoever is behind these attacks is natural in the sense that it is part of our world... But I don't think that it's human."

CHAPTER TWENTY-TWO

Not surprisingly, the media were begging for an interview, and after Abigail did that, she went Live via her own website, not trusting social media this time, to deliver an in-depth analysis of the situation. Then, she announced to her team that they would leave. The plan had always been to go back to Washington in the next few days, but Abigail decided that she wanted to go now; whenever Representative Christensen said *'Now'*, it really meant immediately. Crystal took five minutes to pack before going on the hunt for Greer, who had been acting weird since watching the CNN report. She found him in the garage, checking the car.

"Tom, you okay?" she enquired.

He shot her a dark look from behind the hood.

"Negative," he snapped. "I'm fucking not."

"Yeah, no fucking kidding. What's the problem?"

"You're asking me?" he exclaimed. "Didn't you hear what she said?"

"Sure, I heard," Crystal nodded calmly. "Abi explained that the attacks seem like a coordinated effort by the Global Network to hit on all symbols of government. She reiterated that their end goal is the annihilation of all forms of independent sovereignty. And she concluded that this looks like the first step in an all-out war against the people. Makes sense. I agree with all that."

Greer walked up to her, his face dark with fury.

"You know that's not what I'm talking about," he spat.

"I thought Russ had briefed you and Scott about the rest..."

"But he sure didn't say a damn thing about aliens!" Greer exploded.

Crystal gave a frustrated sigh. She was tempted to ask what planet he had actually been on the past few weeks... Then again, she knew him well. Greer was the kind of soldier who tended to focus on the job at hand, and become deaf and blind to anything else but the mission. It was one of the reasons she had called on him in the first place, to be fair...

"Look," she told him, "I know it's hard to stomach, but just think about it for a minute; if only the White House had been hit, we could look to the usual suspects for who's responsible, right? But everyone's been targeted; at the same time, and in the same way... It all points to a common enemy outside the boundaries of what we know. Abigail is right about the..."

"She's fucking insane, Thor," he cut her off. "And you must be as well, if you believe that crazy shit!"

Crystal started to lose patience with his rantings.

"You did too," she pointed out to him, "before the A. word was mentioned. You thought Abigail's message and her mission were worth risking your life to protect her..."

He stabbed his finger in her chest, hard enough to hurt.

"Yeah," he sneered. "And I trusted you, too, before sex with the client turned your brains into a pile of shit."

Crystal slapped his hand off as he attempted another jab.

"Shut up, Greer," she warned. "And back off."

"Or what?" he hissed.

The argument may have degenerated further if Abigail had not suddenly appeared in the doorway, carrying her suitcase in one hand, and Crystal's rucksack in the other. She instantly took notice of their aggressive stance, and paused.

169

"Is everything okay, Crystal?" she enquired.

She was asking her, but her eyes remained firmly fixed on Greer in a silent but very obvious warning. In reaction, he gave a furious shake of the head.

"Urgh…"

Crystal nodded in response to Abigail, and even though she was the one in charge of keeping her safe, she still felt a rush of warmth and gratitude for the fierce expression of protectiveness in her eyes. Their bond was deep. Strangely, it had always been this way, and it seemed to be precisely what Greer seemed to have such a problem with; or maybe he really hated the fact that Crystal had broken all the rules by getting so close to '*the client*'. And then, there was the other stuff, of course… Crystal returned her gaze to him. What made this situation even harder for her was the fact that she genuinely respected the guy. Even though she felt like he deserved a good punch in the face right now, she did like him, and she did not want him to leave.

"Tom. Come on, let's just talk, okay?" she invited.

"Sorry," he replied. "I'm out. Good luck with everything."

He grabbed his bag, threw it over his shoulder, and walked off down the driveway. Crystal watched him go. He did not turn back once. Abigail came to rest a gentle hand over her shoulder.

"Too much for him?"

"Yeah," Crystal murmured. "Too much, indeed."

She did not have time to dwell on his dramatic departure. Scott was happy to stay on, which was a relief. Other than that, it was still snowing outside; the temperature had dropped during the night, and local roads were covered in a sheet of ice. It would make the drive to the airport difficult at best, although Crystal was quick to remind herself that it would play in their favour. More worrying was some information that Russell had to share, as they all climbed into the car.

"News has started to emerge that a select number of people have been whisked away to secure locations, and this is the case around the world, not just here in the US," he announced.

"What? Like heads of state and important members of the cabinet?" Crystal enquired. "Isn't that normal procedure in this kind of situation?"

"It would be, yes; except that we're talking about the crème de la crème of industry here, along with groups of scientists and engineers, famous Hollywood actors, more politicians, singers, sports people... Anyway, you get the idea."

"Hm. The people who can pay to do it are jumping ship," Abigail remarked.

She was calm, pretty unfazed. Crystal reflected that none of what was happening must be a real surprise for her. It was, after all, the stuff that she, Senator Birch, and a few others had been warning people about all along.

"Looks like it, yes," Russell agreed. "Rich people and those in the know are departing en masse. In fact, I got information to suggest that some of them had started to leave even *before* the series of explosions happened at the White House, the Kremlin, and in London, Berlin, etc."

"Do we have more information about what's happening in all of these places?" Crystal enquired.

"Nope. Just that these symbols of government are no more, now. The National Guard are on the streets in D.C., and a state of Martial Law has been declared."

"Damn," she groaned. "Abi, are you sure that you want to go to Washington?"

"Oh, I'm sure," her lover replied confidently. "I wouldn't be much of a leader if I ran in the other direction when shit starts to happen, right? I know my place is in D.C., standing shoulder to shoulder with our people. Okay with that, Captain Thor?"

Crystal nodded as Abigail smiled at her and squeezed her hand.

"You know I'm with you, Ms POTUS," she replied.

"Thanks, my love," Abigail murmured. In a louder voice for everyone to hear, she added; "Now, we can be sure that this is just the beginning of much worse things to come. The Global Network are stepping up the pace, indeed, taking control. What will they do next?"

"Close the airports," Russell declared.

"Probably, yes; that's why I want to get out quick..."

"No, Abi; I mean it." He was in the front seat next to Scott, who was driving. He turned to look at her. "News just in; all flights have been cancelled. US airports are closed until further notice, and people advised to stay home."

Abigail pursed her lips in sheer defiance.

"Like hell," she said. "We'll drive, then."

∞

They settled in for the long run. Over the rest of the day, Abigail went Live at regular intervals, and she also conducted a series of interviews; Russell was mostly on the phone with their office in Washington, keeping up with their team and getting updates on what was happening on the ground at their destination. News channels ran out of fresh content after a while, although a steady stream of so-called *'members of the public'* came on one after the other to rehash the fear-inducing official narrative: the hour was grave and dangerous; people should stay in their homes; and the troops on the streets were only there to protect them, of course.

"These are lies," Abigail remarked bitterly. "Troops aren't there to protect, but to control. I'll bet you anything that these interviewees are paid actors. It's about twisting perception."

Crystal gritted her teeth at the sickening notion that any of the soldiers out in the streets might be persuaded to turn their weapons against the population. *Their own brothers and sisters...*

"But again, Crys, it all depends on what despicable lies they in turn have been fed about this whole situation," Abigail stated. "Think back to your own experience, and coming to realise that you were being manipulated..."

"Yes, but this is happening at home!" Crystal insisted.

"Regardless; enough brainwashing will give the Network the results that they're after every single time, I guarantee you that. Whether it's at home or abroad, it makes no real difference in the end. Remember what I said to you, though."

"What's that?" Crystal sighed.

"When people realise the truth, everything will change in the blink of an eye. There are more than seven billion of us on the planet now; we've never been more divided. Coincidence? Of course, not. The Global Network thrive on this rule, a *Divide-and-Conquer* principle. Kept apart and in a state of fear, we are easy to control. But what if seven billion suddenly woke up to who we truly are: one race, one people – HUMANKIND. Do you think that the Network would stand a chance, then?"

"No," Crystal admitted. "I know you're right."

"We just need to reach the critical balance point that will tip the odds in favour of the truth, understanding, and cooperation between us all on planet Earth," Abigail concluded. "Everything will change when we get there. I believe it. I know it."

Her passion rolled like a deep ocean wave, all-powerful and irresistible. It was hard to forget though that at the same time, the White House had been destroyed, ordinary law suspended, and the entire world stunned into paralysis. Crystal stared long and hard into her eyes.

"We might have to fight, first," she said.

Abigail leaned over to brush a soft kiss on her lips.

"We always were," she said. "Now it's time to end it."

Crystal replaced Scott behind the wheel for a while. Seven hours later, tired and hungry, they arrived in Lincoln, the capital city of Nebraska.

"Let's take a break here," Abigail decided. "Refuel and get something to eat."

They stopped at the first place they found open, a small steak-house near the university campus. The waitress watched them come in with a bored look on her face. She clearly did not recognise Abigail, as she handed out menus and directed them to a table for four in the middle of the dining room.

"Actually, we'll have that one over there," Crystal declared.

Without waiting for approval, she headed to another table in the far corner of the room. This one was flanked by two solid walls, situated away from a handful of other diners, and offered good views of the front door. The waitress stared hard at her, as if Crystal had just slapped her across the face.

"What-Ever," she snapped. "Yell when you're ready."

"We're ready," Abigail nodded, further confusing her.

They ordered a round of steak and fries and some mineral water to go with it. Once again, the waitress winced, as if the order personally offended her.

"You guys don't want any beer or wine?"

"No, thanks," Abigail said politely. "Could you please turn up the sound on the TV?"

The woman obliged, amazingly, without arguing or rolling her eyes any further. The other people in the restaurant, a young couple holding hands, and two businessmen who occupied two separate tables, all turned to watch the screen, as a sombre-faced news anchor appeared under a flashing-red *BREAKING NEWS* banner.

"What the hell is he going to tell us now?" Russell muttered uneasily.

Crystal braced herself for more bad stuff as the newsreader began to speak, although what he announced was no surprise to her. Indeed, she understood the mechanics of war. She glanced toward her lover to see how she was taking it. Abigail met her gaze calmly, nodded in acknowledgement, and reached out to take her hand under the table. Crystal was sure that she would have anticipated this latest development as well. She understood that for some people though, it would come as more of a shock than anything else that had already taken place... Without a shadow of a doubt, this had the potential to be even more traumatic to a lot of them than watching their beloved White House burn to the ground.

"Now this will provoke a reaction," Abigail said.

"Now," Crystal murmured, "people will start to die."

CHAPTER TWENTY-THREE

They ate quickly and did not linger after dinner. News came that groups of people had started to riot in the streets in protest at the take down of the Internet; a call from Abigail's office confirmed that this was happening in Washington as well. The police were responding with the usual tear gas and water cannons.

"No reports of any live shots," Russell confirmed.

"No, not yet," Abigail said darkly.

If she had been able to, she would have gone Live online instantly to urge everyone to stay safe and be careful. Of course, that option had been taken away from her now.

"People forget that the military invented the Internet," she muttered as they hurried back to the car. "Now they're taking it away... All on par for the course. Russ, can you get me on TV so I can talk? CNN, FOX? Any other network? What about radio?"

Instead of responding, he stopped dead in his tracks, just eyeing his phone with a dumbfounded expression on his face.

"Let's go, Russ," Crystal urged him impatiently.

It was early evening, still relatively busy out in the streets. Martial Law was not in effect in Lincoln, NE, or at least not yet, as Abigail was bound to point out. It would happen before long, no doubt. Crystal was worried about road closures, not being able to travel at night, or at all for that matter. She did not want Abigail to be standing in the middle of the open street either.

"Russell!" she barked. "Come on, man!"

He looked up, eyes wild, staring straight at Abigail.

"Shit!" he blurted out. "The phones have gone dead!"

"That's all right," she reassured him. "Forget about it. Let's just make it to D.C., hey?"

Up ahead, Crystal spotted a young male leaning against the side of the Range Rover, rolling himself a cigarette.

"Matt," she just said.

"On it," he replied, and picked up the pace toward the car.

Crystal pulled Abigail closer against her side, and with her free hand, she grabbed hold of Russell as well and gave him a friendly but firm pull.

"Walk," she instructed. "Talk later when it's safe."

At the same time, she kept her eyes on Scott. She saw him get up to the guy, and as the individual looked up, ask him to move away. Crystal relaxed a tiny fraction as the stranger raised a quick hand in apology, and immediately stepped aside. Scott was solidly built, with an attitude to match. No one with any sense would argue with him, or hover around after he told them to leave. But as the smoker walked away, he turned back once to look directly at Crystal. As she returned his stare, frowning, he smirked, and opened his eyes wide. Her heart skipped a beat.

"Fuck!" she exclaimed.

He was gone, vanished into traffic before she could take a second look, but she knew damn well what she had seen. Blood-red eyes the size of golf balls plunged into hers as if he could hurt her just by looking... *Jesus!* Now, Crystal's sixth sense was yelling at her to get the hell out of this place. *Go, go, go!*

"Abi, get in the..." she started to say.

But the sight of Scott whirling around, weapon in hand and pointed straight toward her head, froze the words right out of her mouth.

"GET DOWN, THOR!" he yelled.

Crystal reacted on pure instinct. She did not think, speak, or argue. She just locked both arms around Abigail and pulled her down to the ground with her, cushioning her fall and shifting her body to shield her from whatever else may be coming their way; a punch, a bullet, or a red-eyed alien, all would have to go through her first. It only turned out to be Russell, in the end, who landed in a heap in the gutter right next to them. He may have been helped along by a swift push from Scott, who fired three rapid shots above their heads before crouching down low behind the car.

"Two armed guys, Crys," he panted. "Managed to hit one in the leg. Hey... What the...!?"

Sig Sauer in hand now, Crystal stared in the direction that he was looking at, and at the same time, she felt Abigail's fingers digging into her side.

"Oh, my God," her lover hissed. "They're here..."

The normal people who had been out in the street before, hurrying home from work, maybe; coming back from the stores; students on their way to and from campus, etc., were still there. Everyone had stopped and sought to take cover at the cracking of gunfire suddenly erupting. They huddled in shops' entrances or hid in between cars. Parents held their kids tightly against their bodies. They shot anxious glances around, trying to figure what was going on, unsure that it was safe to move out of hiding yet... And amongst them now stood other beings who were not hiding, but watching. *Watching us*, Crystal realised. To all intents and purposes, they looked like humans, and could have passed as such. She noticed that they were a little taller, and fitter, with longer faces and of course, those disturbing, unnaturally large red eyes... The more Crystal stared, the more of these creatures seemed to appear. *Not just here*, she thought. *They're everywhere...*

"Let's go," she urged.

She did not add *'before these make a move'*, but she feared a sudden rush. For now, the beings just stood in the middle of the regular people, blending in so well with them that she would never have known they were different if not for those red orbs. In disturbing timing, Crystal caught one of them blink, and she was startled to see a pair of perfectly normal-looking human eyes appear in his face. Then he blinked again, and the red eyes were back, boring into hers with predatory, sickening intensity.

"Crys, get in," Abigail ordered.

Crystal shook herself out of her spell and jumped in next to her on the back seat.

"Go, Matt!" she said. "Get us out of here."

He floored it, peeling out of their parking spot with enough acceleration to make them all feel G-forces. Crystal exchanged a brief look with Abigail, as her lover wrapped both arms around her waist and shook her head in amazement and dismay. Crystal leaned forward to rest a hand over Russell's shoulder.

"Russ, you okay?" she asked.

"I lost my phone," he mumbled, as if in a daze. "Shit."

She gave him a reassuring squeeze.

"We'll get you another one, bud. Matt? How're you doing?"

"We'll need gas in twenty miles," the ever-practical soldier replied. And then, with a wild glance in the rear-view mirror, he added: "What the fuck was that out there?"

"Evidence," Abigail replied, and she sounded angry instead of scared. "Again, proof that we are not alone in the universe, not even on our own planet. Confirmation that our civilisation has been infiltrated by hostile beings!"

"And so many of them," Russell muttered under his breath. He glanced back at her. "You think this is it, then? The final push to take us over?"

Crystal felt her lover tense even more against her side.

"Might well be their final push," Abigail seethed, "but they won't take us over. Goddammit! And here we are in the back of beyond without any means to communicate with people! Russ, as soon as we get to D.C., we have to..."

She never had a chance to finish her sentence, as suddenly, a flash of blinding light illuminated the vehicle from all sides. In the next second, something that she never saw coming slammed into it with devastating force. All at once, it felt like the Range Rover encountered a solid wall in the road, which brought it to a lethal stop. Added to this was another crushing impact from the off-side. Crystal did not have much time to reflect, but a single memory did flash through her mind: *IED!* This sure felt like one... All of a sudden, she was back in Afghanistan during her last mission. She heard a sharp scream. Everything went black.

∞

As she slowly came to, Abigail became aware of a lingering pain down her right side. Then, a blast of frigid air made her shiver violently, and she realised that she was lying on the ground with her face pressed against a patch of snow. *What the hell...?* She rolled onto her hip, managed to sit up; she moved her legs, and checked her side. Nothing broken, but everything was awfully sore... It took her a minute longer to gather her thoughts. The last thing she remembered was kissing Crystal at her house in Denver. *No, wait...* More had happened since then. She racked her brain to put it all together. *Think, for God's sake!* Finally, it all came back to her in a terrifying rush. Everything. She recalled Scott firing shots at some Red-Eyes; seeing them all gathered in the street; speaking to Russell in the front seat. She froze. *We were in the car...* Abigail looked up as her mind finally cleared.

Oh, no... The Range Rover had come to rest on its roof a short distance away. Under the light of a bright full moon, it was easy to see that it had been transformed into a pile of twisted metal now, all mangled into an almost unrecognisable mess. A plume of smoke rose from what was left of the destroyed hood, and it was the only thing in or near the car that Abigail could see moving. All pain forgotten, she half-ran and half-limped toward the stricken vehicle, reaching the rear first. The door on this side was gone, the back window as well.

"Crystal..."

Shaking at the thought of what she might discover, Abigail leaned in over the back seat. The space was empty. *Perhaps she was ejected out of the car like me...* Abigail shot a desperate look around the field that they had landed in. No one was there as far as she could tell.

"Crys!" she yelled. "Crystal, where are you?"

Silence was the only response. Fighting a growing fear that she may be the only survivor of this crash, Abigail moved as fast as she could to what would have been the driver's seat area next. She could not see inside, nor even make out where the actual door should have been from the mass of molten plates in front of her. She banged on the still-heated frame.

"Scott!" she yelled. "Matthew, can you hear me?"

Frantically, she slid to the other side and peered under what looked like the engine block. The car had been reduced to almost half its size by the force of the impact, but she could see inside the front from this angle. Abigail lost her breath at the horrific scene, and a deep wounded moan escaped her lips. The two men were still in their seats; the dedicated soldier who had stuck with her against all odds, and her gentle, generous and kind Russell as well. Both crushed to death by four-hundred-pounds of V8 engine hitting them in the chest at maximum velocity.

"Russ," Abigail murmured. "Oh, honey, I'm sorry..."

His eyes were open and he was looking up toward the stars, but his gaze was fixed and glassy, devoid of any life. Russell was gone, and Abigail pulled away, unable to keep looking. Now the pain in her leg hit her with a vengeance, as well as the freezing cold. She glanced toward the road. Surely, someone would stop? And the police would come? *Maybe in normal times, but now?* The road was all empty, and as it started to snow, thick and heavy, Abigail felt like the only person left in the whole wide world.

"Crys?" she whimpered. *Oh, please, let her be okay...*

The odds that this would be the case were slim, but Abigail went to check the back seat once again. She hobbled around the vehicle a couple more times, looking for any clues of what may have happened to her lover. Clouds had come in, obscuring the moon and making it harder to see. A cold wind began to blow.

"Crystal!" Abigail screamed. "CAPTAIN THOR! Answer me, dammit!"

Anger was one way to keep her energy, although it did not work for long; but it did give her enough of a boost for Abigail to remember the emergency kit that she always kept in the back of her car. The trunk had suffered the same fate as the rest of it, and its contents been blown halfway across the field, but never mind. The kit contained a flashlight, a blanket, water, and a good knife too. *I'll grab that, and go look for her.* Seeking shelter in the wreck, and just waiting for help which may never arrive was not an option. Leaving this awful place without Crystal struck her as even more ludicrous. Abigail began to shuffle across the field, looking for the remains of anything that might look like the first-aid kit. Just at that moment, she also spotted some lights in the distance. Her heart leapt in her chest. *Help...*

"Has to be," she murmured. "Please, just let it be..."

She raised her arms, waved, and drew in a breath to yell.

Sadly, before she could even utter a sound, someone grabbed her roughly from behind. A strong hand covered her mouth. Abigail struggled wildly to free herself, but whoever that person was, they were much too strong for her. Heart pounding in her chest, her blood rushing in panic, she still had the presence of mind to remember the technique that Crystal had taught her in the gym in Iowa. She stepped forward with her left leg, crossed back over with her right, and turned into her attacker's body. She pushed with both hands, giving the move everything that she had, every last ounce of fight that she could still muster. And it worked... Without glancing once behind her, Abigail sprinted off toward the road, running for her life.

CHAPTER TWENTY-FOUR

Crystal caught up with the escaping woman before she could reach the tarmac. She tackled her from behind and brought her down a lot harder than she wanted to, but she did not have the strength for anything else, and she needed to stop her. They fell forward and rolled. Abigail was still in fighting mode. Crystal barely avoided a flying punch, and managed to grab hold of her wrists.

"Abi. Abigail, stop; it's me!"

She tried to keep her voice down, and at the same time, be loud and firm enough that it got through to her. Abigail finally went still, blinked, and stared at her as if she had seen a ghost.

"Crys... What... I thought you were... I..."

The normally talented speaker ran out of words, and she just burst into tears. Crystal got up on her knees. She pulled her tightly into her arms. The embrace sure did feel good to her too.

"Shh. It's okay," she murmured. "Sorry I scared you..."

She had woken up at the bottom of a freezing ditch on the other side of the road, feeling like she had been run over by a truck, which was actually pretty accurate. When she spotted the destroyed Range Rover, still smoking out in the field, she had assumed the worst about her lover... Finally catching sight of her in one piece was a huge relief; although Crystal realised at that same moment that Abigail was about to make a terrible mistake.

She instantly did what she had to do to keep her quiet, and safe, which admittedly may not have been the most reassuring of all moves. Anyway... Only the result mattered. Now Crystal held her hard against her chest, as Abigail sobbed in release of a massive dose of adrenaline and fear. Before long, and despite that reaction, she pulled back sharply to look at her.

"You're hurt!"

"No, I'm fine," Crystal said firmly.

Abigail took her face in both her hands.

"Crys, your hair is wet with blood," she argued.

"Just a scalp injury," Crystal assured her. "Bleeds a lot, but no big deal."

It was probably a lot more serious than just that, given how light-headed and nauseous she had been feeling, but Crystal had more important questions on her mind.

"Abi, where are the guys?" she asked.

Abigail bit so hard on her lower lip that she drew a drop of blood from it. She swallowed hard, tightened her grip over her lover's hands, and broke the awful news to her.

"They didn't survive the crash. They're both dead."

Crystal had seen the awful condition of the car, and part of her already suspected the truth; confirmation still hit her hard, and a wave of grief and deep sorrow threatened to overwhelm her. *Matthew... Oh, man!* She fought bitter tears at the memory of her friend, and tasted vomit at the back of her throat. The nausea became harder to control, but she knew that she could not afford to give in to her emotions. Crystal took a deep breath. *Come on, you can do this...* For sure, it would not be the first time she had to compartmentalise her deepest feelings while she concentrated on survival, and looking after those who depended on her strength and skills for theirs. She mentally said a prayer for her fallen colleague, and focused all on Abigail.

185

"I'm sorry about Russ, Abi," she told her. "I know it's hard, but for now, we really need to make a move. It's not safe around here."

"Is that why you grabbed me so hard before?"

"Yes... Sorry about that. But look over there."

Crystal wrapped a safe arm around her neck and directed her gaze to the other side of the field, where Abigail had spotted the original light.

"I just thought it was someone coming to help..."

"It's not. Check out the wooded area on the left."

Abigail did, frowning hard as she concentrated. As soon as she spotted what her lover wanted her to see, her eyes widened in renewed shock.

"Those glowing dots in the trees," she exclaimed. "Don't tell me it's..."

Crystal nodded as sharply as her killer headache allowed.

"Red-Eyes," she confirmed. "Looks like a bunch of 'em."

"And it looks like they're on the move, too!"

"I'm afraid you're right. Let's get out of here."

Crystal pushed to her feet and felt instantly dizzy. It only lasted a second or two, fortunately. Abigail did not notice. She had a moment of hesitation as well, but not for the same reason. Instead, she glanced toward the car, her face a mask of despair.

"Nothing we can do just now," Crystal said through gritted teeth, knowing exactly what the problem was. "We'll come back for them, okay?"

She was not for a second trying to fool her. This happened to be Congressman Christensen, after all; not a stupid or naïve woman by any stretch of the imagination. Crystal needed to say the words though, if only to reassure herself that they would not simply leave their friends' bodies in the carcass of the car, to be eaten by birds, or worse... Fall into the hands of the Red-Eyes.

Abigail clearly understood. She brushed her fingers against her cheek, and leaned into her for a brief kiss.

"I love you," she whispered.

"Me too. Now, let's go."

They headed off into a cutting wind, so cold it hurt. There had been no need for bulky jackets in the well-heated car, and now, neither of them was equipped to trek across a snowy field, in a near blizzard, and in the middle of the night as well. They managed to get back to the road. Even there on solid ground, Crystal lost her balance a couple of times. She would have fallen if Abigail had not been there to catch her.

"I'm okay," she muttered. "Hard to walk with frozen legs, that's all."

All the symptoms pointed to a severe concussion, but she reminded herself that pain only meant one thing: she was still breathing. Still alive. Neither Matt nor Russ would ever have the luxury of complaining of a headache again. She was the lucky one here, and she damn well was aware of it. She found it hard to breathe once again at the thought of them both. Dead; Gone; No more... Crystal suppressed an angry groan. *Stop feeling sorry for yourself, soldier,* she instructed herself. *Keep going, and don't you dare slow down!*

"They're gaining on us," Abigail announced suddenly.

The Red-Eyes were running parallel to their position now, and actually, they were overtaking fast. Crystal wondered about their purpose. She had no doubt that these beings had caused their car crash. If they had the ability to engineer something like that, and if they wanted them dead, then surely, she and Abigail should not be able to walk by now. Were the Red-Eyes enjoying the chase, the thrill of the hunt? Or was it really the best they could do? Crystal remembered the one that she had encountered in New York. He was tough, sure... But nothing out of the norm.

Concussion or not, she could still fight, and shoot. It looked like ten or twelve Red-Eyes out there. *Yeah, I can handle it,* Crystal re-affirmed to herself. She glanced at Abigail and felt an instant rush of affection and admiration for her. Her lover's lips had turned blue from the cold; she was limping badly. A haunted expression lingered in her eyes, shock and trauma due to not only the crash, the loss of their companions, but also the rate of change of everything else. It was hard to conceive that only the night before, they had been sharing lasagne and good times at her house back in Denver… Traces of tears were still visible over Abigail's pale and dirt-smudged cheeks, and from time to time, her eyes would fill up again. In spite of this, and fear of what might happen next, she managed to keep up the pace, keep track of enemy progress, and keep her from falling flat on her face a number of times. Crystal squeezed her hand.

"Hey; good fighting, by the way."

"Had a good teacher," Abigail replied. "She's hot, too."

Crystal forced a smile even though her head felt like it was nearing explosion now. At least she was not bleeding anymore; the blood had long since frozen in her hair.

"We'll find shelter," she promised. "Get warm, and figure out our next step. I'm armed and I've got plenty of ammo. These beings will not stop us."

The weather conditions might do worse damage anyway, but there was no point in dwelling on that. As she spoke, Crystal shot another glance in the Red-Eyes' direction. Taken aback, she realised that she could not see them anymore. *Gone? Or about to pounce?* She let go of Abigail's hand and reached sharply for her weapon. Holding it tight in both hands, she scanned the empty road and surrounding darkness. It occurred to her that the guy in New York may not have been so special, but he had pulled a vanishing trick at the end that had left her vulnerable to attack.

Crystal may be a great fighter, but she would not stand much of a chance against a troop of invisible soldiers... She spun around as her partner let out a sharp gasp.

"Look!" Abigail exclaimed. "Headlights!"

Crystal spotted the approaching vehicle and her heart rose in her chest at the thought of some help, warmth, and a way of getting out of this nightmare. Only a second later though, it sank again at the realisation that it may be a trap.

"What if..." she started.

"We have to take the risk," Abigail interrupted before she could even finish her sentence. "This could be our only chance tonight; if we miss it... Crys, I don't think I can walk all the way back to Lincoln. I don't think you can either."

She was right, of course.

"You go hide in the ditch," Crystal instructed.

"No, I'm staying with you."

"Abi, there's no time!"

"No, Crys," Abigail snapped. "This is us together now. No damn CPO and her client, okay? I am not going to leave your side, so you can save your breath."

Crystal nodded reluctantly. She hid her weapon, and they both went to stand in the middle of the road, waving at the car. As it got close, Crystal spotted the familiar blue and red lights on the grille and roof.

"Looking good!" Abigail yelled into the wind.

God, I hope so! The officer in the patrol car flashed his lights, and came to a stop in front of them. He rolled his window down, and rested a meaty forearm over the frame. Crystal spotted the eagle, globe, and anchor tattooed on his skin, and she could have cried in pure relief.

"Marines?" she said.

He gave her a curious look.

189

"That's right. You ladies break down?"

"We rolled our car," Crystal just replied.

She would wait to share any more until they were on their way. She shot a nervous glance over her shoulder. Still no sign of those Red-Eyes coming back, but of course, it did not mean that they were safe yet... At least the officer who had stopped was a Marine, and she did trust in that.

"I'll get you guys some blankets," he said.

On closer inspection, after shining his torch over them, he must have realised that they were both in a bad state. He popped his trunk open and jumped out of his seat.

"You need the hospital, uh?" he added.

"Yes, we do," Abigail replied gratefully.

She threw a pointed glance toward her lover which Crystal totally missed, so absorbed was she in her inspection of the dark fields at the back of the road.

"I'll drive you," the officer offered. "It's been one thing after the other out there tonight, and every medic or ambulance we have across the county is tied up."

"What's happening?" Crystal asked in her command tone.

"Oh, the usual; times about a hundred." He shrugged. "I guess losing their precious Internet's got people feeling all kinds of weird and crazy."

He passed her a thick woollen blanket. Abigail seized it and immediately tried to wrap it around her shoulders, but Crystal would not have it this time.

"You first," she murmured. "Please, babe. You've got less layers on than me."

The Marine cop handed her another blanket along with an intent stare.

"You military?"

"75th Army Ranger," Crystal said curtly. "Special Forces."

"Right. Nice one. Sure got that vibe about ya."

She maintained her obsessive scanning as he went on. Her nausea had eased off slightly before, but now it was back with a vengeance. She felt tense; anxious... Almost like right before she used to get one of those terrible panic attacks. And the cop was still talking.

"I'll tell you what else has been happening, Ranger."

He was nervous too, Crystal realised. Probably what made him babble on like this, instead of just getting behind the damn wheel again, and driving the two injured women straight to the place they needed.

"We've been getting an awful lot of calls about red-eyed folks wandering the streets." He grinned uncomfortably. "We're not even close to Halloween... Wonder what the hell's go—"

CHAPTER TWENTY-FIVE

Time came to a complete stand-still for Abigail as she witnessed what happened next. She saw her lover reach for her weapon; she heard her yell an urgent warning. She noticed the look of frozen stupor on the cop's face; it must have appeared to him as if she was going to shoot him in the face... He had no idea that one of those red-eyed folks he had just mentioned was rushing at him from behind, brandishing a blade the size of a machete. In a split second, Abigail recognised the longish face and too-large eyes. She saw what she could only describe as demonic intent behind the red glow; no conscious awareness other than pure evil. Thankfully, Crystal reacted quickly and accurately. She fired a single bullet over the cop's shoulder that brought his attacker down. The killer blade landed at his feet.

"What the fuck!" the man exclaimed, startled.

Crystal lowered her weapon and they all looked down at the entity's body. Almost instantly, it began to dissolve into a dark gelatinous mass. It smelled like rotten fish and ammonia... Abigail felt her stomach turn. The cop continued to stare at the corpse, then back to Crystal; in a daze. This was no Halloween prank, for sure. Crystal gave him a rough shove to wake him up.

"What's your name?" she asked.

"Pearson. Ben Pearson."

"All right. Grab your rifle."

"Who are these people?" he gasped.

"They're not people," Crystal said sharply. "Now move!"

The officer's Marines training kicked in, and he dived inside the car to retrieve his automatic rifle. Abigail had found shelter behind the vehicle's back door. Crystal took up a solid defensive position in front of her; one knee down, weapon raised, finger heavy on the trigger. She could just make out the line of Red-Eyes on the edge of the field. They were back, except that this time there were three times as many; they were closer; armed with silent weapons that fired what looked like thin spikes of light. It appeared like shooting stars from a distance. It would have been beautiful, if not for the fact that a single one burned a baseball-sized hole into the lid of the trunk, of course... The Red-Eyes kept on shooting relentlessly; the patrol car acquired a few more holes; and the two armed humans carried on returning fire in the hopes of stopping the beings' advance.

"We won't be able to keep up," Crystal announced after a few minutes of this exchange. "Looks like we'll run out of ammo before these even break a sweat!"

Maybe she was hoping for a suggestion, an idea, anything else of the helpful kind; but Pearson only swore in reply, sharing his frustration as he observed what she too could see.

"Shit! They're all breaking off in different directions!"

Abigail rested an urgent hand over her lover's shoulder.

"Crys, give me a weapon," she demanded. "I can help."

Crystal shot her a piercing look that did not immediately make sense...

"Jump on the back seat and stay low," she ordered. "Hey, Marine! Give me your rifle and backup. I want you to get behind the wheel and drive."

"What?" he yelled in puzzlement.

"Just get the hell out!" Crystal hissed. "I'll cover for you."

All of a sudden, it dawned on Abigail with stunning, heart-breaking clarity. So, this was what had been lurking behind her earlier glance. *Goodbye...*

"Oh, Crystal," she murmured. "Don't..."

Of all the options to rescue themselves out of this situation that Abigail may have imagined, this one would never, ever have crossed her mind. The idea that Crystal might want to stay behind in order to facilitate her own escape made her want to vomit in disgust. Her brain ached to even contemplate such a thing. Of course, it was not so farfetched when she considered who she was. Captain Thor... A tough and courageous soldier; the owner of a pure and valiant heart. She was a warrior to the core, a true protector. Abigail had always known this about her. Sure, she was attracted to that selfless spirit. If sacrifice was the only choice left, if it was the only way to save the woman that she loved from being murdered by a vicious enemy, then Captain Thor would never hesitate. Abigail knew that she loved her, and this was just Crystal making her choice, now.

"Get in the car, Abigail," she repeated in a hard voice that did not sound like her at all.

She even tried to force her in, but Abigail shoved her back violently. Her vision blurred, as painful and bitter tears filled her eyes. All she wanted to do, even as weapons flashes continued to erupt in the background, was to wrap her arms around Crystal, tell her how much she loved her, and stop this entire world from going mad for just a goddamn minute! Instead, she swallowed back her tears, and glared at her as if she had no feelings for her whatsoever.

"I said I'm not going anywhere," she declared, with a calm and control that she absolutely did not feel. "And I'm certainly not going to leave you behind. So, stop that nonsense; and give me a weapon so I can fight!"

Pearson chose that moment to chime in, in between ducking behind the hood to avoid one of those lethal laser beams, and returning a volley of automatic fire. By then he seemed to have gone from helpful but confused cop to fully reawakened Marine; he also had a useful compromise to offer.

"Hey, I say we all go," he declared. He nodded briefly to Abi. "You can drive." He looked back toward Crystal. "You and I can handle the shooting. I agree with your friend, Ranger. I'm not going to just drive off and leave you here on your own."

Abigail exchanged a loaded glance with her lover. *Please...* Crystal looked tense and furious, but she gave a small nod as it probably dawned on her that Abigail would never leave without her anyway. And of course, Captain Thor was not one to waste anybody's time arguing stupidly in the middle of a firefight. Not when people's lives were on the line.

"Fine," she agreed. "As long as we go NOW!"

Abigail did throw her arms around her neck for a brief but fierce embrace.

"Thank you," she breathed.

Crystal pulled her backup weapon from her leg holster and gave it to her.

"Just in case. It's loaded. Just take the safety off. You know how?"

Abigail was not a complete novice with guns.

"I know what I'm doing," she confirmed.

"Well; all right then, Ms POTUS."

Just for a split second, the stern face of the military officer slipped to allow her lover's warmth to shine through. Love and tenderness twinkled through her deep black eyes. Crystal even flashed that sexy crooked smile that Abigail so loved to see.

"Don't ever leave me, Crys," she exclaimed.

"I won't," Crystal promised. "I love you."

It was a genuinely heartfelt but risky promise to make, and one which Abigail was about to find her lover would not be able to keep, no matter how much she wanted to.

"Watch out!" Pearson yelled suddenly. "Incoming!"

The Red-Eyes had breached their perimeter. They were no longer over there, but *here!* Abigail saw Crystal transform back into Captain Thor in the blink of an eye.

"Stay behind me, Abi," she ordered, and leapt to her feet.

Abigail felt the weight of the weapon in her own hands. She fumbled with the safety catch. Meanwhile, Pearson was allowing his rifle to do the talking, unleashing a nice kind of hell onto the enemy. Crystal took care of the Red-Eyes who were able to slip through his barrage of deadly bullets. There were several... *Too many*, Abigail realised. Her lover was shooting hard and fast, hitting bullseye with every bullet. But more kept on coming, and soon, Pearson let out the dreaded announcement.

"I'm on my last round!" he shouted.

"Same here," Crystal growled.

"We can use their weapons?"

"I tried. Didn't work."

Abigail saw her reach for her dagger, and her heart sank. If it came down to that, a simple knife against laser weapons, this fight would be over in seconds, no matter how skilled Crystal may be. Abigail seized her last chance to make a difference.

"I'm going for it," she yelled. "Cover me!"

It should have been an easy move to go around the car and jump behind the wheel, but it was not, because by that point, they were completely surrounded. Even so, Abigail almost made it. She was nearly there when a dark shape appeared in front of her, blocking her way. She fired two good shots at it, but missed. The gun was unfamiliar, heavy; she had not used one in years, and now she was facing a live target intent on destroying her.

Shit…! Breathing hard, her hands shaking, Abigail tried again as the Red-Eyes raised his own weapon. Her next bullet was better, but still slightly off. She would not get another opportunity to get it right. The being took another step toward her. He aimed. Fired. He did not miss.

∞

Abigail saw the flash of light, but strangely, she did not feel any pain… Just the weight of her lover's body slamming into hers, as Crystal caught her in a protective embrace and spun her around, placing herself in the line of fire. *In between me and the shooter…*

"No, Crys!" she gasped.

Abigail knew she had been hit from the violent spasm that Crystal gave as the shot impacted. She felt the rush of air against her ear as it left her lungs. Horrified, Abigail stared wildly into her eyes.

"Sorry…" Crystal murmured.

Her eyes fluttered closed and she slumped heavily against her. Abigail supported her down to the ground, even though all the strength had gone out of her legs. *This can't be happening!* She was no longer aware of anything around them. She had no idea if Pearson was still shooting, or if he had run out of ammo and gone down too… An alien being could have been standing over her armed with one of the lethal blades that they carried, and it would not have made a jot of difference to her. All she knew was that Crystal had been shot in the back. By some miracle, she was still alive, and the shot had not gone right through her. Abigail hoped that it was a good thing… But her lover was bleeding an awful lot, and she seemed on the verge of losing consciousness.

"Stay with me, Crystal," Abigail yelled. "Can you hear me? Come on, soldier! Open your eyes!"

She ripped off her sweater and rolled it into a ball that she applied against her back. Crystal flinched in pain. She groaned, and struggled to open her eyes.

"Yes," Abigail encouraged. "Look at me."

Crystal reached blindly for her hand. A trickle of blood ran down the side of her mouth as she coughed. Abigail gripped her fingers in hers, fighting tears all the while. *I'm losing her…*

"I'm here, my love," she whispered against her ear. "I'm with you, Crys."

Crystal did manage to open her eyes. Abigail saw what an effort it took for her to focus on her face, but she was finally able to hold her gaze.

"Abi…" she murmured. "Leave…"

"Shh," Abigail said gently. "It's okay, darling."

She looked up, startled, as Pearson suddenly appeared out of nowhere. The grim expression on his face confirmed that it was not good news. Hers must have told him everything that he needed to know as well. They exchanged a silent nod. *So, this is how it ends…* Abigail reflected.

"Drive," Crystal repeated in a broken voice. "Both… Go!"

She started to cry silent tears, exhausted and unable to say anymore; but her eyes never left her lover's face, and all Abigail could do was watch on helplessly, as her blood turned the snow under her body crimson, and her breathing gradually grew more laboured. Pearson laid a large hand over her shoulder.

"Easy, Ranger," he told her. "They've gone now. Help is on the way. Lots of soldiers, and lots of ammo. Just rest, my friend. It's all good."

Abigail knew he was lying. She could hear snow crunching near the vehicle now, the beings closing down on their preys; Crystal was too weak to realise it, and Abigail flashed the man a deeply grateful look before she locked eyes with her again.

"It's okay, my love," she repeated. "Relax; this fight is over and we'll be home soon. I've got you, Crys."

Crystal fought to keep her eyes open. Abigail noticed that their combined words of reassurance seemed to have a calming effect on her. At this stage, it was what she wanted. To be able to give her solace, a sense of absolute safety... And to make her feel all the love that she had for her, of course. She held her tighter against her chest; she cradled her face in the palm of her hand. Crystal gave a small sigh and unconsciously nuzzled her cheek into it. Her breathing slowed. She sank deeper into the embrace.

"Mmm... 'Kay," she murmured.

"Go to sleep, darling," Abigail whispered. "When you wake up, everything will be all right. I love you."

CHAPTER TWENTY-SIX

It felt as if even the skies above shook in sorrow when Captain Thor exhaled for the last time, and died in her lover's arms. In the seconds that followed, Abigail let out a raw, broken, heart-wrenching scream. She stared up at the stars in helpless fury and even worse grief. The tears that she had so far managed to hold back, just because she did not want Crystal to see them, flowed freely down her face. She hoped that death would follow quickly for her now too. She could hear the Red-Eyes coming... Abigail clenched her teeth. *Well, bring it on then!* She no longer cared about pain or anything else. She had no fear either. She just wanted to be gone, out of there, and reunited with her lover; that was all.

"Look at that," Pearson said, pointing at the sky. "Look, dammit!"

Abigail did, when he grabbed her arm and shook her just enough to make her react. On auto-pilot, in deep, painful shock, she noticed that it did appear as if something was happening up there: the sky seemed charged... With what, she had no idea. But it was moving, shimmering...

"What the fuck is up there?" Pearson groaned.

Abigail did not reply. *I don't care...* She returned her eyes to Crystal, breathing harder at the sight of her lying so still. *So much blood...* And yet, her lover looked like she was only sleeping.

Abigail touched her fingers to her cheek and shivered at how unnaturally cold she had become even in such a short amount of time. She suddenly remembered that she had a few shots left in her backup weapon. At least three. *One is all I need…* She ran her fingers through Crystal's still wet hair.

"I'll see you soon, my love," she whispered.

With absolutely zero hesitation, and with steady hands this time, she located the gun and grabbed hold of it. A quick glance toward Pearson confirmed that he was not looking at her. Even if he had, he may not have tried to stop her. After all, who knew what these awful beings would do to them when they finally got up close and personal? This may well be the best solution of all… Abigail raised the weapon to the side of her head. She made sure that it was nice and tight against her temple. She was only a split second away from pressing the trigger now. She tightened her finger over it and glanced at her lover's face for one last time. *I'm coming, Crys.* It would have been all over for Abigail if suddenly, the weapon had not started to heat up in her hand. The heat was such that she cried out in pain, and instinctively let go of it. The gun landed in the snow. She stared at it, shaken. The damn thing was so hot that it was glowing red. Abigail stared some more as the skin on her hand started to blister. *What is going on…?*

"Oh, my fucking hell!" Pearson exclaimed.

She whirled around to look at him.

"What?" she yelled. "What is it?"

He glanced at her in pure astonishment.

"It's a craft… Just look up, for God's sake!"

Abigail did raise her eyes finally, and even though she was numb through and through, her mouth still dropped at the sight. It was a mix of awe, disbelief, and reluctance all wrapped into one. There, about three-hundred feet above their heads, a giant metallic disc hovered silently… All black and perfectly smooth.

She could see no cockpit; no windows. Come to think of it, the thing seemed to be made of a single block of seamless material. Abigail could not identify or even hear a propulsion system, and yet, it just floated up there seemingly effortlessly. Other than the Red-Eyes themselves, it was by far the most alien thing she had observed in her entire life.

"Do you see it?" Pearson insisted.

He sounded terribly excited... Why the hell did he sound so excited when the woman that she loved lay dead on the ground? Abigail was stunned. She could not understand his reaction. She felt a hot river of tears start to run down her face again that she absolutely could not stop.

"What are you talking about?" she cried.

"This, my friend," he replied intently, and pointed to a spot on the hull.

Abigail followed his line. She blinked to clear her vision. Once more, she froze.

"You see it now?" he yelled. "Uh?"

She nodded. *Oh, my God...* The craft that did not look quite so alien now began to emit a deep humming sound that made the hairs stand up on the back of her neck. The vibration felt like a low-level electrical charge; slightly unpleasant, uncomfortable, but nothing worse. At least not to Abigail, that is. It had a much worse effect on the Red-Eyes: one by one, they began to smoke, and catch fire. As they did, a series of blood-curdling screams echoed across the field. Abigail shivered all over again. Such a terrifying thing to hear... And it sounded like hundreds of them were out there. Pearson punched his fists through the air.

"Get some!" he shouted. "YEAH!!!!! Come on!"

Abigail looked back toward the silent ship in the sky. She narrowed her eyes at the engraved seal on the bottom that the Marine had pointed out to her; it was clearly an American flag.

This is ours, she thought, her heart beating out of her chest at the sudden realisation. *It's ours, and it's come to help us now...* Abigail wanted to remain cautious with her conclusions, although the results spoke for themselves. She and Pearson were alive; and the Red-Eyes were burning. It was all pretty simple, really. She thought of Russell, her heart breaking into a million pieces all over again. *If only you could see this, Russ! And you, my darling, Crys...* Abigail felt scorching anger flood through her at the injustice of it all. If only this ship, this high-tech military plane, whatever it may be, had shown up a few minutes earlier! Crystal would still be alive; she would still be with her! Abigail gripped her hand in hers, unconsciously trying to keep her warm. She heard her voice inside her head, as clear and strong as ever; *'You're not done here, Ms POTUS. Keep going, Abi!'* Abigail was not sure that she could do it, or even wanted to. Suddenly, the humming stopped, and the ship rotated on itself. It came down to hover just ten feet up above the road.

"Hey..." Pearson crouched down next to her and he rested a gentle hand over her shoulder. "You're Abi Christensen, aren't you?"

Abigail nodded silently. His jaw tightened as he looked at Crystal.

"I'm really sorry about your friend. Hell of a fighter."

Abigail squeezed his fingers. She was struggling to breathe. If she allowed herself to think of Crystal too much, to remember her brilliant smile, her soft kisses, the way that she always held her so tightly against her chest... If she did that, only to be struck again and again with the realisation that her beautiful lover had left this world for good, she suspected that she would lose her mind completely. She was not far from it as it was.

"Thank you for what you said to her in her last moments," she just replied. "It helped."

"I really hope so." Pearson looked intently into her eyes, as if he could guess what she was thinking. "I won't ask you how you're doing, Ms Christensen. But your friend took that hit for you. She wanted you alive. It'll be okay eventually."

Abigail gritted her teeth and she did not reply. *Not okay*, she thought. *Never will be. But I won't let you have died in vain, my love.* Her heart bleeding, but intent on staying alive now, for Crystal if not herself, she once again returned her gaze to the ship. A line of bright lights suddenly came on around the hull. A large panel slid open underneath.

"Whoa…" Pearson muttered.

He was tense, too; Abigail could tell. What would appear in front of them now? Would it be Friend, or Foe? Would it even be Human? As it was, she heard his voice before she even saw him in person.

"Abigail? Abi?"

Abigail swallowed hard. She went extremely still. So much had happened in just a couple of hours' time; so many horrible things that had pushed her to the edge of her limits and what she thought she could handle, and then beyond that... *Why would this be any different?* Still, she struggled to make sense of this next development.

"It can't be…"

But her ears told her it was, even if her mind answered that it could not be real. A solid ramp materialised under the ship out of thin air. And then she watched him stroll down the length of it, looking as fresh and familiar as the last day she had seen him. Instead of his usual attire, he wore military combat boots and an olive-green uniform that looked like a flight suit. Two patches on his chest included the US flag on one side, and a star-like design that she had never seen before on the other. *Focus, Abi!* Her eyes shot back to his face. He smiled encouragingly.

"James?" she cried. "Is that you?"

US Senator James Birch walked pretty fast for a dead man... He quickly closed the distance between them, holding her gaze intently all the while. As he came to stand in front of her, he took her hands firmly in his, and flashed her another warm, gentle, reassuring smile.

"James," she repeated.

"Abigail, my dear. Are you all right?"

"I don't understand," she said roughly.

Another delusion... Another goddamn lie! If he had to fake his own death, then why didn't he at least tell me? Discovering that the man was still alive was such a huge relief for Abigail that it was beyond words for her to express... But holding on to some anger really was the only way that she could stay in control. She was still shaking, and her teeth were chattering now. It seemed to be getting worse. He must have felt it, how could he not? He laced his arm around her waist and kept hold of her hand at the same time.

"I know. I will explain everything," he promised.

Pearson came to attention as Birch turned to him next.

"Ben Pearson; Lieutenant, US Marines, Sir," he introduced himself.

"Officer," Birch nodded. "There is no time to explain, but police duty or not, I would strongly suggest that you come with us now. Of course, it is your decision."

Pearson flashed an intent smile as he glanced at the ship.

"Oh... Yes, sir! You bet I'm coming!"

Birch noticed Crystal next. His face turned grave, and he let go of Abigail to take urgent steps toward her. He actually knelt down next to her body, and laid his hand over her forehead.

"Who is this?" he asked. "One of your group?"

"She's my partner," Abigail murmured. "My love."

"What happened, Abigail?"

"She jumped right in between me and the shooter," Abigail stammered. "I should have died. It should be me lying there, James, not her... She gave her own life to save mine!"

Birch stood up briskly at that, turned back toward the ship, and raised his hand. Immediately, two other guys dressed in the same uniform as he was ran down the ramp.

"Pick her up," Birch instructed. "Take her to the infirmary. Lieutenant Pearson, help 'em out."

"Yes, sir," Pearson said.

"She's dead, James," Abigail repeated, her voice breaking.

He gently took her arm and started to lead her up the ramp.

"So was I, my dear," he murmured. "So was I..."

Abigail shot him a wild and terribly confused look, but she could not ask anymore. She was fast losing the ability to speak. Birch half-led and half-carried her inside the ship. It was bright in there, busy. Lots more people in uniform, soldiers, one would assume, were onboard. Birch and Abigail followed close behind the two men who carried Crystal to the infirmary. Once there, they laid her down on an exam table, and left. A team of people dressed in scrubs who looked like regular doctors began to undress her.

"Hurry up," Birch instructed.

They certainly did. Abigail watched in absolute disbelief as they literally ripped the clothes off her body. In her haste, one of the doctors lifted her arm and let it drop back down on the table, hard.

"Be careful with her!" Abigail cried. "What are you doing?"

The doctors carried on without paying any attention to her. Abigail knew it did not matter anymore; she knew that her lover could not feel anything anyway... But no matter, she could not help her reaction. She turned toward Birch, in absolute turmoil.

"Why are they doing this?" she snapped.

"It's not guaranteed, Abigail," he murmured in reply. "You have to understand, it never is. But we will try."

She shook her head, not understanding.

"What?" she repeated. "What are you saying?"

The team of doctors lifted Crystal's now naked body onto a flat rectangular board, and they carried her to a water tank of the same shape. It was deep, filled with a bluish-green liquid. Birch held her back as Abigail tried to step forward and intervene.

"Shh... Abi, please. It's okay. Let them work."

"But what are they doing to her?" Abigail almost screamed.

"Trying to bring her back," Birch finally answered. "Just like they did with me."

CHAPTER TWENTY-SEVEN

Crystal stared at the ceiling for a long time as she began to come to. There was no pain, no sensation of anything. Her mind was totally empty, just a blank slate of pure awareness. She did not have the slightest notion of who she was, or even *that* she was. A body, a person... She could remember none of it. She drifted in silence, floated in a sea of nothingness for a long time; until a quickening occurred, a tensing of her whole being. A thought pierced through. *Where am I...?* She suddenly recognised the ceiling for what it was, and the rest of the room came into focus as well. White walls; white floor. She was lying on a narrow bed. White sheets, military-issue rough. *Ugh... Dammit... Not again.* It occurred to Captain Thor that the only places that looked so sterile and cold were the kind where she usually landed after things had gone badly wrong in her job. Where was it this time? Iraq? Afghanistan? She found an intravenous needle in her arm connected to a bag of fluids. She pulled it out, ignoring the line of blood that trickled down to her wrist. *What the hell happened to me?* She took slight comfort in the fact that she could feel her legs and arms. Her limbs were still attached, which was always reassuring. She moved her hands over her torso, frowning when she discovered the tight bandage wrapped around her chest. Not so good, perhaps. *Did I get shot?*

"Hello?" she called, and glanced across the room.

It looked just like a typical medical facility, although no one was around. Well; at least no damn doctor was going to tell her to stay put when she had other ideas. She pushed the light cover off her legs, pleased to find that she was wearing scrubs, top and bottom. A definite improvement on the usual. Now if she could only find her boots... Crystal slid off the bed, unprepared for the rush of light-headedness that hit her as soon as her feet touched the ground. She groaned, quickly grabbed onto the side of the bed to maintain her balance. *Take it easy, soldier.* She took a few deep breaths and waited for the feeling to pass. It got better. She shuffled forward, and as she moved in front of it, a lighter panel on the side became transparent. *Okay... High-tech infirmary...* She still had no idea where she was. She looked through the newly-appeared window, but it was pitch-black on the outside.

"What the hell is this place?" Crystal muttered.

Vague images of an empty field and patchy recollections of being on the road broke through her mind. Anger at her inability to figure things out began to simmer too. *Was I in some kind of crash?* She stared hard at the floor, fighting hard to remember. *Get your brain in gear, for God's sake!*

"Crys!"

Crystal looked up sharply at the sound of a familiar female voice calling her name. Her heart lifted in pure joy at the sight of her.

"Abigail..."

Her memories came flooding back in the five steps it took for her lover to rush across the room, and throw her arms wildly around her neck; the campaign, the car crash, Scott and Russell, the red-eyed beings... And one in particular, as he levelled his laser weapon straight at Abigail, and pulled the trigger. Her joy forgotten for the time being, Crystal started to breathe faster.

"Shh, it's all right, my love," Abigail said quickly.

Crystal remembered grabbing hold of her and turning her around to shield her from the deadly hit.

"Are you okay?" she gasped.

"Yes, darling. Everything's fine. Just calm down, okay?"

Crystal attempted to, but now the details were coming back to her at the speed of light. She would never forget the flash of blinding pain that followed the hit, which felt as if her entire body had been blown up from the inside. She could recall falling down, and the paralysing cold that settled over her as she lay in the snow, bleeding. She could still hear Abigail's voice repeating the same thing over and over; that they were safe now, and that she loved her. Nothing else after that... The realisation that she must have fainted, leaving her partner without protection, was enough to send her into full panic mode.

"Crys, don't do this," Abigail said. "It's okay now."

Crystal heard her but as if from a long way away. *How long was I out? Where are we? Are you really okay?* She tried to say the words but her breathing would not allow it. Her vision blurred. Her heart was racing. She pressed a hand against her own chest, unable to escape the panic. *Fuck!*

"Abi..." she panted. "Abigail!"

Crystal managed to catch a single glimpse of her face before heavy black dots obscured her vision again.

"I'm here," Abigail promised. "Relax. You can do it."

But Crystal could not. She heard voices in the background. She felt extra hands on her, grabbing hold of her, and something cold was applied over her face.

"No..." she moaned.

"Don't fight it, my love," Abigail said. "Just breathe."

Crystal fought it, whatever and whoever it was, but she did not win. She felt a sharp sting on the side of her arm. Everything went black.

∞

Waking up the second time was harder, somehow, although this time Abigail was there, and her brilliant smile was the first thing that Crystal saw when she opened her eyes. No panic ensued.

"Hey..." she murmured.

"Hey, you," Abigail said gently. "Welcome back, my love."

She leaned over her and pressed her lips against hers. The kiss was tender, warm, reassuring. Crystal closed her eyes again briefly, and she sighed in pure pleasure.

"Feeling better?"

"Yeah. Sorry about before. I got caught in it."

"No, Captain," Abigail argued quietly; "I'm sorry I wasn't there when you first woke up to give you that grounding kiss you needed."

Crystal shot her a groggy smile.

"'S'okay, Ms POTUS..."

She was back in bed now, tethered to that bag of fluids, and perhaps it was a good thing, because she felt spectacularly weak. But as she returned her gaze to Abigail, she noticed the unusual brightness of her eyes, and this instantly became a much bigger concern to her than her own condition.

"What's wrong, Abi?" she asked.

"Nothing, don't worry," Abigail replied, a bit too quickly.

"But you're crying," Crystal insisted, only to wince as she suddenly remembered Russ. *No wonder...* "Sorry. Head's still a bit fuzzy, I think."

"That's okay. And stop apologising."

"Are you sure that you're all right?"

"Yes," Abigail promised. "I'm just emotional because I'm so relieved to have you back... You saved my life, Crys."

211

"That's what CPOs are for, hey…" Crystal joked. She wiped a tear from her cheek with the back of her knuckle. "Please, don't cry, Abi. I'm here; all in one piece."

Abigail flashed her a loaded, intense, lingering look.

"I missed you," she said intently. "I love you so much."

"Love you too, babe," Crystal murmured.

As if to demonstrate her point, Abigail treated her to the sort of fiery kiss that never failed to make Crystal tremble, and which always left her feeling a little breathless too; but in a good way, with a happy, blissful smile on her face. It worked a treat this time too.

"Now tell me straight, soldier. How do you feel?"

"Ah… The usual," Crystal shrugged. "Tired. Sore. I'll live."

"Yes," Abigail nodded; her expression fiercely serious once again. "You most certainly will. Crys, we need to talk. A lot has happened since that night on the road."

"A lot? What do you mean? How long was I out?"

"Two full days and nights, my love," Abigail replied.

"What?" Crystal exclaimed, shocked. "You're kidding!"

"It's not that bad, considering… I was also in bed recovering for most of that time. Ben's with us, by the way; he's doing fine. He's been in to see you a few times, but you were unconscious, and I don't think it would have registered with you."

"Ben?" Crystal frowned, struggling to place the name.

"Pearson. The cop we met on the road; remember?"

"Oh, yeah," Crystal nodded with an instant smile. "Marine Pearson, uh? Great. Glad to hear he's okay."

As she continued to look at her, as her mind cleared a bit more and her normal focus returned, she noticed that Abigail was wearing a military uniform. Or at least, it sure looked like it; brand-new combat boots, black fatigue pants with lots of pockets that looked a size too big for her… *Maybe the Army rescued us.*

Crystal barely glanced at the US flag embroidered on her long-sleeved shirt, a thick base-layer type garment. Nothing unusual there, and she must have owned thousands of these tops over the years. But her eyes stumbled over the patch on the other side of Abigail's shirt. Three highly-stylised yellow stars in a circle, one big and two small ones, with a sign that looked just like a Nike swoosh through the middle, and an acronym that she did not recognise: **H.I.G.A.** *All right,* Crystal thought, frowning in wonder. *So, perhaps NASA came to save us...?* She sat up straight, determined to find out what was going on; but before she could ask Abigail about the meaning of the letters, the uniform, and request that someone please give her some real clothes to wear, and a pair of boots too, a deep male voice echoed from the other side of the room.

"Captain Thor! How wonderful to find you fully awake and talking at last! Welcome back to the world of the living, my dear friend!"

Taken aback, Crystal turned her attention to the newcomer. He was tall and trim, with bright, intelligent blue eyes, and thick white hair neatly combed back. A distinguished-looking kind of guy, quite a bit older, and dressed in the same uniform. Crystal narrowed her eyes at him; she was pretty sure that she had never met this man before in her life, even though he called her a dear friend. He came to stand next to the bed, kissed Abigail on the cheek like they were best buddies, and held out a firm hand to her.

"I'm Congressman James Birch. It's an honour to meet you, Captain."

Crystal shook his hand as the name slowly registered. *Oh, that's right,* she remembered; *the dead guy... Am I still dreaming or something?* She threw a confused glance toward Abigail which Birch obviously did not miss either. He laughed easily.

"I know, I know; but reports of my death have been greatly exaggerated."

"No, they were not, James," Abigail murmured.

He chuckled, eyes twinkling as he held Crystal's gaze.

"You and I do share a special bond, Captain."

Fully awake now, her faculties restored, Crystal could feel her impatience growing, as well as irritation at being given more riddles than answers. The congressman seemed to be having a good time with this; she definitely was not.

"First of all, call me Crys," she replied. "I'm retired."

"As you wish," he nodded, smiling as if he knew something that she did not.

"And tell me what you mean, a special bond?" she asked.

The crazy thought did cross her mind that he might tell her he was her father, who Crystal had never met. Her mother had died when she was only three-years-old, leaving her to be raised by an aunt who was never happy about it. She had no clue who Crystal's father might be, as she told her often, *'otherwise I'd ship you off to him'*. Crystal had tried to learn more about him, and to find him when she was old enough, but without success. During the lonelier times of her childhood, she imagined that he must be a James Bond-type officer on a secret mission who would come back for her one day. Crystal had not thought of him in years. She wondered unhappily what sort of powerful drugs they must have given her to trigger such unusual, unhelpful memories. She stared at Birch, frowning hard all the while. At this stage of the game, she was convinced that nothing, no matter how crazy it may be, could surprise her anymore. Of course, she was wrong about that too.

"I died," Birch said to her. "I was murdered, actually."

"Did the Secret Service help you to fake your own death?" Crystal enquired.

To her, as it had for her partner upon discovering that her good friend was still alive, it made perfect sense. The man knew more about the Global Network than anyone else alive, and if he planned to reveal all, then… But Crystal was surprised when he shook his head, no longer smiling now.

"No; I mean, I was *dead,*" he insisted. "And so were you."

Crystal turned toward Abigail once again to find her staring at her intently, her gaze razor-sharp and full of genuine dismay. She remembered her tears from just a few minutes earlier, which still struck her as unusual. Representative Christensen was not the kind to burst into tears at the drop of a hat. There was what she had told her as well; *I'm so relieved to have you back…* The stricken look on her face now also hinted at a darker part of the story. Crystal held her lover's gaze.

"I just passed out," she said. "Right?"

Abigail swallowed hard, and she shook her head.

"No, my love," she replied. "You died in my arms."

CHAPTER TWENTY-EIGHT

Finding out that she had been a corpse for two full hours before being brought back to life was not the most difficult thing for Crystal to process. She had not been conscious of any of it; there had been no pain for her once she was through. If she had not come back, she would never have known. She did feel a hint of sadness about that, sure; but much worse for her was witnessing the expression of pure devastation in Abigail's grey eyes when she explained what had happened to them during that night, and how her partner had died. It was something no one ever had to witness, Crystal reflected bitterly, the pain and sorrow of their own death reflected in a lover's eyes. *And what a good thing that is too...* Once the first moment of surprise and dismay over, she wanted to find out more, of course.

"How did you bring me back...?" was her first question.

Abigail squeezed her hand warmly, and exchanged a brief glance with Birch.

"What is it?" Crystal enquired with an instant frown.

"Well, just that we would normally give you a bit longer to recover before we throw you right back into the thick of it," the man replied. "Your body's just gone through a really traumatic event..."

Crystal shrugged impatiently, ignoring the pain in her chest when she moved.

"Yeah, well," she grunted, "I can tell you that the body will feel a lot better once it's given boots to wear, and food to eat."

Abigail grinned at her typical reply; Birch simply nodded.

"It's true we have no time to waste," he agreed. "You'll find boots and clothes in the bathroom. See you on deck when you're ready; I will have food and some answers for you."

Crystal had a quick shower; she got dressed. She could feel some of her normal energy returning, although she was grateful for her partner's help as she got ready.

"Sure, you're okay to do this?"

"Yes. I'll be fine, babe."

Abigail shot her an amused glance, a perfect mix of irritated and tender.

"For your information, I have never let another woman call me that before, you know?"

"Of course not, Ms POTUS," Crystal replied smugly, as she wrapped her arms around her. "Since no one is allowed to do it but me."

They exchanged an intimate and spirit-warming hug, and a similar kind of kiss. Abigail lingered into the embrace afterward, smiling, with her eyes closed.

"Mmm…" she sighed. "I love the way you kiss me."

"Not bad for a dead soldier, uh?" Crystal joked.

"Not funny, Ms Thor."

"But you chuckled."

"No," Abigail corrected. "I choked."

She led her through the automatic sliding doors and into a large curved corridor. There were no windows anywhere. It was busy. People in uniform walked fast on their way to wherever. No one paid attention to them, and Crystal glanced curiously all around her. Abigail had mentioned the starship in her account of the events of that night. This place sure had a military vibe to it.

"Reminds me of a Navy ship," she said. "Only bigger."

"From the outside, it looks like something right out of *Star Wars*," Abigail commented.

"Damn! Wish I could have seen it!" Crystal exclaimed, and just barely refrained from making another bad joke.

"You will, I promise," her lover assured. She took her hand, and smiled as they reached a new set of doors simply labelled as: *DECK #1.* "Now get ready for something else that's even more breath-taking, my love."

Crystal followed her through the doors, curious yet unsure of what to expect, and she instantly came to an abrupt halt at the otherworldly sight that greeted her.

"Oh... WOW!" was all she could say.

The room was spacious and circular in shape. All around it, the same grey metallic structure as in the corridor could be seen, but here, the walls in between each support beam were made of transparent glass. In essence, this was a 360-degree observation deck which had been made to look like a typical meeting room, equipped with a large oblong table, chairs, a water-cooler, and smart screens. The word *'typical'* could never be applied to the outside view; it was at once breath-takingly beautiful and mind-bendingly strange. Crystal gave a soft chuckle.

"Wow," she repeated in pure amazement. "I never thought I'd see this in my life..."

She barely glanced toward Birch when he walked in. The man was accompanied by Ben Pearson, who cracked a brilliant smile as soon as he spotted Crystal standing in the room. He did not look the least bit fazed by this view... He just walked over to clamp a steady hand over her shoulder. He shook her hand, and gave a delighted chuckle.

"Hey, Ranger! You're a bit warmer than the last time I saw you, uh!"

Without missing a beat, Crystal flashed him a mischievous wink.

"Shame no one could resurrect your sense of humour at the same time..."

"Guess I'd need more than a miracle for that," he laughed.

"Well; it sure is good to see you smiling and in one piece, Marine," Crystal concluded.

True to his word, Birch had brought her some food: bacon, eggs, pancakes, fruit, orange juice, coffee... A real feast, the sort that Crystal had been hoping for. Now though, she found herself drawn to the astonishing view instead. She struggled to take her eyes off the huge expanse of black sky outside the panoramic windows, lit up by a million twinkling stars in the background; and on the ground below, all this dark-coloured rock, boulders, and huge craters scattered everywhere... Birch stopped next to her, and he patted her on the shoulder.

"Pretty spectacular, isn't it?"

"Yeah, you could say that," Crystal nodded. "So; now we're on the moon... I mean, above it. We're all onboard a US starship, floating above the surface of the moon. Jesus..."

"I think we can safely leave him out of this one," Abigail remarked, and she rested her hands firmly on her shoulders. "Sit down, my love. You need to eat."

She placed a full plate in front of her, put a fork in her hand, and sat down by her side. Pearson poured them all some coffee, and Birch simply took a seat in front of Crystal.

"That's right," he approved. "Eat, and find your strength. Meanwhile, I will answer your questions; starting with this ship, and how you were brought back to life, since the two happen to be linked."

Crystal started eating, but she kept her eyes on him.

"I'm ready," she nodded. "Let's hear it."

"So, this is the USS Eisenhower II," Birch declared. "Named in recognition of the first of our Human representatives to make contact with an interstellar civilisation in 1955. The starship was built two years later with blueprints that these beings, known as the *Shanayael,* gave us. To this day, this technology is still far in advance of anything that we have available…" He gave her a fierce look. "Well… At least, officially; you understand."

Crystal certainly did. It was more tin-foil stuff, but she was past worrying about that now. And of course, she was familiar with the strange rumours regarding the Nellis Air Force Base, also known as Area 51, where the so-called reverse-engineering of E.T flying craft may have been going on behind closed doors. *Not so crazy rumours now, that's for sure…*

"Is this technology what also allowed us both to be brought back to life, James?" she asked.

"Yes, it is," Birch agreed.

Crystal shot a hopeful glance toward Abigail.

"What about Matt, and Russ? Can we…"

"I'm afraid not, darling," Abigail said gently. "Their bodies were too damaged for it… But we were able to bring them back, at least, and take care of them the way that they deserve."

Crystal nodded, not allowing her emotions to rise.

"And you say that these beings, the *Shanayael…* They're the ones we thought had made contact only once, and disappeared, never to be seen or heard from again?"

"That is correct," Birch nodded. "Although now we know that it was not only once. Now, right before my, uhm… Let's call it my *'assisted'*, fateful plunge into the waters of the Potomac River, I was about to be introduced to another organisation, this one called *HIGA.*"

Crystal glanced at the patch on her uniform.

"Which means…?"

"The acronym stands for the *'Human Inter-Galactic Alliance'*. To cut a long story short, you can think of them as the good-guys counterpart to the Global Network."

Crystal sighed in frustration, and unconsciously reached for her partner's hand.

"Another parallel offshoot, uh?" she groaned. "Our normal world feels less and less like the real thing."

"I know," Abigail admitted. "And I know that this is a lot to digest all at once… You're right, Crys. Our *'normal'* world no longer has much to do with actual reality anymore. Looking at it from this new perspective, I'm sure you can appreciate fully the effect that so many years of perception control has created."

Crystal forced a small smile for her.

"That's for sure. I always felt constricted in the world, and like there was more to it than I was being told… But yes. This is huge." She turned back to Birch. "What about the Red-Eyes in all this?"

"Deep infiltration is their game," he replied. "Through the Global Network, they've been influencing and moulding our experience with increasingly sophisticated means; if you thought that Google was just a search engine, for example, you can think again. Same with all the social media sites. None of them ever were about communication; but censorship, control, and turning human beings into slaves, certainly."

"I've heard that before… But how?"

"Easily. At the beginning, you had *'holdables'*: your phone, laptop, tablet, etc. Then, it moved to what are called *'wearables'*: fitness trackers, all kinds of reality-augmenting gadgets, smart watches… And lately, we've been down to *'implantables'*: I mean, people are allowing themselves to be chipped! They think it's cool that they can open a door or pay for their lunch with just a wave of the hand!"

Crystal stared hard at Birch as a note of anger crept into his voice. She had completely forgotten about her food now, and the lunar landscape no longer held her attention either.

"Are you saying that eventually, the entire population will be chipped? And that we will be remotely-controlled by this race of ETs?" she asked.

"I'm saying that's the system they *want* to put in place; not that it will definitely happen," Birch replied, looking intently at her in return. "But they're stepping up the pace."

Crystal had started to feel nauseous all of a sudden. Abigail quickly poured her a glass of water.

"Here, darling. Crys, it's fine if you need a break..."

"No," Crystal insisted. "Keep going. What's the situation on Earth?"

Abigail kept a firm hold of her hand as she explained it.

"Over the last twenty-four hours, there have been several more targeted explosions. The pyramids of Egypt are gone. So is the temple complex at Angkor Wat, the Eiffel Tower, parts of the Great Wall of China... Basically, they are attacking our symbols of humanity one after the other."

Pearson suddenly chimed in, eyes flashing in fury.

"False flag operations," he declared. "It's happening!"

"Yes," Birch concurred. "Now I'm sure you can easily guess what follows next, Captain Thor."

Crystal swallowed; unfortunately, she could.

"Military rule everywhere," she murmured. "Is that it?"

"That's right, Ranger," Pearson muttered. "Martial law is on now, from Moscow to New York, Paris and Hong Kong..."

"Our people are scared, Crys," Abigail added. "Begging for these extreme measures, demanding military protection against an invisible threat that they do not understand... Of course, the Network is delivering exactly what they want."

Crystal shook her head, trying to make sense of it all, but it was not. Something was missing.

"Hold on a second," she exclaimed, dumbfounded. "What are they telling the people is behind these false flag attacks now? Not Al Qaeda again, right? Who are they pinning it on this time?"

She was losing track, breathing harder as stress started to take hold, and Abigail reached out to rest a soothing hand over her thigh.

"Relax," she murmured.

Birch answered the question.

"It's the craziest thing," he declared.

"Tell me something I don't know," Crystal growled.

"The Network," Birch nodded, "is telling people that a race of hostile extra-terrestrials is responsible; which is what they are, of course. They're flipping reality, distorting perception, twisting truth to serve their own purpose. There have been convenient sightings of the Red-Eyes to support the official story. After this, do you think that anyone on Earth will object to being chipped if it means being identified as a genuine Human, and having their safety guaranteed?"

"Goddammit to hell!" Crystal exclaimed.

A range of emotions threatened to overwhelm her; rage and frustration mainly... Outrage, and a deep sense of helplessness too. She dropped her face into her hands and took several deep breaths to calm down. When she looked up, she was astonished to find that Birch was smiling.

"Now, Captain," he said. "Shall I give you the good news?"

CHAPTER TWENTY-NINE

The headquarters for the *Human Inter-Galactic Alliance* that Birch had mentioned briefly before were located on the far side of the moon. This was the reason why the Eisenhower II was stationed there in the first place.

"Not a PR stunt, I assure you," he confirmed.

"Didn't think it was," Crystal said sharply. "Let's go."

The base was a huge sprawling complex that covered over five-thousand hectares. It might have taken an entire day to visit the installations, but Birch took her on a far more concentrated tour. Everything looked brand-new; it was incredibly high-tech. Of particular interest to Crystal were the military installations. Massive flight hangars housed the sort of futuristic combat craft that many a fighter-pilot back on Earth would have begged to be allowed to fly. The officer who always insisted on calling herself *'retired'* could not help but grow quietly excited.

"Are you a pilot, Captain Thor?" Birch enquired.

"I can move a chopper around," Crystal replied with a light shrug.

A conservative self-assessment, for sure... In truth, she was a certified and experienced Apache pilot. She had flown combat missions whilst in the Middle-East; but Crystal was instinctively cautious about revealing too much of her military background, even now. Birch surprised her with his next question.

"Would you like to take one of the jets for a quick spin? Mr Pearson has been begging for an opportunity."

Pearson glanced at her, eyes bright and already grinning in anticipation. Crystal immediately turned to Abigail.

"Is it okay?"

"If you feel up to it... You don't need to ask, Crys."

"I know I don't; but my mission is to stick to you like glue, remember?"

Abigail leaned in to whisper in her ear.

"You'll get special access later, Captain."

"That's not what I meant, Ms POTUS," Crystal pointed out with an amused smile. "Although I look forward to holding you to that promise."

"Good. For now, I think I'm perfectly safe here with James," Abigail assured her. She smiled, and pressed a soft kiss over her lips. "Go, my love."

Crystal did not need further encouragement. Flying a non-reactionary propulsion craft for the first time was a life-enhancing prospect for any pilot. Crystal wanted to be given a proper trial, and with this goal in mind, she was a lot more forthcoming about the details of her experience. Once the *HIGA* lieutenant in charge of her induction realised her level of qualification, and what she could do with a traditional aircraft, he was pretty happy to teach her the basics of this much more advanced vehicle, and let her play with it to her heart's content. Crystal learned fast and well. Only twenty minutes into her test flight, she was comfortable enough to take the gravity-powered jet beyond the moon's orbit, and afford them some magnificent views of planet Earth from space.

"Fucking astounding!" Pearson yelled.

Crystal nodded, laughing in pure joy at the sight.

"Hell, yeah!" she replied. "Fucking awesome."

After practicing a whole series of evasive manoeuvres that made Pearson turn either green or grey, depending on how aggressive she decided to make her moves, Crystal also got the chance to test the weapons system onboard.

"I find there's nothing like blowing up a few asteroids to make you feel properly alive," the *HIGA* pilot declared. "Give it a try, Captain."

With his expert guidance, Crystal soon got the hang of the laser weapons at her disposal, and several pulverised asteroids later, she was in full agreement.

"Yep," she grinned. "Life-affirming, for sure."

Once back at base on the ground, she met with a few more pilots, talked to a bunch of soldiers and their commanders, all volunteers from the regular services, and managed to get a much better sense of *HIGA's* capabilities as a whole. Their army was only small, just under five-thousand soldiers in total; but they were definitely advanced in terms of motivation, commitment, and technology.

"So, what do you think?" Pearson enquired.

"I like it," Crystal replied. "I like it a lot."

She could easily tell what was on his mind simply from the look of pure excitement plastered all over his face; he would be joining the ranks of *HIGA's* professional army before long, no doubt about it.

"I wasn't ever too happy as a cop in Lincoln, you know," he confided in her. "Had no family, no girlfriend, no real buddies; At least not like the kind I had in the Marines. You understand, right?"

"Yes," Crystal nodded. "I know what you mean."

"This *HIGA* setup feels right to me," he added. "And I think that with the situation on Earth as it is now, a full-on war may be on the cards pretty soon..."

Crystal managed to engineer a few minutes to speak to her partner alone after this, right before Birch took them to meet with the members of the *HIGA* Council. This would be Abigail's first time with them as well.

"Ben may be right," Abigail reflected when Crystal shared his ideas with her. "One thing's for sure, we won't be able to go back to Earth and just pick up where we left off. Everything's changed now, for us, and for everybody else on the planet."

She sounded wistful, and Crystal reached out to caress her cheek softly.

"How are you doing, Ms Christensen?" she asked.

Abigail wrapped her arms around her shoulders. She rested against her as Crystal held her close, and she looked up into her eyes.

"So long as I'm with you," she replied, "I'm great. And just let me rephrase what I just said; two things have not changed in my world. The first one is; I love you, Crys."

Crystal flashed a gentle smile.

"I love you too, babe."

"Secondly," Abigail added, "I'm still on a mission to reveal the truth to our people. Let's face it, we've not done such a great job of being human so far, have we? We make war, destroy our planet, live in fear of one another... In our current limited and fearful mindset, we're probably a lot closer to the Red-Eyes than the *Shanayael*..."

"Mmm. I guess that's true," Crystal agreed reluctantly.

"But once we finally wake up to our amazing potential, and become a united civilisation, one people," Abigail said fiercely; Above all, Human! Then, it will be impossible for the Global Network to keep controlling us. The Red-Eyes will disappear. It may sound crazy as hell, I know. But hey; you died, and here we both are now, at a secret base on the far side of the moon..."

"Yeah," Crystal chuckled. "We're pushing the boundaries, for sure."

"Exactly right, my love!" Abigail exclaimed with a brilliant smile. "And that's what we need to keep on doing. Stay focused, continue working, hold on to our faith and each other. I know we can do this!"

Her passion alone was enough to make Crystal shiver. And then, there was all the rest of her... For the first time in her life, Crystal was a hundred-percent clear on her purpose, and where she belonged. It was right here, right now, with this one woman.

"Roger that, Abigail," she nodded. "Always with you."

∞

Just like Crystal had taken the measure of the *HIGA* army earlier, it was Abigail's turn to have an opportunity to meet with their Council. Birch had described the group as *'the good guys'* to them both earlier, and now he elaborated on that.

"The *Human Inter-Galactic Alliance* is a group of individuals whose purpose is the protection and development of Humanity as a whole; they work to ensure a peaceful existence for us, and fair, meaningful cooperation with our interstellar neighbours."

"They're in touch with the *Shanayael*," Abigail stated.

"They have been, on and off over the years. Not a lot, I have to say... The *Shanayael*'s first rule of contact is non-interference in the affairs of other civilisations."

"But what about the technology that they gave us?" Crystal remarked. "That's not exactly non-involvement, is it?"

"They gave us a few pointers, yes," Birch agreed. "But we had to figure it all out; it took many years to develop *HIGA*, this base, and our starships. We had to do the bulk of this work, for sure."

"So, does that mean that they will not help us fight against the Red-Eyes?" Crystal insisted.

"We don't know yet," Birch replied.

Crystal was not happy with this enigmatic reply, and it was not hard to guess by her expression. Abigail rested her eyes on her, and just had to suppress a smile. Her partner had recovered fast from her brush with death. Her natural toughness was back now, on full display once again, reminding Abigail of the first time that she had met her; *Sizzling good looks and a bad attitude...* Here was the dutiful soldier with the rebellious streak that she had described to Russell once. Captain Thor, fearsome owner of what really had to be the sexiest grin in the universe... Abigail gave a soft sigh. Here was her lover and protector; her friend; her partner. She flashed her a soothing glance.

"Let's just see what happens next, uh?" she murmured.

Crystal nodded; she relaxed. They walked into the Council room. Abigail was soon delighted to discover that the mix of nations represented in the group did not just mirror that of the current G20 organisation. This council was not simply a show of economic power by the biggest and more powerful countries of the world. The members of *HIGA* included Maori people from both islands of New Zealand, and Australian Aborigines; Native American chiefs; African tribal leaders; a united contingent from all the nations of Europe; and envoys from the ancient cultures of both China and Japan.

"True representatives for planet Earth," she concluded with a beaming smile, after meeting each and every one individually. "United in friendship to safeguard the future of our planet, and the freedom of our people... My friends, it is such a great honour to be introduced to your group."

She meant it. Her intensity was palpable. The members of the Council were obviously extremely pleased to meet her too.

Abigail saw Crystal flash her a firm thumbs-up from the back of the room, and Birch stepped forward to take centre stage. The atmosphere was charged, electric.

"Ms Christensen," he declared with an eager smile, his eyes flashing in anticipation. "I know that you were in line to become the next President of the United States…"

Abigail did not betray any emotion. He was right to put it in the past. She was not sad about this, only aware that the time had come to step up to her bigger purpose. The only question was, which form would it now take? She suspected that she was about to find out.

"The situation with the Red-Eyes and the Global Network has reached critical levels," Birch continued. "We were hoping that it might resolve itself with people like you at the helm, and a bit more time… But it hasn't, and now we need to take full-on action." He glanced briefly toward Crystal. "This may mean we have to fight; but diplomacy will play an important part in our efforts as well. We must show our friends from the Cosmos that our civilisation is worthy of help and assistance in this time of great danger, but also opportunity and transformation."

Abigail took a deep breath to relax, as it began to dawn on her where this may be going.

"For this job, we need a strong individual, determined, clear of mind and spirit. This person will be able to negotiate for peace on behalf of the people of Earth, but they won't be afraid of war either. We need someone who's already well-known around the world; a woman that a lot of people already trust, and can relate to." Birch paused to grin at her. "Sound familiar, Abi?"

"Go ahead, James," she nodded with a quick smile.

"We are ready to push for disclosure," he concluded. "And if we have to fight, we will. Abigail; we hope that you will agree to become *HIGA's* new Ambassador, and our leader."

The sheer significance of the moment was certainly not lost on Abigail as she considered her answer. Here was a brand-new government in the making, the kind of evolved organisation that she had always imagined might come into play after disclosure. It was her dream, in other words, manifesting right in front of her eyes, and she was being asked to lead. Abigail took another deep, steadying breath; it was not a commitment to make lightly, she knew. Then again, it felt as if she had spent her entire life preparing for it. She glanced toward Crystal, who was watching intently from the side. Her lover looked strong, alert and focused as usual. *My gorgeous bodyguard…* Abigail felt a sure quickening in her chest. *I love you so much, Crys!* Crystal met her gaze, coal-black eyes burning bright with the same light. She flashed her a discreet wink, and a single nod of approval. Abigail turned back to Birch, and to face the entire group, all waiting expectantly.

"Yes," she simply said. "I will."

∞∞∞∞ EPILOGUE ∞∞∞∞

They started to plan their return to Earth. It was a different place by then. Army tanks were on the streets of every major city. The government had been replaced by a Global Network-controlled military. Combat troops were out in growing numbers, curfews were in effect and strictly enforced. Schools, banks, restaurants, gas stations, etc. were closed, and only a few stores remained open for food. All constitutional rights had been suspended, which included freedom of speech, of course...

"The Network always did everything they could to control the official narrative, but at least, alternative opinions could be expressed and shared via the Internet," Abigail remarked. "Now you should expect anything that you see or hear on the so-called News to be propaganda, only what they want you to hear; and this includes a bunch of damn lies about my death, *again!*"

She was determined to make it back to Washington D.C., to check on her team, and address the nation. No doubt the return of murdered Senator Birch would grab people's attention, and facilitate the rest. Abigail had her mind set on delivering their speech from 1600 Pennsylvania Avenue, which of course was the prestigious site where the White House had once stood. *HIGA's* tech wizards could hack into the Internet, and broadcast their message to the rest of the world. Everyone would get to hear this. Birch supported the plan, but was reluctant about location.

He argued that they could deliver their message from the moon, where it would be a lot safer. Abigail insisted that they had to go home if they wanted to make a real impact.

"Come on, Abi, that's crazy," he exclaimed. "You think that broadcasting from the far side of the moon, or from the cockpit of a US starship, won't have even more of an effect?"

"But you know that some people still don't believe that we landed on the moon in 1969," she countered. "They're convinced it was all made in Hollywood! Unless they can see both of us on the ground, James, real flesh and blood, they'll never believe a word of what we have to say."

They could not agree, except to disagree. In the end, in pure exasperation, Abigail turned to Crystal.

"What do you think, Captain?" she enquired. "Can we pull this off, or not?"

Crystal was very much aware that this was not her partner asking for her opinion here. If it had, she may have agreed with Birch. Abigail's idea, although appealingly flamboyant, was also amazing in its level of insanity. To hold any kind of meeting on the street of the US capital, political or otherwise, when it was under Network-military control could have been viewed as plain suicidal. There was also another sobering fact to consider: if the troops did not arrest her and throw her in jail, which they would be perfectly allowed to do under the rules of Martial Law, then the Red-Eyes might find a more permanent way to silence her. If Crystal had listened only to her heart, based on this, she might have asked Abigail to stay on the moon, and be safe. But as it was, she too had made a significant decision the previous day. Once again, Crystal was a soldier on active duty, this time with the *HIGA* forces; as such, this was her new Commander-in-Chief speaking now, asking her professional opinion about what was possible to achieve. She gave a brisk nod.

"I think you both have a point," she declared. "But we may only get one shot at this, and Abigail is right; we have to make it count. It's a dangerous idea, but it's my job to make it work, and safe for you both. Leave it with me."

She decided that what they needed was a solid diversion to take the Network's troops away from Pennsylvania Avenue, and keep them occupied for the duration of the address. As a skilled strategist with plenty of relevant experience, it did not take her long to work out a plan of action, assemble a squad of qualified *HIGA* soldiers, and link up with Abigail's people on the ground. Birch was impressed with the speed at which she made it all happen, and also much happier about it as well, once she briefed him on the details of her plan.

"Great job, Captain," he approved enthusiastically. "Now, we're ready. I can't wait to go back home!"

∞

Dawn found them onboard the USS Eisenhower II, ready to start on their way back to Earth. The journey would not take long. They were accompanied by a full squadron of soldiers to help with the job at hand, seventy-five men in total, and Marine Ben Pearson in the lead. The ex-cop had won himself the job fair and square, with no help at all from Crystal or anybody else. In many ways, he reminded her of Matt Scott, and the guys from her old unit; all men that Crystal said a prayer for every morning upon waking up. Her brothers, in a sense, never to be forgotten. She felt just the same about Pearson. She had total confidence in his judgement and abilities.

"So, Captain Thor..." Abigail said quietly, as she joined her lover on the observation deck. She was intent on stealing a few moments alone with her before the mission started officially.

235

Crystal turned around and flashed her a gentle smile.

"Ms Christensen," she nodded. "So; once again, we go."

"That's right." Abigail came close, and wrapped her arms around her neck. "How does it feel to be in command of your own starship?" she enquired.

"Oh…" Crystal chuckled in pleasure. "It makes me want to giggle my head off pretty much constantly, at the most awkward moments. Unofficially, you understand."

"Of course. I won't tell your boss."

"Thanks, babe."

"And if you ever call me that in front of people," Abigail added, pretending again that she did not adore it, "I will have to silence you."

Crystal grinned harder, and raised an interested eyebrow.

"Oh, really?" she laughed. "And how will you do that?"

"Thanks for asking," Abigail shot back. "Let me show you."

She tightened her embrace and kissed her. Long and hard at first, then more intimate, and slow, just the way that she knew Crystal enjoyed the most. She ran her fingers through her hair, teased the back of her neck with her nails. She leaned into her aggressively and slid her leg in between hers, loving the grunt of arousal that the gesture elicited from her lover. Crystal seemed to struggle to gather her thoughts after the kiss, and certainly to open her eyes.

"You're beautiful," Abigail murmured.

"Thanks," Crystal chuckled. "You're not a bad kisser for a politician."

"Just reminding you of what you're fighting for, soldier."

Crystal smiled at that, although she grew thoughtful too.

"That's not what I'm fighting for," she said. "I have another dream; you know? There's something else I hope I get to do with you someday."

"Really?" Abigail was genuinely intrigued. "Tell me."

Crystal held her gaze, eyes flashing in anticipation.

"There is such a lot at stake today," she reflected. "No one can predict what will happen after your talk. You're the leader of *HIGA* now too, and I am a ship's Captain in their military. Who knows…? One day in the near future, we may have to travel to some other galaxy on the other side of the universe; to meet with our friends from the Cosmos, and ask for their help in saving Humanity."

Now, Abigail looked more puzzled than curious.

"Space travel is your dream?" she asked. "Is that it?"

"Ah, it'd be fun," Crystal replied with a crooked smile and a light shrug. "But this is the real thing: once all this crazy stuff is over, I'll buy that campervan I've wanted for so long, and take you on a road trip."

A slow, loving smile appeared on Abigail's lips.

"You'd trade your starship for a campervan?" she teased.

"Hell, yeah!" Crystal grinned. "Don't tell the ambassador, okay?"

Abigail laughed in pure delight and mounting excitement.

"Where will we go?" she asked. "Montana?"

"Why not? Or we can just see where the wind takes us."

"Just the two of us, and the open road…" Abigail mused.

"No duty, no hard mission," Crystal agreed. "Just you and me, babe, never going any faster than 45mph. I think that's the kind of life I'd like to have."

Abigail hugged her with everything she had.

"Sounds like a great dream," she approved. "Thank you for sharing it with me and giving an extra reason to give it my best shot out there today."

"I love you so much, Abigail."

"I love you too, Crys."

They exchanged a silent, close and intimate embrace; it was several long minutes later when Abigail finally forced herself to pull back, and meet her lover's eyes. Crystal exhaled softly. She looked happy, ready, quietly confident; just the way that Abigail felt as well.

"We have important work to do before we can leave it all behind," she declared. "First, we save the planet. Then, we go. Deal, Ms Thor?"

Crystal nodded, smiling as Abigail took her hand.

"Deal," she replied. "Always with you, babe."

THE END...

ALSO

BY NATALIE

DEBRABANDERE...

UNBROKEN

"I couldn't stop reading. Heart-warming love story, full of intrigue, suspense, and a touch of terror. Loved it."

STRONG

"Raw and heart stopping action in Afghanistan. As a Marine, the main character deals with the stress of battles and loss. Great story, highly recommended."

ASHAKAAN

"What a fantastic book! I love a good Sci-Fi adventure with a strong female lead who can kick butt, outsmart the bad guys but not totally, and fall in love."

FELUCCA DREAMS

"Excellent writing! Awesome love story! The sensuality between the characters is palpable. Natalie Debrabandere keeps hitting hit out of the park!"

LOOKING FOR ALWAYS

"One of the purest love stories I have read. Original and captivating story line, amazing characters. This book keeps you hooked until the very last word. Great job!"

BEYOND THE QUEST

"Fast-paced, addictive, full of twists and turns! A riveting, exciting tale of love and adventure!"

OF SCARS AND DUTY

"OMG, Major Williams rocks!"

"A kick-ass Sci-Fi military Lesfic!"

THYRA'S PROMISE

"A wild and epic tale! Passion, action, suspense…
This book has it all!"

COAST GUARD RESCUE ONE

"Classic Lesfic – Hugely entertaining!"

AMAZON #1 BEST-SELLER

CONTACT 2020

"One hell of a good Sci-Fi!"

"Spectacular!"

(Book I in the best-selling _Contact_ Series)

A SOLDIER FIRST

"Sexy and action-packed!"

"A definite winner!"

(Book II in the best-selling _Contact_ Series)

WARRIOR 3.0

"Awesome Sci-Fi! Brilliant romance!"

"A fitting conclusion to an exciting trilogy"

(Book III in the best-selling _Contact_ Series)

RIDING ON HIGH

"Vintage Lesfic… Couldn't put it down!"
"Suspense, tension, a thrilling romance… Brilliant!"
AMAZON #1 BEST-SELLER

AS FAR AS IT TAKES

"Sizzling hot! Keeps you guessing until the end!"
"Smart, tender funny – a Lesfic delight!"
AMAZON #1 BEST-SELLER

**Keep up to date with Natalie's work on Twitter and Facebook
On Instagram: @natalie.debrabandere.author
And on the web: www.nataliedebrabandere.com**

Thank you for reading and reviewing!

9 781693 009549